Sisters
of
Arden

D1452425

Judith Arnopp

Published in 2018 by FeedARead.com Publishing

Copyright © Judith Arnopp.

The author or authors assert their moral right under the
Copyright, Designs and Patents Act, 1988, to be identified as
the author or authors of this work.

A CIP catalogue record for this title is available from the
British Library.

Cover photo: © Alexander Cherepanov | Dreamstime.com

Cover design by Covergirl

Edited by Cas Peace

www.caspeace.com

Dedication:
For Temujin and Christian,
who carry my genes into the future.

1537 - Yorkshire

We run, heads down through the darkness, away from the cries of our dying friends and the sickening thud of their falling bodies.

Ducking through a garden gate, I cast about for a hay store or a tangle of bushes that might conceal us. Grabbing her wrist, I pull Frances into a briar patch, the thorns snagging and tearing at our robes and limbs. As we crouch in the dark, she trembles and wipes her wet cheeks on my sleeve. I can just distinguish her bone-white face and the stark terror in her eyes, and I am sickened with guilt that I have led her to this. Her life is now forfeit to my mistaken conviction that simple folk can make a difference.

I grope for God in the faithless void of my mind, begging that the king's men grow tired of the hunt and ride away, back to their warm hearths, their laden tables, and their fragrant, sinful wives. Frances' teeth begin to rattle, her breath faltering as her courage dwindles. I give her a gentle shake and put a warning finger against her lips, beseeching her to be silent, to be brave for just a little longer.

As the stealthy hooves draw closer to our hiding place, we hold our breath, sinking deeper into the undergrowth when he halts just a little way above our heads. The dank aroma of rotting vegetation rises; the tang of frost tickles my nose and pinches my toes. Frances trembles so violently it is indistinguishable from the juddering of my own body. I fumble for prayer, nausea washing over me as I fail to recall a single one.

A creak of harness as the rider shifts in his saddle. I cannot see him but when the horse snorts, in my mind's eye his breath mists the darkness, rising wraith-like in the night. I can feel the rake of the man's gaze as he searches, seeking out our hiding place. My lungs strain fit to burst, my chest is aching, and I am ready to relinquish my freedom for just one blessed breath. The horse stirs, turns and moves away, and we fill our lungs with fresh damp air. We clutch hands as the vague hope of escape returns.

Then noise erupts with a harsh yelp. A hound is loosed and, with a furious growl, it crashes through the hedge. As I fall backward, I glimpse a lolling tongue, and yellow eyes stare briefly into mine; cold, murderous eyes. Frances' scream shatters the night as the jaws clamp down upon her wrist.

"Let go! Let go!" I strike out with my bare feet, feeling the crack of bony ribs beneath a silken coat. The hound yelps but holds on fast, screaming aloud as I kick out again, hammering his head with my heels. The air fills with a confusion of hooves, screaming women, and triumphant male laughter as they lay hands upon us. As they drag me to my feet, Frances gives a loud unintelligible sound that breaks my heart.

"Please," I beg, as my hands are wrenched behind me and roughly held. "We are nuns from Arden. My sister has done nothing. Take me, but ... let Sister Frances go – she ... she doesn't understand."

A white dagger of agony flashes through my skull as my captor clouts me around the ear. My head rings and my vision blurs. Through a fog of pain, I realise they are hauling Frances from the ground, dragging us both rudely forward.

"Hold them," the man on the horse orders, and their grip tightens as he slides from his saddle, hawks and spits on the ragged skirts of my habit before slowly unfurling a rope from his belt.

The knots are tight about my wrists; my hands are numb. I cry out as the horse jolts forward and, tethered to the saddle, all we can do is follow him. Agonisingly, we retrace our route back the way we have come, through the hamlets and homesteads that earlier offered us shelter.

Our cause is lost. Our peaceful mission to bring England back to the true church has failed; doomed by the promises of a false king. In the lightening dawn, the slack-limbed, sightless bodies of those who aided us sway as we pass. The voiceless, lifeless men, women and children who dared to share our questioning of the king's wisdom gape blindly at our passing.

We will join them soon; our useless lives cut short, our fruitless existence ended in ignominy.

My throat grows tight. How have we come to this?

Two years earlier – St Andrew's Priory, Arden

Bitter winds blast across the heath; I hold my lantern high and peer into the gathering dusk. Although I have searched for hours, there is no sign of Marigold. I am so cold I have lost all feeling in my fingers and, beneath my habit, my skin is shrivelled and lumpy like that of a plucked bird. At the thought of food, my belly rolls, and saliva rushes into my mouth. I have not eaten since Terce and even then not enough to satisfy.

As I climb higher, hoping for a sign or the sound of lowing, the pain in my lower back stabs like a devil's fork. I can go no further. The prioress demands punctuality and whether I abandon or continue the search, it is long past Vespers. I will be punished either way.

I turn and squint into the distance, barely able to discern the darker shape of the ramshackle priory buildings nestling in the bowl of the hills. It will soon be too dark to see at all and I must return empty-handed, my quest failed, to face the displeasure of my superiors.

Frozen, wet and daubed in mud, I stumble and slide, retracing my footsteps down the rough heathery hillside, berating myself for this ill-advised mission. Instead of exhausting myself out here on the heath, it might have been better to remain in the meagre comfort of the priory and pray for Saint Brigit's intervention, as my sisters are doing. Or better still, just wait and see if Marigold could find her own way home. Patience has never been one of my virtues; in fact, Sister Dorothea would say I have no virtues at all.

I burst through the kitchen door, throw off my cloak and turn to Sister Juliana, who is struggling to light the fire. She looks up from the hearth, a smudge of soot on her cheek.

"Where have you been? The fire is out, supper is not prepared and the prioress is in a towering rage."

"I was searching for Marigold. Ooh, but I am frozen. All the way home I was dreaming of the fire that I imagined awaited me."

The kitchen is the only place in the priory to ever offer warmth. I gaze wistfully at the cold hearth. Sister Juliana stands up, staring despairingly at the pile of damp wood.

"Fires are like our souls; left untended, they grow weak. At least you have brought Marigold back and there will be a little milk for Sister Mary's supper. She has been calling for it. She isn't very well at all."

Sister Juliana always finds a spark of comfort in the dark but, like finger and thumb pinching out a flame, one look at my expression extinguishes it. "Oh, pray do not tell me you didn't find her!"

I raise my hands and let them drop again before moving to the hearth, sinking to my knees in the cold ashes. I take up the tinder but my fingers are yet too stiff to strike, so I let it fall again. There are few luxuries within our community but milk is one of them. We preserve what little we have for the aged and the few poor souls in the infirmary who crave the warm nutty goodness of Marigold's teat. It will be hard for them to go without. Failure swamps me again. I fumble for excuses.

"I searched for hours. My voice is hoarse from calling. Had I lingered any longer I'd not have found my way back in the dark. I promise I will try again in the morning, as soon as it is light enough to see my way." I rub my palms briskly, wincing at the pain as the feeling returns. "As soon as I can use my fingers I will have the fire lit in no time. Will you help me with supper?"

"Gladly. The broth is stone cold and the bread is two days old but … things could be worse. Things can always be worse."

I'm not so sure. Sister Juliana's face is pinched, the bones of her skull clearly discernible beneath paper-thin skin. Her nostrils are red and crusted with a rim of snot, but her eyes are kind. Unlike the older nuns, the hardships of life at Arden priory have yet to take their toll on her goodness.

We are an impoverished house. A family of six nuns, a few lay sisters – of which I am one – and two orphan boys who make a home in our stables and run errands for us … when we can find them. Our community is aging; three out of six of us are too old and infirm to undertake an equal share of the burden. Arden priory is remote, set apart from the world of men so that we may dedicate our lives to God, but life on the Yorkshire moor is so harsh that survival often demands precedence over piety.

We are not rich. Not like Fountains or Rievaulx, which I've been told are vast, their treasuries overflowing with riches. I doubt they'd even notice the loss of a single cow, or struggle to keep food on the refectory table. Arden suffers while the great houses thrive. The gentry do not grace us with their daughters who have heard God's call, or their sisters who have fallen by the moral wayside. The noblest and richest in the land decline to send even their most inconvenient female family members here. Our lack of beneficiaries is bringing our house down, stone by stone; our fields and outbuildings cry out for maintenance and our tiny church is almost empty of plate. There is far too much work for the three remaining able-bodied women to carry out, so we pray and bide our time in the faith that, one day soon, God will notice our plight and send salvation.

I have been here at Arden since infancy. I know no other world, no other way of life. The only man I have ever seen is the stout abbot who comes to officiate at Mass. He takes note of our poverty, shares a huge meal with the prioress, and then rides away again, back to his sumptuous hall and hearty dinners.

Sister Mary, who often entertains us with her tales, says I was found one winter's evening at the priory gate, a newborn infant bawling for the comfort of my dead mother's teat, a large golden ring clutched in my furious fist.

"So, my mother was rich then; gentry?" I ask when she tells me of it. "Perhaps I have a wealthy grandfather or an uncle, maybe even a brother somewhere in the world."

She cackles, her gnarled hand patting my head as she douses my hopes, pouring cold reality onto my golden dreams.

"Nay, child. The ring was wrought of base metal, the jewel just polished stone. It had no value. Most likely your mother was seduced by a rogue. From the looks of her corpse, she was little more than a child and a poor woman by her clothing. Such innocence is too often ruined by the lies of a rich man and many a poor maid has been deceived by false words of love. She'd not be the first to fall for the tricks of a honey-tongued cheat."

The bitterness of her words fires my imagination and I wonder if Sister Mary ever fell foul of such a man. But before I can enquire, the door opens and the prioress strides into the room to stare down her long nose at us. I sink into the shadow and creep away to escape the reprimand I know is due to me.

The sorry tale Sister Mary tells of my origins confirms that I am not after all the misplaced daughter of a comfortable squire, but sprung instead from the loins of a villain and the womb of a fool.

A few hours later, the fire is giving off meagre heat and supper is served. The prioress, having partaken of a meal in her private chamber, joins us. She clears her throat, drawing our attention, and we lower our heads to hear her prayer. She gives thanks for the provision of our food – irreverently, I hope she will add a codicil begging that the next meal be larger, with perhaps a little meat to flavour it.

By the time we begin to eat, our supper is congealing in our bowls. Luke and Mark, tired and filthy from the barnyard, slurp like swine over their bowls in the far corner. We eat quickly, the only noise the clattering of spoons, the gasp and grunt of hunger teased rather than appeased. I finish too quickly and smear a morsel of bread around the bowl, forcing myself to chew the last mouthful slowly for many hours of prayer and toil lie between now and my next meal.

"I could eat that ten times over and still be famished," I murmur to Sister Juliana, who sits beside me.

"We must give thanks for all we receive," she replies, speaking from the corner of her mouth, her eyes rolling in mockery of her own words. On my other side, Sister Frances slurps contentedly at her food. She is the one companion in this place to leaven the darkness and warm the chill that seeps into my bones. She is simple; a great lumpen thing with a foot that turns inward, giving her a strange loping gait, but it does not impair her usefulness. Despite our limited diet, she is strong. I have seen her carry half a tree to the logging place and she can swing an axe like a warrior. In the spring, using just her bare hands, she brought forth a malformed calf from a labouring cow – the poor thing perished but the cow was saved and, for a while, she was everyone's champion.

The dishes are cleared in silence. In the kitchen, I hover near the hearth, giving the appearance of toil when in truth I am stealing what little heat I can. Reluctant to leave the meagre comfort of the kitchen, I must venture outside to secure the hens for the night, and milk the cow – but then I remember that Marigold is gone. There will be no milk, not tonight and, should she not return, there'll be none until the prioress can find enough coin to seek a replacement. Poor Marigold's unmilked teats will be agony. I think of her lonely and lost on the moor. No doubt she is sorry now for slipping her tether and wandering off. With a sigh, I put down my broom and reach for my cloak.

"I will not be long, Sister Juliana. I forgot to shut the hens up and it is now almost too dark to see. Poor Sister Mary will dearly miss her milk and honey this evening."

"Do not tarry, Margery, it is cold out there."

When I open the door, the cold locks my face in its icy blast. I lower my head and hurry across the wet yard, dodging puddles and muck. Freezing water seeps through my shoes and my fingers are so numb that I struggle to operate the latch of the barn door. As it finally clicks open, I hear a noise at the gatehouse. I cock my ear in disbelief and tiptoe across the yard to peek through the chinks in the wooden gate. I can see very little, but the clatter of hooves ceases and a voice calls for admittance. I cannot recall this ever happening before. No one visits Arden. Who on earth can be seeking shelter here, and at this late hour of the day?

The next morning, Sister Juliana hands me a tray and tells me to take it to the guest quarters. "Who is it for?" I ask, looking at the meagre offering. The few visitors who come to Arden usually dine with the prioress in her chambers and are plied with the very best food we can find. This tray bears the same watery gruel with which we all break our fast.

"Ask no questions, you'll hear no lies."

I know Sister Juliana well enough to understand that she doesn't know. She is just following orders, the same as we all do.

The guest quarters are situated close to the gatehouse, set apart from the chapel and cloister. Fine misting rain blows into my face as I hurry across the quadrangle. I screw up my eyes and clatter up the stairs to knock timidly on the door. When nobody answers, I turn and push it open with my back, squinting into darkness. The shutters are closed and the chamber is in shadow, but I can just discern a hump on the bed, a fine gown thrown over the back of the chair. I firm my lips disapprovingly. Whoever has come to stay has not bothered to rise for morning prayer.

Wedging the door open to let in more light, I clear my throat and crane my neck toward the bed.

"I have brought you a tray, madam. It is well past dawn."

A groan, and the bed ropes creak as an arm appears from beneath the covers.

"Mistress." Her voice is clipped and cultured to my ears, which are attuned to the rolling accents of Yorkshire. She speaks so loudly and so suddenly that I slop water onto the tray.

"I beg pardon?"

"I said, 'Mistress'. I am Mistress Grace, not madam, not my lady, not your grace. I am just mistress."

A fair head comes into view; tousled hair, a small white face with a tight mouth, and wide, dark-shadowed eyes.

"I am sorry, mistress. I'll leave your tray and ..."

"Stay."

I halt and turn back from the door.

"I will require help dressing ... I do not ... My maid did not accompany me."

She sits up, holding out her arms for the tray. When I do not respond straight away, she glares at me, forcing me to comply. At length, I pick it up and place it bad-temperedly on her knees. She regards the rapidly cooling gruel with distaste.

"What on earth is it? I cannot eat this."

I shrug my shoulders. "I just brought what I was told. This is the same as the nuns eat. Guests usually dine with the prioress, or have their food prepared by their own servants."

She pokes the thin slop with her spoon, then pushes the bowl away.

"I'd rather starve." She casts herself back onto the mattress and buries her face in the covers.

"Very well, madam ... mistress." I pick up the tray and prepare to leave her, but once more she calls me back.

"Wait. What am I to do? When will a fire be lit?"

"There is no fire, miss. Only in the kitchen and sometimes in the chapter house if 'tis 'specially cold."

"No fire? But it is freezing. How am I supposed to wash and dress?"

"We manage all right."

"Do not be so impertinent."

She glares at me; I scowl back.

"I must go, any road. I was told to bring you the tray. I will be in trouble if I tarry."

I turn away.

"Please ..." She is more penitent now, attempting pleasantries that she can't quite manage. "At least help me dress, I am unable ..."

She makes a strangling noise. At first I think she is choking, but then I realise she is fighting back tears, trying not to weep. I've never been given to crying, I don't see the point of it, but there are some at Arden who cry readily. I can't see it has ever gained them anything but sore, red eyes.

She lowers her head, pinches the bridge of her nose and takes a shuddering breath. Reluctantly, I put down the tray.

"Very well, but we have to hurry. I have chores to attend to."

I pick up her gown, pausing to caress the unfamiliar softness of the material, the fine lace at the collar, the embroidery on the edge of the sleeves. I've never seen the like before and it takes all my effort to resist the urge to rub my cheek against it. When I turn around to help her dress, I almost cry out aloud, for she has pulled off her shift and is waiting by the bed, as naked as the day she was born.

When we change into a fresh shift in the dormitory, the nuns and I wriggle modestly beneath our habits. I have never seen an unclothed person before; in fact, I have never even looked upon my own nakedness, but I cannot help but look at her.

My face burns and my ears pulse with shame as I slowly absorb every inch of her. She is not very old, fifteen perhaps, her cheeks still bearing the fullness of childhood. I see a long supple neck, skinny arms, high, pink-tipped breasts. I look past the round bowl of her belly and falter at the dark triangle of hair between her thin thighs.

"Don't stand staring," she snaps. "There is a clean shift in my bag. If you tarry much longer I will freeze to death."

My ears are still burning as I throw the gown on the chair and search out her linen.

"I will need water to wash my face and hands."

Her voice is muffled as I ease the shift over her head and inhale the warm chamomile scent of her hair. When I offer her a damp cloth to wash she does not take it from me. Instead, she tilts back her head and waits for me to do it for her. Her eyes are closed, dark half-moon lashes on her cheek. Unsure why I comply so readily with her orders, I gently draw the cloth over her skin, noticing the soft flush of her cheeks, the swell of her pink lips. I have never seen anyone like her. She is clearly a lady; she may even be a princess.

What is she doing here?

At her direction, I ease the gown over her head, and struggle with the unaccustomed task of tying the laces. It takes me a long time to thread the ribbon through the eyelets and she grows impatient at my fumbling attempts to tie the knots, but finally she is fastened into her sleeves.

"Now, you must pin on my coif." I turn it this way and that, trying to decide which way up it goes, and place it on her head, tucking her fine hair out of sight. She accepts my help as if it is a given, offering no word of thanks or even a smile of gratitude. When I am done, she smoothes her skirts.

"Now, if you will take me to the prioress, I would like to have a word with her."

It is not my place to argue. It is clear from her fine clothing that she is high born and as used to issuing orders as I am to obeying them. With difficulty, I balance the tray on my hip and open the door for her while she sails through and descends the stair. Careful not to step on her hem, I follow her to the bottom, moving in front to show her the way, faintly despising of the manner in which she tiptoes through the puddles. At the foot of the stair that leads to the prioress' chambers, I halt.

"You will find her up there," I whisper. "But it is not my place to accompany you. I don't want to get into trouble."

"Very well." She begins her ascent but halfway up she pauses, one hand on the bannister, and looks over her shoulder. "What is your name? I may need to summon you again."

"Margery," I reply.

"Very well, Sister Margery, I shall see you later."

"No, mistress. It isn't …"

But she has already turned away and knocked loudly at the door. I hurry away.

"Not sister, not madam, not mistress. I am just plain Margery," I mutter furiously as I make my way to the kitchen.

Sister Juliana is scrubbing furiously at a pile of plates. I put the tray beside the sink.

"You've taken your time," she remarks.

"She didn't want it," I reply. "She is an awkward miss if ever I saw one."

Juliana's lips tighten. "Scrape it back into the pot; waste not - want not. I warrant she'll be glad of food come supper time."

Sister Dorothea enters, waving a piece of parchment.

"There you are, Margery, I've been looking for you everywhere. When you've attended your morning chores, I would be glad of your help in the infirmary. Sister Mary is being very awkward again."

She sighs, failing in her attempt to hide her impatience of the old woman in her charge.

"Yes, Sister. I will be with you as soon as I can."

I pick up the bucket of slops and take it outside to feed the pig and poultry. The rain has ceased but the mud is thick in the byre and slippery underfoot. As I scatter the leftovers, the chickens come running from all directions, heads down, wings outstretched, to scrabble in the mire at my feet.

I have secretly named the hens; there is Dory, a fat white bird who likes to hide her eggs away and who will go broody given half a chance. Then there is Aggie, a straggly-looking thing who lives in a constant state of anxiety, given to squawking and flapping at the slightest disturbance. Dotty lays speckled eggs; on first appearance she seems a plump bird, but after a shower of rain when her feathers are damp, she is reduced to a bag of bones. I like Dotty though. She is fearless, and nosy. She pokes her head into ...

"Margery!" The voice cuts through my musing. I spin on my heel to discover Sister Frances. She is pointing across the kitchen garden in the direction of the meadow. "Marigold!"

Sister Frances isn't given to words. She is slow in both thought and action; Sister Dorothea swears she must have been dropped on her head as an infant. Today, however, she is making herself perfectly clear. Following the line of her finger, I see the elusive Marigold grazing at the edge of the wood as if nothing untoward has happened. Grabbing Frances' hand, I drag her toward the gate and we splash through the waterlogged field, squealing at the shock of the cold water that soaks our feet.

At our approach, Marigold lifts her head and lows mournfully, scolding me for my neglect as if I'd been the one to abscond. I untie my belt and hoist my robes clear of the mud as I edge toward her. Her ears twitch. I reach out and scratch behind them, finding the place she particularly likes to be rubbed. Blissfully, she stretches her neck and I loop the girdle around her in triumph.

"You are a silly girl, Marigold. Look at your udder, so swollen with milk it could burst. Come along, let's get you home; come along now."

Frances lopes alongside, her raised skirts revealing sturdy muddy legs. Every so often she gives a little skip and points at the cow's teats.

"Milk," she says, with a wide grin. "Sister Mary."

The men of the crusades could not have been welcomed home with more joy than when we appear in the barnyard with Marigold in tow. Luke and Mark perform a demonic dance, holding hands and leaping in a ragged circle, while the sisters cluster at the gate. The clamour even brings the prioress from her lair to see what the fuss is about. Observations of silence and contemplation forgotten, they cluster around us, their questions falling as rapidly as sudden rain.

"Where was she? Where did you find her?"

"She came home of her own accord. Isn't she clever? And it wasn't me who saw her first, it was Sister Frances."

Frances beams at the gathering, drinking in the praise, and with sweeping hand movements begins to describe our adventure.

"I'll take Marigold to the shed and dry her off," I say and begin to lead her away. On reaching the barn door, I notice the girl I had helped dress this morning. She is standing apart from the others, watching, her eye darting from one nun to another, a crinkle of disbelief on her brow. She is clearly wondering what the fuss is about and has no idea of Marigold's worth. Once she has lived here a while she will come to understand such excessive joy at the cow's safe return. Once she falls ill and is in need of a milky posset, or tastes her first sample of rich creamy cheese on a feast day, she will value Marigold too.

Marigold's return has lightened our mood. The world seems brighter as, one by one, we drift away to carry out our allotted tasks. An hour or so later, Sister Dorothea finds me searching out eggs in the barn. "The prioress wishes to see you," she says and, from her expression, I can see she is as surprised as I am.

"To see me? Are you sure?"

Sister Dorothea shrugs her shoulders. "'Tis not my place to question." She folds her arms and waits for me to go face my punishment, for that is surely the only reason I am summoned. Dread washes around my belly. It must be because I allowed Marigold to stray; I had hoped the triumph of her return would negate my punishment, but it seems my hope was a vain one. Depositing the egg basket in the kitchen, I follow Dorothea through the cloister. As she strides ahead of me, I watch the flash of her sandals appearing and disappearing beneath the hem of her robes. A great daub of shitty straw is stuck to her heel, picked up unawares in the yard, but I do not tell her. She will notice soon enough.

The last time I fell out of favour with the prioress, she ordered my palms to be lashed with a length of knotted rope. Remembering the sharp sting, I clench my fists, swallow a clot of fear from the back of my throat, and pray silently and desperately that, this time, she will show leniency.

The prioress keeps me waiting. I stand near the door while she scratches on a piece of parchment. The richness of her apartment bears down upon me, the rich colours of the tapestries making me feel like a toad at a winter feast. I shift from foot to foot until her ugly little dog, a nasty yappy beast, jumps from his cushion and comes to sniff at my ankles. Before he can piss on my feet, I nudge him away, the resulting yelp causing the prioress to pause and give me a dark accusing look. She lowers her head and writes again.

At least it is warm in her chamber. A fire burns in the grate and her candles are of wax, not stinking tallow like the rest of us have to make do with. My gaze moves about the room, taking note of the good cloth of her robe, the books on the table, the tapestry on the wall. When she has done, she puts down her pen and slowly and silently reads her words from beginning to end. I am forced to wait for so long that when I notice her cool eyes have turned upon me, I almost jump from my skin.

"Margery. I understand you made the acquaintance of our *guest* this morning."

She emphasises the word 'guest,' turning it into a sneer, a faint wrinkle of displeasure on her nose.

"Yes. She didn't want her breakfast."

She smiles stiffly without comment and laces her fingers together.

"The young woman in question will be staying with us and will require someone to instruct her as to … our arrangements here. Sister Dorothea indicated you might be the appropriate person."

"Me?" My eyes widen. "Pardon me, but she is staying as a guest? For how long?"

Surprise makes me forget who I am speaking to. By way of apology, I turn pink and bob a curtsey. The prioress gets up and paces to and fro before the hearth. As she moves, her skirts whisper, and I remember the rumour among the nuns that she wears a silk shift beneath her habit. My recent discovery of fine linen enables me to imagine the slippery softness of it and envision the rich embroidery on hem and cuff.

"She will remain here as our guest until she has recovered from her malady; then, if she wishes, she will take holy orders and join our community."

Holy orders? Join our community? Her words echo in my head. The prioress sighs impatiently. "Please close your mouth, Margery. Before she begins her novitiate, you are to assist her; teach her the rudiments of living, instruct her how to wash and dress herself, how to pray, how to work … her education has been very much neglected."

She doesn't know how to wash and dress? I am full of questions, full of curiosity, and overflowing with doubt as to my ability to teach the girl anything. She didn't seem to like me and I fear she will never listen. The prioress clears her throat. "I shall provide Sister Dorothea with a full list of instructions for you. Should you need clarification or advice, you must go to her. Now ... you may go, I have other matters to attend to."

I am so taken aback by her orders that I forget to feel relief at having escaped a thrashing. I bob a hasty curtsey and fumble at the door latch, glad to escape into the fresher air. Before descending, I lean on the balustrade, frowning down at the cloister where last week's snow is still piled in the north facing corners. My mind wanders, conjuring a hundred different answers to the questions teeming in my mind. A scatter of freezing raindrops blows across my face, rudely shaking me from my musings. I realise Sister Dorothea is calling from below, her tone sharp.

"Come along, Margery, you can't linger here all day."

I hasten down the steps.

"Who is she, Sister Dorothea? Where does she come from?"

"You'd best ask her that yourself," she replies as we approach the cloister door. Then she halts and turns sharply, waving a long, chilblained finger beneath my nose. "And no gossiping with the other nuns. Whatever you learn about our ... *guest* ... you are to keep to yourself. Do you understand? I will not have gossip."

*

"The prioress says you are to wear these." As I place the pile of clothing on the counterpane, she turns with a rustle of silk and moves toward the bed. Tentatively, she reaches out and tests the quality of the material. Then she closes her eyes with a grimace.

"It is so rough," she whispers. "How will I bear it?"

"You'll get used to it. It is what we all wear."

"The prioress doesn't. Her habit is much finer, and I've noticed her linen is of the finest weave. So much for humility."

I make no reply; it is not my place to criticise my betters. She looks down at her gown, soiled now after too much wear.

"Would you like me to help you?"

She turns to look at me, blinking away tears. I see her throat move, testament to her inner agony, and pity tugs at me.

"Oh, heavens, when I replace this gown with that beastly habit, it will be like stripping off my skin and wrapping myself in someone else's." Her shoulders droop as she stares into an empty corner. "I am not sure I can do it. I am not sure I am strong enough to go through with this."

I step closer.

"Of course you are. It's only a change of clothes. Here, let me help with the laces."

Her head is bowed, exposing the wisps of hair at the back of her neck, and my fingers graze her skin as I struggle with the knots. I tug at the strings that bind her, pull off her sleeves and unlace the bodice. Our faces are so close I can feel the hush of her breath on my cheek.

"Oh Margery," she whispers and I look up, startled. She has never used my name before. I shake my head, screwing up my eyes.

"I don't understand, Mistress. Why are you here if you still long for your old life? Why have you come to Arden?"

She spins away, tripping over her loosened skirts; her fingers are like claws, her throat a network of agonised sinew.

"Do you know anything of the world out there, Margery? Do you think women like me are free to choose where we go or what we do? Do you think we have a voice, or an opinion? Do you think our wishes mean anything?"

I shake my head.

"I wouldn't know, Miss. I've never been anywhere; not even as far as Hawnby."

She stops, plumps onto the bed and stares at the rough habit as if it is unclean.

"And I will probably never leave here now, either. I will end up old and wasted; wizened like the rest of them."

Her voice breaks. She balls her fists, presses her knuckles into her eyes and sways back and forth while I look on, not knowing what I can do to make her feel better. Her shoulders shudder, and when I can bear it no longer I sit beside her on the bed and place a tentative hand on her arm.

"Perhaps ... if you tell me about it, it will ease you."

She raises her head, a string of spittle on her parted lips, her lashes separated and wet with tears. My own eyes prickle in sympathy. For a few moments, she blinks ferociously and I think she is not going to reply, but then she clears her throat.

"My family comes of gentle stock. We are well born but not immensely rich, but my father is – was – an ambitious man. I was set to be wed to a neighbour's son. At first, I protested and didn't like it at all but then ... as I came to know him better, I came to love him and we were both happy with ... the arrangement ... more than happy. We were ... impatient to be joined, but last summer, when the sweating sickness came, my father took ill and died and my ... my betrothed died also ..."

I gasp, making her look up, and her hand tightens about my fingers.

"I am my father's only child. Had he lived, I should have inherited the house and lands and my son after me, but ... because I am unwed, by some cruel facet of the law the property goes to my cousin, William, who is a cruel and ruthless man. When I wouldn't … comply with his demands, he sent me here, with orders that, afterwards, I must take the veil."

"Can he do that?"

She nods and weeps again, her body shuddering as she clings to my hand. My arms slide around her and she falls upon my breast, where I let her scour the sorrow from her heart; sorrow that I see now has been repressed for too long.

After a while, I find I am rocking her back and forth, as if she is a child in need of comfort. She sniffs and shudders while my mind considers the story she has shared. I rest my chin upon her head and wait as she begins to calm. By the time she pulls away, my arm has grown numb and there is a pain beneath my ribs from the awkwardness of our position. She sits up, gropes for a kerchief and dries her eyes, smiling ruefully, embarrassed by her outburst. "Come," she sniffs, "you'd better help me into this beastly thing."

She pulls off her shift and I avert my gaze as I drag the fresh rough linen over her head, tugging it down to cover her nakedness. Next comes the habit that swamps her frame, dulls her beauty, but somehow also serves to accentuate her fragility. When I notice how she struggles to knot the girdle, I kneel at her feet and do it for her.

"What did you mean when you said, 'afterwards, I must take the veil' – after what?"

She looks down at me and our eyes meet, hers full of disbelief at my question.

"Margery! Are you truly such an innocent? Is it not clear to you that I am going to have a child?"

In the weeks that follow, I instruct her in the tasks we must perform each day. She leans against the barn wall and watches me lay my face against Marigold's haunch and encourage her to let down her milk. She sprinkles feed to the hens, backing off and squealing if they come too near, afraid they will peck her toes. Afterwards, she carries the basket of smooth brown eggs to the kitchen, where I show her how to trim the vegetables, stir the broth and stoke the fire.

"We have no servants here, apart from a pair of wastrel boys in the barnyard. We do most of the menial work ourselves," I say. "You will soon learn."

She pulls a doubtful expression, pokes a scalded finger into her mouth and shakes her head.

"I shall never get used to this," she says, and she is proving so incompetent that I fear she is right.

Yet, to my surprise, as the weeks go by she does learn and as she slowly becomes accustomed to the imagined terrors of the barnyard and the vagaries of the kitchen, she educates me in return.

For the first time, I learn something of the world outside Arden. She tells me of her life before her father died, when they dined three times a day, had servants to wait on them, slept in goose-feather beds and filled their days with leisure. Her face lights up with the remembered thrill of riding to hounds, of archery practise, of dancing on feast days. She rarely speaks of her mother or her betrothed, but she knows all about the king and his new queen. For the first time, I hear court gossip of the enchanting new queen, Anne Boleyn, whom Grace despises as an upstart and a whore.

"Poor Queen Catherine," she says. "She was his queen for more than twenty years and bore King Henry many sons, although she lost them all. It breaks my heart to think of her cast aside and forbidden to see poor Princess Mary."

"Have you ever seen the king?"

"No." She shakes her head. "But I once saw his portrait in the town hall. He is magnificent, but I'd not want to wed him. He is not for the likes of me, yet Anne

Boleyn is a commoner just as we are, despite the king's attempts to better her status."

"Really?" I look at Grace kneeling at the hearth, raking cold ashes into a basket. Her robes are soiled, her nails are broken and filthy, and her cheek is smudged with soot. She sits back on her heels and waves a burnt stick at me.

"Anne Boleyn is quite old, and not very pretty by all accounts. The king raised her, of course, made her a marchioness so she'd be fit to marry. They say …" As her voice drops to a whisper, I move closer. "… that the king was besotted, some say bewitched, and he would not rest until he had her. But now, of course, the pair of them argue, like every other man and wife in England."

"Do husbands and wives argue? I hadn't realised …"

"Well, you wouldn't, shut away in here, would you? My parents argued every day of their lives until my father moved his things into a separate wing of the house. Mother hated his mistresses, his drunkenness, and his constant absence, and called him ungodly. When Mother died, it was almost a relief; once she was gone, the peace was almost palpable and my father and I did very nicely … until the day the sickness came."

Her shoulders droop and I sense she is about to revert to her former sadness. Grace's moods are as changeable as the weather; one minute wet and moody, the next sunny and blithe. To distract her from growing too maudlin, I lean over, pass her a basket of kindling and instruct her how to set the fire.

She never talks about the child she is carrying. I don't know when it will come or how it will get here. When I think of how the animals in the barn push and strain to bring forth their young in a spurt of birth water and shit, I know it can be nothing like that. I imagine some sort of miraculous unfurling of the belly button, or a mystic opening of the rib cage. With a sideward glance at her belly, I consider how huge the child must be to make such a mound. How it will make its entrance into the world I can't imagine. It is all a mystery to me and, although Grace does not seem to dwell on it, the matter often keeps me awake into the small hours.

In the end, I even broach the subject with Sister Maude who, since she oversees the infirmary, seems the appropriate nun to ask. It is a difficult subject to raise. I linger in the doorway, shifting from foot to foot, twisting the end of my girdle until she grows impatient and snaps at me.

"I have work to do. What do you want, child?"

"I – I ..." My face contorts as my belly squirms with embarrassment. "I want to know about babies ... how – how they get here."

I've never seen such an expression. Her eyes open, her cheeks turn the colour of a turkey's wattles, and she pulls her neck in, making her many chins increase.

"That is not something that should be discussed." She moves to Sister Mary's bed and twitches the sheet tight, tucking it in so hard poor Mary can barely move. "Now, run along about your business. Time is not for wasting."

She strides away but, having come so far, I am determined not to be so easily dismissed. I trot along after her.

"But ... I need to know. Mistress Grace is going to have a child – how will we know when it is ready to be born? Is there something we need to do – some preparation? And how will we tell when it is ... done?"

A chuckle from the corner and Sister Mary's bed ropes creak as she struggles to free herself from her blankets. I thought she had fallen asleep. She wrestles to sit up, fixes me with a twinkling eye.

"You make it sound like a cake, lass. God will let us know when the mother is ripe. Do not fear."

Sensing Sister Mary may prove to be the more fruitful source of information, I take three steps closer.

"Is it like when the anim–"

My shoulders are seized from behind; strong hands spin me round. Sister Maude pokes her face so close to mine I can see the coarse hairs sprouting on her chin.

"Out! Now!" She grabs my collar and propels me from the room, sending me tripping down the stone step. Before I know it, I am outside, where the sun is doing its best to shine through the dreary grey clouds.

May 1536

After weeks of wind and rain, the first day of May dawns bright and still. As soon as I open my eyes, I can tell from the smell in the air that there has been an early frost. Yet by mid-morning the sun is warm on my neck as I poke at the soil in the infirmary garden, extracting weeds and plucking snails from the lush spring growth. My back aches and my knees are cold from the damp grass. At the first opportunity, I abandon my chores and drag Grace out onto the moor.

"I'm so tired," she complains. We have been working since sunrise but I am not weary; instead, I am invigorated by the change in the weather. I quickly outstrip her, hastening up the hill, away from the confines of the priory, to embrace the freedom of the hills. At the top of the rise, I pull off my coif to feel the air on my head, throw open my arms and embrace the buffeting breeze.

"What are you doing?" Grace calls as she puffs behind me and, my conscience pricking, I wait for her to catch up. She places one hand on my shoulder, the other to her back, her belly jutting out before her while she catches her breath. Her skin is pale, a sheen of sweat on her brow.

"I love it out here," I shout into the wind. "It is the only place I ever really feel alive!"

She flops onto the ground, arms and legs wide, her belly as round as the kitchen cauldron.

"Perhaps it is easier to feel 'alive' when you're not burdened with a child."

As I squat beside her, she struggles upright and, putting a hand to her brow, squints into the distance. "It is pretty, though," she adds grudgingly.

"When I was a child, I used to think I could see the whole world from here. I thought England was the world then, but now I know better."

"How old are you?" Grace stretches out her legs, pulling up her skirts to reveal puffy ankles and pink, swollen toes. It is warmer in the dip in the heather she has found where the wind cannot reach. I sit down beside her and tilt my face to the sky.

"I don't know. Sister Mary reckons I must be more than twelve."

"Have your courses started?"

I shake my head, hug my knees and turn away so she cannot see how hot my cheeks are burning. I know very little of such things but I'd be blind not to have seen the other nuns dealing with the curse. I've scrubbed the blood from their shifts and run to the infirmary often enough to fetch something to ease their gripes. It looks a sordid, uncomfortable business and I am not in the least eager for womanhood and all it entails.

"It's nothing to worry about." I feel her hand on my knee and shrug my shoulders.

"I'm not worried, and if I were what'd be the point? Worrying wouldn't change it."

"No." She laughs softly and, pulling a piece of bread from her pocket, breaks it into two and hands me a share. "You are very wise, Margery. It took me a long time to realise that."

"Aren't you worried … you know … about the child?"

She closes her eyes, turns a little pale, and shakes her head.

"No. As you say; what'd be the point?"

We linger for an hour. I pull up my skirts to let the air lick my knees, and lie down beside her. After a few moments, I point out a cloud in the shape of a dog, and shortly afterward, spy another that resembles a fish.

"Oh look, Margery," she says. "That one looks like Sister Dorothea, do you see?" We break into giggles, and soon every cloud resembles something, or someone. I am still laughing when her sudden scream startles me. She leaps up, slapping at her leg until a large black beetle falls from beneath her habit.

"Horrid things; why did the good Lord create beetles? What benefit do they give?"

Burrowing in the heather, I hunt the creature down. Trapping it between finger and thumb I hold it aloft, watching its legs vainly treading the air. Grace leans away from me. "Urghh! How can you, Margery?"

For a moment, I consider tormenting her with it, but I've heard that a fright can bring a child early and I'd certainly not want her to give birth up here on the heath. Reluctantly, I let it go, watch it scurry out of sight before I lie down again with my head close to hers. The sun is warm on my limbs, easing my bones, kissing my skin, making me languid and lazy. Our voices grow quieter, our minds drowsy in the afternoon sunshine.

"It won't do to fall asleep," I murmur, turning my head toward her, but I am too late. Her eyes are closed, her lips gently parted, her breath ticking in my ear.

The sun moves slowly across the sky, taunting my laziness, reminding me there are chores to be done, and the trouble that will befall us when our absence is discovered. Giving her a gentle shake, I sit up, pull the skirts of my thick dark habit over my knees and peer down the valley, where a ribbon of road threads across the moor. I narrow my eyes. A cloud of dust informs me a party of horsemen is approaching. The valley road leads only to Arden.

"Look," I say, pointing. "Someone is coming." With a groan, Grace sits up and rubs her eyes before sleepily following the line of my finger. She squints into the distance.

"Visitors?"

I shake my head. "Nobody makes social calls to Arden, and the prior came last week." I get up and offer her my hand, hauling her to her feet. As we descend the slope, she clings to my arm, the rasp of her breath buzzing like a wasp in my ear. I want to walk faster, to discover who it is that rides so speedily to Arden, but I force myself to go slowly, helping her over the rougher parts of the way.

Anxious not to encounter Sister Dorothea, we enter through the farmyard gate, treading warily through the muck. As we pass the byre, Frances appears from behind one of the haystacks. Her face is white and she runs toward me, clings earnestly to my hand. "Where were you?"

She is agitated, upset.

"I hide."

"What's the matter, Frances? Has Sister Dorothea missed us? Are we in trouble?"

She shakes her head and points in the direction of the porter's lodge.

"Strangers! Men!"

"Men? What men?"

I shake off her hand and peer around the corner of the barn wall. The prioress is standing at the foot of her stairs with a man, a gentleman by his dress, and they appear to be arguing. Her upper body thrusts forward, anxiety in every sinew, and she is wringing her hands, her mouth moving rapidly. I cannot hear her words or those of her sturdy companion, but something about his stance, the dark hue of his clothing, fills me with fear. Everything about his unwarranted presence is intimidating, although I don't know why. He rummages in his pack, takes out a roll of parchment and waves it beneath the prioress' nose. She puts her hands behind her back and refuses to take it. I turn back to my friends.

"Frances, take Grace to the infirmary and claim you are ailing. Stay there. I will join you as soon as I can."

"Why?"

"Just do as I say."

I paste a smile onto my face and nod reassuringly, pretending a confidence I do not feel. I cannot imagine what is wrong but I am consumed with a strange, non-specific fear. Once my friends are out of sight, I tuck my hands up my sleeves, lower my head and, as unobtrusively as I can, make my way around the cloister in the direction of the kitchens.

Before I reach the door, a great crash rings out, followed by a cry. I stop dead, crouch below the window and, when I can breathe again, I raise my head to peer above the sill. Sister Juliana is standing with her back against the wall while two strangers search methodically through our meagre store of foodstuff. Another man is piling pots and pans upon the table. Every so often, one of them makes a mark upon a roll of parchment. As if she senses somebody watching, Juliana slightly turns her head. Her eyes meet mine and, with a brief shake of her head, she warns me not to enter. As quietly as I can, I duck down and back away.

When I approach the farmyard, a great squawking informs me there are men in the byre, too. I peek around the corner in time to see one of the king's men cuff young Mark around the ear. His brother Luke is nowhere to be seen, and I have no doubt he has crept away to hide. I wish I could do the same but it is my duty to act, to attempt some act of bravery that will drive these men away.

Should I try to protect Marigold and the hens, or should I investigate the uproar issuing from the church? I hover in the cloister gateway until, deciding the Sacristan is worthier of my rescue if not my love, I sneak quickly through the west postern door into the nave, my heart banging hard.

Sister Christiana stands braced across the treasury door, denying access to a man in a torn jerkin. Knowing her well, I can detect the slight tremor in her voice that betrays her fear.

"There is no need for you to enter. I can list our possessions for you. We are a poor house and have just one gilt chalice and a silver tray – their worth is very small and will do little to replenish the king's coffers."

He leans forward, growling into her face.

"I can't take your word for that. You're probably hiding something to fund yourselves when you are all thrown out of here."

He pushes her aside, sending her staggering across the floor, but she rights herself in time and faces him again, her chin knotted, the sinews of her throat tight with anger. As he takes an iron bar to the lock, she clasps her hands, shaking her head righteously.

"The good Lord sees all, young man. You remember that. He witnesses everything you do and can see deep into the darkness of your heart. You will be punished in the hereafter."

I hold my breath, leave Sister Christiana to her fate and creep from the nave. Outside, I gulp in cold air and crouch against the wall before slowly circumnavigating the cloister in the direction of the infirmary. Crouch-backed, I hobble through the garden, disturbing early bees, the scent of warming earth heavy in the air. Lenten lilies nod benignly in the sunshine, belying the sudden violence of the day. As I approach the door, the sounds of commotion grow louder, and I recognise the booming voice of Sister Mary calling down a curse upon the king and all his men. With my back to the wall, I slide beneath the lintel. The men have not ventured here, but the younger sisters have taken refuge and are gathered about Mary's bed.

"Hush, Sister Mary," Grace implores her. "Do not shout so loud!"

"Shout? Who is shouting?" Her hirsute lips are disapprovingly pursed.

"Come now, Mary. Remember your heart …" Sister Maude takes hold of the old lady's hand. On hearing my footstep, they all look fearfully toward me. I creep forward. "Margery, what is happening, do you know? Is it the king's men?"

"Yes, I think it must be. They seem to be taking stock of our possessions … the byre, the treasury, even the kitchen store room."

We exchange glances, fear surging in my gut when I realise they are as terrified as me. Even at Arden, we have heard of the ruthlessness of the king's men.

"So, it has come." Maude releases Mary's hand, crosses herself and silently begins to ask for God's assistance. The others follow suit, bowing their heads and, after swallowing a sudden irritation at the futility of prayer, I do the same.

"What do you mean, 'it has come'? What has come?"

Grace's voice breaks into our prayers. I raise my head and meet her terrified eyes, her bone-white face. She places a shaking hand on her belly. Sister Maude ceases to pray, and wets her dry lips with her tongue before explaining.

"Some months ago, we had news that the king is … has been persuaded to close some of the smaller religious houses. I feared we would be among the first. It looks as if the news was right ..."

"Close them? Why? What will he gain?" My voice comes out in a squeak. "And what about us; where are we to go?"

It was bad enough when the king broke with Rome and we were forced to accept him as head of the church in England. We obeyed then and paid – still pay – lip service to the crown but, in our hearts, we love the pope more; far, far more than the king. But to leave Arden ... is unthinkable.

Arden has been here since the time of the second King Henry; long before the Tudors were kings over England. It has survived war and pestilence. Sister Mary took her vows here over sixty years ago and I – short as it is – have been here my whole life.

"I don't know – our fate isn't their concern." Sister Maude pushes past me, bustles to the door and looks anxiously across the precinct. "Look."

I go to her side. The king's man is still attempting to gain access to the prioress' chambers. As we watch, he pushes her to one side and she follows at his elbow, speaking rapidly, her hands clasped. Although I cannot hear their words, it is clear he is deaf to her plea.

I nudge Sister Maude when my attention is drawn to a group of men entering the cloister through the far gate. She draws in a sharp breath, sliding an icy hand into mine.

"The prioress will stop them ..." Grace has crept unnoticed to my shoulder; the glances we exchange are ripe with unspoken thoughts.

"I am not so sure ..."

"Quickly!" Sister Maude turns and propels us back to Sister Mary's bed. "They are coming this way, conceal yourselves ..." But she is too late. Before we can hide, the tramp of feet disturbs the silence, the door is thrown open, and we turn, standing stiffly as they invade the sickroom.

Sister Maude stands very straight, her hands concealed beneath her habit, her erect body shielding us from the full assault of their gaze. We cringe cravenly behind her. My heart is racing but I am glad of Grace's fingers gripping tightly to my arm. Yet sick as she is, Sister Mary will resort to no such cowardice. She strains forward in her bed, her voice slicing through their menace.

"Get out of here, you rat-shite! How dare you enter a lady's chamber?"

Bolt upright, her face puce with fury, she waves a crooked finger, presenting such a terrifying picture that the fellow pulls up short. Momentarily fearful, he runs his gaze over her, taking note that his assailant is nothing but a crone. He emits a bark of unpleasant laughter and holds a flickering torch aloft, lighting the gloom, revealing the shabbiness of the infirmary. Through his eyes I see the unswept corners, the threadbare blankets, and the four frightened women huddled around the bed.

He pushes back his cap and comes closer, his gaze travelling impudently up and down Grace's body. To our astonishment, he leans closer and prods her belly with a filthy finger.

"Well, well, well," he sneers. "A pregnant nun. That is interesting. Very interesting indeed. Our master will be wanting a word with you."

Grabbing Grace's wrist, he tries to haul her from the room. She fights against him, twisting and turning, but she lacks the strength to best him. As he drags her from the infirmary into the garden, we scuttle after, Sister Mary's curses billowing in our wake – as futile as mist. I run after them, suddenly fearless.

"Please, be careful," I try to reason. "Think of her child."

Ignoring me, he drags her up the stair. I scramble after them, just managing to slide through the door before it slams shut. The prioress looks up and the gentleman turns at the sudden intrusion, his eyes widening when he notes Grace's condition. He starts to slowly roll the sheet of parchment he is holding. The prioress blanches.

"What is the meaning of this?"

The minion drags off his cap and leers horribly.

"I've discovered a pregnant nun, my lord. I thought you'd be interested."

The prioress stands very still, her wrists clasped, her lips tense while, like a cat stalking a mouse, the man moves toward Grace. His eye travels rudely up and down her frame. He snorts. The prioress lifts her chin.

"This girl is not a nun; she was sent here by her family for the duration of her confinement."

Ignoring the prioress, he moves with menacing lethargy.

"Yet she wears a nun's habit."

"Merely for convenience. Life in the priory is unsuitable for the silk gown she wore on her arrival ..."

He raises a hand, silencing the prioress. Her face pales. Her lips clamp together.

"Her condition will be noted." He unfurls his papers and makes some marks with his pen before standing and casting one more disdainful look about the chamber. He does not acknowledge me. To all intents and purposes, I am not here.

"You shall hear from us again in due course. Do not attempt to remove or conceal any of your treasures. We have taken note of every last piece. All church property now belongs to the king."

He treads quietly across the room, pausing while his man opens the door. Closer proximity allows me to examine him in more detail. I notice his hands bear the signs of labour, and the hair on his chin is coarse, his skin pit-marked and grimy. It is merely his clothing that marks him as a man of gentility and, as Sister Mary is always telling us, you can't make a silk purse out of a pig's ear.

Without taking proper leave of the prioress, he passes across the threshold, leaving us alone and mercifully unharmed. Grace sinks to her knees, her breath ragged with fear.

"I thought he would take me and throw me in the Tower."

The prioress sneers.

"Why would he do that? In the greater scheme of things, you are nothing and nobody in this world."

With small hope of offering much comfort, I squeeze Grace's shoulder before addressing the prioress directly.

"What will happen to us? What is to be done?"

She turns toward me, as astonished as if her lap dog had sat up and begged a question. Her eyes are cold and hard – like stone.

"Pray, girl," she says at last. "All any of us can do is pray."

After the king's commissioners have ridden away, an unstable peace settles upon Arden. As we restore order to the kitchens and the barn, Sister Maude tries to appease Sister Mary, whose righteous anger quickly degenerates into fearful tears.

Luke creeps back through the priory gate and helps Mark to round up the hens, herding them into their coop for the night. In the physic garden, I weep over the trampled seedlings and cuttings that have been trodden into the soil. We work silently, feverishly salvaging what we can and setting aside broken shoots in the hopes of re-rooting them later on.

"That man." Grace stops what she is doing, her anger startling me from my reverie. "That bully; he was so full of hate I'm surprised it didn't knock him over backwards."

I straighten up, my back stiff from stooping.

"As Sister Christiana told him, God witnesses his evil and will punish him."

"Do you believe that? Do you believe in evil? Is it some separate thing or is it within us all? Are we born cruel or do we learn to be? Perhaps such things are passed on to us by our parents."

I hope not. I have long believed my own mother must have been a fool, and my father a rogue. I have no wish to grow to be the same.

"I think we learn it," I say after further thought. "Look at me. I know nothing of the world outside Arden and I am no different to any of the sisters here. I don't know how to be anything other than what they've made me."

She shifts her position, resting her back against a stone wall.

"Exactly. You have experienced only good and so are kind and sweet, but had you been raised among evil people, ill-treated or exposed to dishonesty, you may have learned to be the same."

We stare at each other for a long moment.

"So, life is just a matter of chance then?"

She nods, her eye distracted. "Yes. I think so. We enter the world innocent of sin, and absorb what is around us."

"Like a dry flannel in a puddle."

She laughs. "If you want to put it like that."

"Yet the Bible teaches we are conceived in sin, or so the sisters say."

Instinctively, she places her hand on her belly.

"Not always."

For a long moment, our gazes lock. When I wrench mine away and lower my chin, her hand comes out to cover mine.

"What is it, Margery?"

I clear my throat.

"Your eyes," I say, squinting past her as if there is something in the distance that fascinates me. "They are very blue."

She laughs softly through her nose.

"So are yours."

I look up, startled.

"Are they? I had no idea. I've no idea what I look like."

"But ... surely someone has told you, surely you have seen your reflection."

I shake my head.

"Only in the bucket as I draw it from the well, but the water slops around so much it isn't clear. I dare say I wouldn't know my own face if I bumped into myself coming through the cloister."

She shuffles forward on her knees, grasps my hands and peers closely at me. Heat begins to burn my cheeks.

"Then I shall tell you how you look. Your face is quite thin. Like I said, your eyes are blue, not blue like a summer day but paler – grey blue ... like those little butterflies that live on the heath, and your lashes are short with hints of gold. Your nose is long ... distinguished, and your mouth is wide and generous. Your skin, if it wasn't so dirty, is paler than mine, with a few freckles on the bridge of your nose. Your chin is well defined, determined and strong, and your hair ..." Before I can stop her, she pulls off my veil. "... is light brown ... and dearly in need of a good wash."

I put up a hand to the short coarse strands and, with sinking heart, wish it was golden like hers.

"Like a gargoyle on the church."

Her laugh is louder this time, and so unrestrained it draws Sister Maude's attention to us. She looks up, trowel in hand.

"I can't imagine what you two have to laugh about," she says. "Get on with your work. Use the time to commune with God."

Obediently, we resume our task and, as we work, instead of 'communing with God' I try to put together the parts of my face that Grace has described. Of course, I know that looks are unimportant and that it is sinful vanity to dwell upon one's appearance but ...oh, instead of a small brown nut, how I wish I were beautiful ... like an iris or a lily, or a rose.

<u>June 1536</u>

As Grace's pregnancy progresses, Sister Dorothea instructs me to leave the nuns' dormitory and sleep instead on a narrow truckle bed in Grace's chamber, in case she should need me during the night. I very quickly discover that Grace snores worse than Frances. She interrupts my rest so often that I wake heavy-eyed and irritable in the morning. But I am too softhearted to disturb her when I have to get up for Lauds. She has not yet shaken the habit of sleeping late into the morning but today, as I quietly grope for my habit in the dark, she turns heavily on her mattress.

"Margery. I thought you'd never wake. I think ... something is wrong."

She heaves herself up onto the pillow, her fat gold braids resting on her swollen breasts, her hands cradling her huge stomach.

"What do you mean, wrong? Are you ill?"

"No." She catches her breath. "I think, perhaps, it is the child."

Fear plunges through me.

"I will fetch Sister Maude." I spin round, fumbling beneath the bed for my shoes.

"Margery!" She grabs my hand. "Don't leave me. I am afraid."

I rest for a moment at the side of her bed.

"I have to leave you, just for a short while. I must fetch help ... I cannot deliver your child. You need Sister Maude, she is ... she is skilled at such things."

I pray she will not recognise the lie. It has become clear to me over the last few months that Sister Maude has no more idea about birthing than I have. What can nuns possibly know of such things?

"I will be as quick as I can, I promise."

I prise her fingers from mine and toss her a confident smile before I dart from the room.

As I approach the quire, I can hear the nuns singing, praising the Lord for the dawning day. The voices of the prioress and Sister Maude are tuneful and fine. Sister Dorothea's is flat, her words a little out of time with the others. Sister Frances has her head thrown back as she joyfully joins her discordant notes with the others. After paying brief respects to the altar, I creep to Sister Maude's side and tug at her sleeve. She jerks her arm away, frowns at me and shakes her head as she continues to sing.

I pull a face and resort to mummery in an attempt to convey my mission without the use of words. In the end, I stick out my belly, ape the gait of a pregnant woman and point earnestly in the direction of the guest chamber. She looks at me blankly until the gist of my message filters through. Then she puts down her prayer book, whispers in the prioress' ear and hurries with me from the chapel.

"How long since she felt the first pain?"

"I don't know, Sister."

We cross the quadrangle and pass the dormitory building toward the guest chamber. Throwing open the door, we discover Grace straddled on the bed, her expression contorted with fear and agony ... and shame.

"Margery!" she cries when we enter. "I am so sorry. The bed, my shift – they are wet."

Sister Maude casts an eye about the room, assessing the situation, and places a tentative hand on Grace's brow as if she suspects a fever. She smiles uncertainly and, with great hesitancy, places her other hand on Grace's belly. Her face slackens, fear blossoming. She clears her throat, fumbling for composure.

"Fetch help, Margery. Ask Sister Christiana and … and perhaps Sister Dorothea too, and tell the others they must pray."

As I turn to do as I am bid, Grace makes a sound I have heard only in the cowshed. With a last desperate look at her, I flee the room. This time, I burst unceremoniously into the church and shout across the nave.

"Sister Maude needs help. She begs that Sister Christiana and Sister Dorothea be allowed to join her in the guest quarters."

The lyrical voices dwindle away. The prioress lowers her prayer book.

"What is it, girl?"

"It is Grace. Her child is coming. Sister Maude sent me to fetch help."

She closes her eyes and breathes audibly through her nose.

"Very well, do as she asks."

She does not look at me again and before we have even left the confines of the church, the singing resumes, reminding me I have not passed on Sister Maude's entire message. I turn around, my voice echoing to the roof:

"Sister Maude also suggests you pray for a safe delivery!"

With a sharp flick of her wrist, the prioress orders me from her presence and I flee from her sight.

Softly, I close the door and creep to join the nuns at the bedside. The moment she notices my presence, Sister Maude takes me by the shoulders and tries to propel me from the room.

"This is no place for you. Go to the kitchens and heat some water, and fetch something to wrap the child in when it comes."

Beyond her, I just glimpse Grace's terrified face. Our eyes meet and she reaches for me, shrieking my name. I strain away from Maude's grasp.

"She needs me!"

"The birthing chamber is no place for a girl," she repeats and my knees crack, my palms stinging as she hurls me through the door to sprawl on the tiled floor. Fury fills my heart.

"It's no place for a nun, either!" I yell and, with the worst words I can think of on my lips, I do as I am bid and hurry to the kitchens.

To my joy, I find a vat of water already warming on the fire. I heave it off and fill a jug, snatching up a handful of the linen cloths that Sister Juliana uses to strain the cheese. As fast as I can I hasten back to Grace. Women die from childbirth. My own mother perished from it.

This time, they do not heed me when I enter. The number of nuns in attendance has increased to five. They crowd the bed, offering useless advice to one another. Sister Dorothea suggests that everyone loosen their girdles, for she's heard that knots in the birthing chamber can hinder the progress of the delivery.

"I've heard the queen wore the Virgin's girdle to ensure an easy birth," Sister Dorothea says.

"Little good it did her," answers Sister Juliana, sorrowfully shaking her head. I could scream at their incompetence. Why did nobody prepare for this?

Grace moans and we watch helplessly as she writhes, arching her back, her heels digging into the mattress. Through a fog of fear, I recall that earlier in the year, Queen Anne was delivered of a dead son.

"Perhaps it is time?"

Nobody moves. We cannot take our eyes from Grace's agony, the torment that has her in its grip. It may well be time for the child to come, but none of us knows what that might mean or what to do about it. Grace twists and screams. Someone must do something. I open my mouth, but before I can speak, the door opens and Sister Frances hurries in with a ball of twine. As her almond-shaped eyes move anxiously about the room, I suddenly realise she is just the person we need.

I spring forward and, pushing the nuns aside, hustle her closer to the bed.

"Sister Frances has saved many a calf and lamb in her time. It – it can't be much different, can it?"

Fear fills Frances' eyes. She shakes her head and tries to back away, but I hang onto her sleeve and point to the bed.

"Frances, if you don't help her, Grace may die! You don't want her to die, do you?"

Grace is grunting now, her face turning puce. Slowly, Frances' body relaxes and the nuns cluster about her, nodding and speaking all at once.

"Yes, yes, Sister Frances, you must help her; you simply must. It is your duty to do so."

They are glad, I realise, to be spared the duty themselves. They'd rather leave it to a simpleton than soil their own hands.

I cannot bear to listen or to look, but my gaze remains fastened to the bed, witnessing things I'd rather not see. I cannot tear them away. Grace's body is contorted, her screams loud enough to rouse the dead. As Frances takes her place at the foot of the bed, the nuns fall back and resort once more to prayer. Lacking any holy relics, we place our prayer books and crucifixes on the mattress.

"Please don't let her die."

I have forgotten how to pray properly, the English words of my made-up prayer interlace strangely with the Latin intonation of the nuns, but I do not stop.

Our voices rise and fall as Frances rolls up her sleeves. Grace groans and growls, arching her back, and when she emits a foul word, the praying nuns falter at the shock of it.

"Don't stop," I urge them. "Keep praying. She needs our prayers. Don't stop."

They begin again with increased urgency. I creep forward, crouch at Frances' side and whisper into her ear.

"What is wrong, can you tell?"

She shakes her head.

"Stuck," she says. "Child big. Grace little."

I wring my hands and begin to beseech God more fervently than before. I feel so helpless watching Grace's body convulse, the veins on her neck standing proud like ropes. She has become my friend, her initial sharpness softened into something compelling, something foreign. Indispensable. I cannot lose her now.

As I watch, the memory of Frances hauling a calf from its mother refuses to leave me. It was a large ugly beast with a malformed head and it perished soon after … but the cow survived. That is all that matters. Grace must survive. My lips move as I resume my former prayer, chanting the words of a rosary.

"Can't see." Sister Frances pushes Grace's bloodstained shift higher and eases her knees apart. I look away to where the nuns, their eyes tightly shut, implore God with renewed vigour. It is as hot as hell in here.

Elbowing past them, I throw open the shutter and carry a lantern closer to the bed, holding it high above

Frances' head. Time passes so slowly that I lose all track of how long I wait with my arms aching, my belly churning, my knees trembling. It could be a little after Terce or it could almost be time for None; I do not know. It feels as if I have stood here my whole life, with my ears filled with prayer, my body wracked with fear, watching as one dear friend fights for the life of another.

I have just about lost hope when Grace finally lets out a savage growl and falls back on the bed, her face as white as a winding sheet. Silence falls, even the sound of her breathing is hushed. With one hand, Frances fumbles for the knife. Blood spurts before she grabs a blanket and, wrapping something in it, thrusts it into my arms. I turn rigid with horror.

"Dead," she says, and turns her attention back to Grace.

Slowly, I turn toward the door. My heart is aching, my dry eyes riveted on the bed, not knowing if Grace lives or not. Once she learns of the death of her child, I doubt she will wish to. I look down at the burden I am carrying and wonder what I am to do with it.

The tiny body weighs nothing. I hold it close to my chest, afraid of harming it, although it is beyond injury. I reach out and open the door. With each step I take farther from the birthing chamber, the ache in my chest increases. Agony.

In the kitchens, the fire has burned away, our breakfast bowls still litter the table, and one of the farmyard cats is lapping milk from the jug. I remember I haven't yet milked Marigold, or fed the hens, and nobody has begun to prepare our evening meal. The birth and death of this child has set our whole day awry.

I hiss at the cat, scaring it away, and look down at the bundle I am holding. Tentatively, I draw aside the covering and force myself to look at it. I expect to find a monster, like the deformed calf, but instead I discover I am holding a tiny miracle in my arms.

He is finely wrought; his perfect features tinged blue as if he is made of marble. His lips, his nose, his mouth are quite perfect but he has no hair, and the delicate tracery of veins on his skull reminds me of a decaying autumn leaf. If he were to open his eyes, I know they'd be blue, the exact shade of his mother's ...

I feel heavy, overwhelmed with sadness, the futility of it all. I think of the things he'll never do, the smiles he'll never give, the kisses he'll never receive, and in those moments, I feel love for the very first time. Somewhere inside the cavity of my chest, the sharpest pain I have ever known flares and burns, forging a link with this dead child that will never be broken.

I place my lips on his temple and close my eyes, breathing him in as my heart slowly cracks. When I open them again, I imagine I see a faint pulse beating on the top of his head. Fearfully, I place my fingers over it and sense a weak throb of life, a pulse of hope so faint it is scarcely there. But it is enough.

With a shriek, I tear open the blanket and give him a gentle shake. I scream his name, although none was ever chosen. With tears of terrified joy on my cheek, I recall Frances breathing life into dead lambs, forcing breath into the lifeless corpses of newborn calves. Brushing the plates and bowls from the table, I lay him down and begin to rub his body, chafe his limbs, crying and shouting as I do so.

"Live, little boy," I cry, as power surges through my body. "You have to breathe! You have to live! Come on, Andrew! Come on!"

I lean over him, cover his mouth with mine and blow gently, watching his chest rise and fall. Then I gently rub him all over, afraid I am too rough for he is so delicate. I fear I'll break him.

Slowly, oh so slowly, his skin appears a little less grey, his lips a little less blue and a little more pink. An age later, his body moves and stiffens, his features contract and he grimaces, opens his mouth and sucks in his stomach. I stand back.

"Oh God, oh God, oh God, *please!*"

His tiny chest heaves and he spews up something foul, coughing and spluttering before opening his mouth and giving vent to unholy rage.

During my fearful, joyful, desperate rush back to the birthing chamber, I imagine the elation of the nuns when they realise what I have done. In my mind's eye, I see Grace's face opening with elation, I see the nuns falling to their knees, weeping prayers of thanks to God in His great mercy. I imagine myself hailed as His instrument – a saviour of this tiny almost lost soul. But my reception is very different.

Nobody even notices I've returned. I have to push my way to the side of the bed, shake Grace's shoulder to make her look at me. Her face is wan and grey, her expression dull, and when I raise my shaking arms and offer her son to her, she makes no exclamation of joy. Instead, she rolls away, and the world turns a little colder and darker.

Despite my pleading, she refuses to look at him; she will not hold or nurse him.

"Grace, Grace, I know if you held him just once, your heart would open to him."

How can she resist him? I look down at his pinched, disgruntled face and love pours afresh into my heart. "Sister Maude, you speak to her. He will surely die if he is not nursed soon."

She shrugs. "If that is so, then it is God's will."

Speechlessly, I watch her gather up her basket and quit the chamber. They all leave us, one by one, tiptoeing away, leaving the child to perish in my arms. For the first time in my life, I see them as they really are: ruled by the narrow stricture of the church; iron-willed, intractable, and hard.

"Is it because he is a bastard?" I call after them. "I am a bastard too but you didn't leave me to perish on your doorstep. Why is it different for him?"

A hand falls on my arm and I turn to find Sister Frances. There is a tear on her cheek; her usually dancing eyes are downcast with sorrow. Pitifully, she shakes her head.

"What can I do? I can't just let him die."

My voice is no more than a whisper. She pats my arm and her round face stretches into smiles.

"Marigold," she says. "Milk!"

For weeks, the child jousts with death. Some days I think we will lose him; other days I think he will thrive. He is grizzly, unhappy to be apart from me. When I try to lay him in an old produce crate to sleep between feeds, he screams so hard I fear he will rupture something. In the end, Sister Dorothea suggests I strap him about my waist as the peasant women do. After that, he accompanies me about my working day. Soon, I grow so used to him that he is like an extra limb I can neither use nor dispense with. Sometimes, I hate the hold he has over me and rue the day he ever came into my life. His red, roaring face and ever-questing mouth fills me with the sinful impulse to leave him to his fate, return him to his mother, refuse to dedicate hours of my time to trickling Marigold's goodness into his ungrateful mouth. But at other times – usually when he has just been fed and has fallen into peaceful slumber, I look down at his bone-white skull, the tracery of veins on his temple, the purplish hue of his eyelids, and wonder what my life was without him.

Somehow, with God's help, I manage to pull him through the first few weeks of life. The nuns ignore his presence but they do not chide me for tardiness when my chores are neglected, or scold me when I am late to prayers. As he grows and his personality develops, I realise I should probably give him a name and persuade the nuns to christen him. Henry, perhaps, after the king, or James or John after the apostles ... but then, a memory sparks of those furious moments I spent wrestling for his life on the day of his birth. I addressed him then as Andrew and it seems to me now that God, or some guardian angel, had placed that name on my tongue.

I lift him up, dangle him in the air, and he regards me though slitted, disapproving eyes. He is an ugly little thing. I smile and anoint his forehead with my lips.

"You shall be called Andrew, after our patron saint," I tell him, and as I kiss him again, his face turns purple, as if in judgement of my choice. His whole body stiffens while he strains every muscle and releases the contents of his bowels in a great explosion.

"Andrew! I have only just changed your linen!" I cry as I go in search of a bowl of water and some fresh clouts.

July 1536

The month draws to an end. The last few weeks have been warm and the physic garden is burgeoning with growth. Taking advantage while Andrew slumbers, I gather marigolds and chamomile to take to the still room. As I work, I keep one eye on the position of the sun. He will wake soon and clamour to be fed and cleaned, so I must make the most of the quiet sunlit garden while I can.

His bottom is often red raw and it took a great deal of wheedling to persuade Sister Maude to show me how to prepare a soothing salve. It is a great pity she cannot make him a sleeping draught so I can get the rest I need. Although I managed to gain permission to be excused from attending the night services, the nuns often wake me on their way to quire – usually when I have just slipped into an uneasy sleep. My eyes are constantly tired and sore from lack of sleep and my mood is scratchy, as if I have burrs beneath my shift.

Now that she has no further need of a private chamber, Grace is ordered to sleep in the dormitory with the rest of us. But while Andrew shares my bed at one end, she chooses to sleep at the other. These days, she will not even look at me, and I am hurt by the withdrawal of her friendship. I wonder what I have done to deserve such treatment. I miss her and the glimpse she provided of the outside world, but she behaves like a polite and chilly stranger, not at all like a fellow member of our community. Joy has vanished from her soul and in its place lurks a serious, often unpleasant demon. It is Sister Juliana who informs me that Grace is studying to take the veil.

"Grace is to become a nun?" I frown. I know she has no vocation and it is clear to me, if no one else, that her decision to dedicate her life to God is because she believes there is no other choice.

There is always a choice, I grumble angrily to myself. She is young and beautiful and should ride far away from Arden. Hiding away behind the cloister will deny her the things she needs to thrive – like depriving a flower of water and light.

As if my thoughts have summoned her, Grace enters the refectory in the company of Sister Dorothea and Sister Christiana. She doesn't even glance my way as she takes her place at the far end of the table. I watch as she gives thanks for her food and, with eyes downcast, begins to nibble at a crust and daintily sup her pottage. This is not Grace. She was never so constrained. Am I the only one to see there is something wrong? Is she ailing; hiding some infection picked up in childbed; or is she purposely hiding her real self, concealing her inner spark in case it should be perceived as sin? Is she afraid someone will see it and try to stamp it out?

My mind drifts back to the afternoons we used to spend on the heath, airing our knees to the sunshine. In those days, the world seemed a fine place and we spoke of foolish, girlish things. For a few short months I had a friend, a companion and confidant, and it breaks my heart to have lost her. I miss her wit, her humour, and the stories of the outside world that seemed so far-fetched. It is a stranger who sits in her place at the table now, not the girl who arrived here all those months ago, or the mother-to-be who pondered with such longing on the shade of her unborn child's eyes. What has happened?

A murmur of voices pulls me from my reverie, drawing my gaze along the length of the table. Sister Christiana is whispering in Dorothea's ear, her gesturing arms testament to some upset. Surreptitiously, I shuffle along the bench, the better to hear.

I catch the words 'queen' and 'princess', and from the sorrowful shaking of their heads, I guess they are speaking of the death of Queen Catherine, who passed a few months ago. It took time for word to reach us but, although it is forbidden, we remember her in our prayers. We are instructed that we must no longer think of her as 'queen', but she will never be anything else, not to us. She was a pious, devout woman who bore witness against the torment of the king and his concubine. In death, she has become akin to a saint and I can easily picture her sitting at God's right hand. I wonder what report she will carry to Him of the king ...

The murmur swiftly rises to a hubbub that is quickly extinguished by the entrance of the prioress. I put down my spoon.

"Sisters." She clasps her hands together and I notice her eyes are bright with unshed tears, her face as colourless as linen on laundry day. "We have had some … rather startling and distressing news from court. It seems that the queen … back in May … Queen Anne was executed…"

The silence roars. The prioress entwines her fingers, knuckles white. "… and the king has taken a new wife. We now must pray for Queen Jane and hope that she bears the king a living heir … very soon."

She leaves us without another word and the voices in the refectory rise to a babble. "Jane who? Does anyone know? What happened to Anne? Oh, poor, poor woman. What did she do to offend the king?"

"I cannot imagine. The king was besotted with her for years … I cannot *believe* this has happened…"

The conversation clamours in my ears. Dully, I pick up my spoon and ponder life's uncertainties. What security do any of us have if even a queen can be riding high one day and cast low the next?

Our humble, gossip-starved souls continue to speculate on the events at court. It has been a perilous year for the king. In January, his estranged queen perished; he suffered a fall from his horse, which caused Anne Boleyn to give birth to a stillborn son; and then he learned he'd been the victim of sorcery, tricked into the marriage by way of witchcraft! Her execution followed swiftly, as did his subsequent wedding to Jane Seymour, a woman whom they say is different in every degree to her predecessor.

How hard it must be for so great a king as Henry to fail in the begetting of a male heir. What a blow to his virility. I look down at Andrew, who slumbers on my chest with milky drool on his chin. I dab it dry with my cuff. How effortless this child's conception was. It is cruel that bastards are so cheaply begotten while royal heirs are so dearly bought. The sisters of Arden pray fervently that this new queen, Jane, will produce a prince quickly, for the sake of England, before she too falls from the king's favour.

Summer peaks in a blaze of sunshine, giving way to persistent rain that lingers throughout August. We battle on, harvesting what we can between downpours, bottling fruit and brewing cures and possets in readiness for winter. I dread the onset of autumn, the slow, uncontainable return of winter ailments, bone-grinding cold and long dark evenings. I determine to make the most of the summer, try to grasp hold of it before it slips resolutely away.

One morning, finding myself between chores, I encounter Grace in the cloister and step into her path, barring her way.

"Walk with me on the moor," I say. "The rain has ceased, we should make the most of the sunshine … I can leave the bairn with Sister Frances if his presence offends you."

She frowns, looks away and folds her arms.

"I have to help Sister Maude…"

"She won't notice if you are late."

"I can't."

Refusing to let her mulish face dissuade me, I tilt my head to one side.

"I won't talk about Andrew. I swear I won't even mention him or tell you what I think you should do … or not do."

She pushes past me and stalks across the cloister. I wish I knew what was wrong with her. Why has she changed? As she reaches the garden door, some instinct makes me call after her. "I miss our friendship, Grace. You are like a sister to me; a blood sister, I mean."

She stops dead, balls her hands into fists and turns abruptly to face me.

"I can allow you ten minutes in the physic garden, if that will suffice."

Joy floods through me. "I will just take Andrew to Sister Frances who is in the kitchen, and then I shall meet you there."

My feet skim along the diagonal path across the cloister garden and in through the door that leads to the kitchens. As I run, my fingers fumble at the knots that hold Andrew snug against my back. I discover Frances sitting on a low stool, a chicken held upside down in her lap while she tends its injury. My sudden calling of her name startles her and she lets it go, yelping as the bird flutters indignantly away in a shower of feathers.

"Please, look after the child. I shall be ten minutes, no more, I promise."

I plonk him on her lap and she takes hold of him warily, bouncing him inexpertly on her knee when he wails at the abrupt separation. Determined not to be swayed by his infantile manipulations, his cries dwindle as I hurry away. Once I near the garden, I slow my pace and force myself to be calm.

Grace is waiting by the crumbling sundial, her form diffused by the light that filters through the ancient apple tree. She looks wraith-like and insubstantial, as if at any moment she may dissipate into a cloud of mist. The sound of my feet draws her eye; the faint smile, which in reality is just a lightening of her habitual frown, reassures me.

"Grace." I reach out to her and she looks down at my fingers resting on her sleeve. "I am so glad to see you. We never speak anymore, not since ..."

"You promised not to speak of it."

"I am sorry."

Yet, how can I not speak of him when his very existence lies at the heart of our problems? He may be anathema to her, but does she not understand that he has become the centre of my world? "I wish we could find a way for us to continue as before. You are the only friend I've ever had."

After a long moment, we turn and stroll between the flowerbeds, where plants beaten down by the recent rain loll across the path. We step over them, the aroma of damp earth and roses rising in a heady perfume.

"Things are different now," she says. "I am to take my vows soon, and you are still a novice. We all change and grow, Margery, nothing remains the same forever."

I gaze about the garden that looks exactly as it always has.

"Nothing ever changes here. Arden has always been the same. People come and go, some seeking God, some seeking solace, but Arden itself is unchanging until the end of days."

"A comforting thought," she says, and I think she has relaxed a little. There is less chilliness in her tone. "But *I* have changed. The birth ... altered something in me. Something I never even knew was there."

"What? What did it change?" I speak softly, so as not to scatter her thoughts.

"Oh." She shrugs, narrowing her eyes as she searches for the correct words to express her meaning. "I am empty of happiness, of life; like a tree in winter, all my joy has fled. There used to be lightness in my soul. It dimmed a little when I was sent away from home but when I came here and saw how ... *uncowed* you were by circumstance, I grew brave again. Through you, I thought I'd learned all there was to be learned, but then when the child came, oh ... such pain, Margery! It seems such a harsh punishment for so small a sin. It taught me that God is not to be trifled with. He has laid a path before me and I dare not veer from it. I must follow His every command or ... suffer the consequences."

"What path, Grace? What do you mean?"

I grasp her wrist and pull her onto a turf seat beside me where we are engulfed by the scent of camomile and roses. We clasp hands. Hers are cold as I force myself to wait patiently for her reply. For a long moment, she stares at the path, before lifting her head and beginning to speak.

"Sister Christiana says my arrival here was not by chance. She believes I was sent here for some purpose known only to God and I must follow it, whether I want to or not."

The breath rushes from my body. As I struggle to keep a rein on my temper, I inwardly curse Sister Christiana for a fool. I count to ten while I compose myself.

"But, if that is the case, why does He keep you from your son? If God sent you here then He also gave you Andrew. Why won't you even look at him? Aren't you even curious?"

She plucks a rose that has balled in the recent rain and begins to peel away the upper layers, stripping away the dead and decaying outer petals to reveal the soft white beauty beneath.

"At first, I think I was too shocked by what had happened to want to look at him. My body was sore, and I was traumatised by the … the indignity of it all. But … after a few days, when I'd begun to heal, when I heard him crying in the night … my breasts would ache." She looks down. I expect to see tears but somehow she regains her poise and lifts her chin. With a ghost of her old smile, she shrugs. "It was too late, Margery. I had turned away from him and I saw that you had taken my place. You are his mother now."

She looks away, her throat working as she struggles to contain her sorrow. When she speaks again, her voice is hoarse with unshed tears. "One afternoon, Sister Christiana found me weeping in the dormitory and she took pity on me. Her certainty and faith in God's plan has been my salvation. She has set me on a new path. I can only trust that her teaching is right."

"Grace." Something is lodged painfully in my throat. I try to swallow it. "He is still your son. I have brought him this far and hope to always have a place in his life, but *you* are his mother. You would feel differently if you just held him. Let me bring him to you."

She shrugs off my arm, stands up and takes a few agitated steps along the path. Then she stops and half turns back to face me.

"I will consider ... what you say. I will pray and seek guidance. I have to try to work out how, as a mother, I can live as a nun, or – or more importantly, how as a nun, I can live as the mother of a bastard. It seems there is a choice to be made. I can never have both."

She hurries away, her skirts skimming across the flowers at the edge of the path, sending a cloud of dandelion seed floating across the garden.

Grace has changed. I miss the vibrant, brave girl I used to know. She reminds me of a flower deprived of water, wilting, her youth fading. The nun's habit drains her face of colour and she has lost weight since the birth, her cheekbones are sharp, her jaw tense, her lips pursed. There is no joy in her now and the worldliness I once found so fascinating is tarnished, her vivid tongue giving voice only to prayer. Grey and black, pale and beaten, she is turning into one of us, and I don't know how to stop it.

I am in the garden gathering herbs to leaven the blandness of our supper. Andrew is lying on the grass, clutching at butterflies, laughing at something I cannot see. My thoughts have drifted far away when I hear the sound of rapid footsteps on the gravel – someone is running across the cloister. I look up sharply, scrambling to my feet as Frances hurtles through the gate.

"What is it, Frances?"

She catches her breath, panting, her muddy habit clutched in one hand, her knee bleeding where she must have tumbled on her hasty journey.

"Men back." Her finger wavers in the direction of the priory gatehouse. My heart leaps sickeningly.

"The king's men?"

She nods, her face stark with fright. Handing her my half-filled basket, I pat her shoulder.

"Don't worry," I say, with more conviction than I really feel. "Take this to the kitchens. I will discover what is happening."

Scooping Andrew into my arms, I hurry across the precinct, encountering Sister Juliana approaching from the direction of the church.

"Did you hear? The king's men are back. They are closeted with the prioress in her chambers."

Together, we raise our eyes to the closed door and wonder what is happening within. Knowing yet dreading the reason for this second visit from the king's commissioners. All across England, the smaller abbeys and priories are closing. We are lucky to have lasted this long.

"There is no stopping it," she says. "Arden will be dissolved, and we shall be sent away, our sisterhood dispersed."

It is unthinkable. It *cannot* happen. Arden has stood for hundreds of years; never affluent, never offending either pope or monarch. What possible benefit can our closure bring the king? We have no treasures. We are not like Rievaulx Abbey or Fountains – we are *nothing.*

'We must alert the others." Sister Juliana's feet skim across the untended mead. I am about to follow when the door to the prioress' chamber opens. Too slow to conceal myself, I stand very still and watch.

The prioress appears suddenly elderly, as old as Sister Dorothea; she holds her body stiffly, her expression stricken. Beneath her elbow, her little dog wrestles for freedom, but she ignores him, clamping him to her side while the fingers of her left hand unconsciously burrow in his fur. I wish she'd release him that we might witness his needle-like teeth sink sharply into the ankle of the man before her; a man clad all in black, who holds the fate of Arden in the palm of his hand.

His lips are moving but I cannot hear his words. From the prioress' face, it is clear he addresses her with discourtesy. His gestures are sharp, his expression scarred with hate. She says something in return and fury passes over him like a storm, then he clatters loudly down the stair. The prioress stands so still, it is as if she is made of stone. I move toward her, and she looks at me with empty eyes.

"You must summon the others," she says. "I must tell them ..."

Her voice breaks as she turns away and I reach out, breaching convention by tugging at her sleeve.

"Tell them what? What is going to happen?"

At first, I think she is going to ignore me as she always does. I am, after all, the lowliest of servants here.

"Oh." She pauses, her throat working as she struggles to find her voice. "Arden is to be closed. We all have to leave."

Rumour runs across the country like a plague, reaching even the cloisters. We hear that parish churches have been robbed of plate and taxed heavily, unaffordable levies for marriages, christenings and burials. Wilder rumours circulate of a new tariff placed upon white bread, goose and capon, and every man in the realm forced to give account of his property and income. It is not just Arden that lives in fear; it is the whole of England. Everyone resents change.

The sisters and I, who have lived and worked and prayed together for so long, cleave to one another in the final days. Only the prioress remains aloof, shut away in her chamber, doing only God knows what. We gather at the infirmary to be close to Sister Mary. We arrive in ones and twos, on the pretext of searching for a posset to ease our aching heads, or to soothe our palpitating hearts. But the thing we really crave is company; the reassurance of our sisters.

Sister Mary clutches at Dorothea's habit.

"They won't really send me away, will they? I've been 'ere for sixty year, I am far too old to undertake a journey."

Sister Dorothea removes the clinging hand and places it gently on the counterpane.

"Whatever happens, Sister Mary, you can be sure God will be with us."

The old woman's face falls and her skeletal fingers grasp the covers as a single tear begins a convoluted journey down the furrows of her cheek.

"God will have his vengeance on them, on the king and those who do his dirty work." The loose skin of Sister Maude's jowl quivers in outrage, her lips a bitter slash of grief while, at her side, Sister Christiana shakes her head.

"It is a sorry time. The sorriest England has ever known. I could almost believe God has forsaken us…"

"God would never abandon us," Sister Maude cuts in. "Sometimes, his ways are mysterious, but in the end, if we are steadfast, all will be well. It is perhaps a test … of our worthiness."

Andrew stirs in my arms. I rock back and forth, soothing him back to sleep, envious of his oblivion. I look at the nuns gathered around me, faces I have known my whole life. Between them, they've played the part of parent, teacher, advisor and friend. Despite frequent feuds and ill-feeling, they are my family, all I have. Sister Frances slips her hand into mine and I turn to look into her frightened eyes. How much does she comprehend of our situation? How much of her fear is triggered by our own?

A footstep on the threshold announces Grace's arrival. She takes a seat between Sister Christiana and Sister Maude. I wish she had chosen to sit with me. I try to catch her attention but her glance flickers away. As his fractious cries begin again, I jiggle her child on my knee.

"Where've you been?" I ask, forcing her to acknowledge me.

"Praying," she says.

Anger gushes from my mouth as if some devil is working my tongue. I lean forward, surprising even myself with my venom.

"As if that will do any good. We've prayed for years, before all this happened, and since the king's commissioners first came we have prayed harder and more frequently than ever before. I think the time for prayer has passed ..."

While the sisters regard me with horror, Andrew squirms, opens his mouth and begins to scream. I shift him to my shoulder and pat his back a little too roughly, making his voice waver. Grace rises to her feet.

"What do you suggest then, Margery? Taking up arms and marching on London?"

There is misery in her eyes that cannot mask her contempt before she moves away to sit by herself. She is the picture of loneliness but I turn away, too angry to relent. If only we *could* march on London; if only every monk and nun in the land could stand up to the king and put a stop to this with a loud and final 'NO!'

We have no alternative but to pray, of course, but, despite the hours spent on our knees, the orders giving details of our departure arrive. The prioress calls us to the chapter house, where we sit in a circle to listen as our fate is revealed. She coughs, her throat constricting, the skin slack beneath her chin.

"The elders of our community, sisters Juliana, Christiana and Dorothea, are to join the sisterhood at Wilberfoss Priory, just a short distance from York."

The three nuns exchange tense glances. Christiana crosses her chest and begins to pray. The prioress smiles at Dorothea.

"Sister Mary, who is in your care, is to receive a pension, so she may live out her days in comfort."

Dorothea nods her understanding. "I will tell her when I return to the infirmary."

"Where is she to live out her days?" I stand up, speaking out of turn, without first seeking permission. "And what about me? Where am I to go? And what is to become of Grace and Sister Frances?"

"There is no further instruction."

"So, we can stay?"

The prioress lets the parchment fall.

"Oh no, I very much doubt that."

My stomach twists.

"So, we are to be cast out? Offered no support, no shelter? You know what will happen, don't you? We will likely be taken up as vagrants, beaten from town to town, shunned and reviled by decent folk everywhere!"

The prioress is broken. Her eyes close and a tear trickles from beneath her lashes, but I am not moved to pity. I cannot allow this to happen. I pass Andrew roughly into Frances' care. "Hold the child, Frances." I push my way forward and the prioress takes a step backwards, not disguising her annoyance. Clasping my damp hands and struggling to swallow the tears that threaten to suffocate me, I summon my courage and school my tone to a more subservient level.

"Where are Grace, Sister Frances and me to go? I have a child to care for; what is to become of us?"

"It is beyond my control, as is all of this sorry … mess." Her voice is placatory, her expression passive, accepting.

"Why has Sister Frances not been offered a place with the other nuns?"

She looks beyond me, to a spot high on the wall, her face lined with fatigue, all trace of her former haughtiness vanished.

"No house would take her; her ... difficulties ... make her strange, people may find her ... off putting."

"So she is to be abandoned, and Grace also, whose family paid good coin when they placed her with you for protection. And I, who have been cared for by this house since infancy, am to be cast off?"

"It is not my doing."

"But we are *your* responsibility. You cannot just wash your hands of us, as if we are of no account."

Her bloodshot eyes dart in their sockets as she searches for an excuse, something to justify her lack of action. Throughout my life, she has seemed as spotless as the Virgin. I have obeyed her, made excuses for her often harsh treatment of the nuns, but now I realise she is weak. Her status, her blood, her position is wholly tainted by selfishness; there is nothing truly pious about her at all. She was born of wealthy stock; that is all. Her status as prioress was purchased, and all these years the lives of the nuns of Arden have been overseen by someone unworthy of her position.

Involuntarily, my lip curls with contempt. If I were in her place, I'd fight to my last breath for the safety of those in my care. She is nothing but a spoiled, privileged coward and it no longer matters that she knows it. I slam my right fist hard against my left palm, and she jerks back as if afraid I will strike her. Her annoying little dog leaps from beneath her habit, barking like a devil, his teeth snagging on the hem of my habit. I kick him away and, with a yelp, he slinks back beneath her skirts. I regard him with a mirthless laugh. Like his mistress, he too is all bark and no bite.

I take a deep breath. I must try to reason with her; perhaps there is still time for me to instil a little starch into the weak fabric of her soul.

"You *must* assert your authority. You might not be able to influence the king, or save the priory, but save your servants you must – remember, God sees into your heart. He knows your cowardice and you will pay for it come Judgement Day."

In turning her own words back on her, I have never been so earnest. It is as if I am watching an effigy of myself from somewhere high up on the wall. I speak with the tongue of a stranger; someone strong and determined. Someone with influence.

I wait, hoping for a change of heart, a sudden decision that will alter everything, but when she speaks, her voice wavers ... supplicating my pity. From the corner of my eye I see the other sisters turn ashamedly away, leaving me and the prioress alone. Her grandeur has faded completely away.

"Margery ... I can't bear it. I don't know what to do. This situation is unprecedented ..."

Her hands tremble, her head droops onto her palms and, to my surprise, her shoulders heave. But I feel no pity, only sickness at her weakness. She has been raised in comfort; even here at Arden her life has been cushioned, unchallenging. Making no attempt to conceal my disgust, I reach for her quill, dribbling ink across her desk as I thrust it into her hand. I will have to make the decision for her.

"Write a letter. When the sisters leave for Wilberfoss, me, Grace, Frances will travel with them. Hopefully, the prioress there will have some pity and grant us shelter; we can offer to earn our board by servitude ... as we have done here."

To my surprise, she reaches obediently for a clean sheet of parchment and I listen to the sound of the nib scratching across the page. I take the letter from her without thanks and, on reaching the door, heave it open so violently that it slams back against the wall. The dog's courage is restored by my retreat and he rushes after me, snarling and snapping at my ankles. I take great satisfaction when the door swings back on him, and his agonised yelps follow me down the stair.

When I wake the next morning, the birds have just begun to herald the dawn. For once, Andrew is still sleeping, his body curled around me, his cheek hot and moist on my breast. Carefully, I ease my arm from beneath him and creep away for a few moments, escaping to the freshness of the cloister garden. It is perfect. Dew clings to the flower heads and beads the leaves of the ladies mantle, and the sweet cicely that froths like a lace collar around the sundial. I follow the path to the medicinal beds and begin to gather more chamomile to ease Andrew's colic. If our departure is imminent, I must dry some to take with me on our journey. When my basket is half-full, I pause at the gate and notice how gently the sunlight plays upon the flowers, the soft fall of spent petals on the grass. My heart catches.

This may be the last time I ever walk here, yet the scent of the blooms, the gentle decay of earth and moss and sun-warmed stone will forever linger in my heart. Blinking moisture from my eye, I tread softly along the gravel path to where the chamomile mingles with the sweetbriar and the last of the roses. My step falters. My hand flies to my mouth and, for a moment, I cannot believe what I am seeing. I fall to my knees, my anguish keening in the silence of the garden.

"Sister Mary." Her robes are sodden with dew; she must have lain here all night. My heart twists. Gently, I try to turn her, but she is heavy and I am forced to heave her onto her back. As I look upon her cold, stiff face I know the worst, but I reach out to touch her hand, hoping to find it warm. Something slips from her fingers. Tentatively, I reach out and pick it up, the truth dawning slowly and horribly.

"Oh God, forgive you for such wickedness," I begin to pray, my words falling over themselves in my haste to secure her entry into Heaven. "I beg you take poor Sister Mary's soul into Heaven." As I repeat the words over and over, I search the garden to ensure I am not being watched. Hurriedly, I tuck the damning phial away in my pocket so none but God and me shall know the truth. And then, with a leaden heart, I reach out and close her lids and rest my cheek upon the stilled breast of the woman who raised me.

We lay Sister Mary to rest beneath the soft sward of the priory churchyard. Rain has fallen overnight but, as we lower her inch by painful inch into the grave, a watery sun emerges. It glints on the leaves, the sodden roof of the church. When the service has been read, we go about our duties. As the others tiptoe away along the puddled path, I linger and watch as Luke and Mark fill the grave with earth. After the boys have gone, I sink to my knees in the long, damp grass. "Nobody can displace you now, Sister Mary. You are, and forever will be, part of Arden."

As I whisper this final message, my fingers are busily pushing newly rooted cuttings into the stony soil, cuttings I struck in calmer days: rosemary for remembrance; sage for wisdom; violets, both blue and white, for loyalty and purity. When I am done, I say a final prayer and leave the churchyard; with each step, the phial concealed deep within my pocket bounces against my thigh. I can only hope that God forgives me for concealing her crime and allows her a place in Heaven.

October 1536

The day has come. Once, I would have been glad of the adventure of leaving Arden. I would have set off eagerly to discover the world beyond the valleys and moors of my tiny slice of Yorkshire. Then, I would have been safe in the knowledge that the priory and everything within it would be waiting to welcome me home. But today, each step that takes me farther from it is like a tether around my heart. There can be no return.

Andrew is a weight on my back, his head nodding on my shoulder, his feet swaying at my hip. At my side, Sister Frances stumbles beside me, one hand clutching my girdle, the other clasping a sack containing a few meagre possessions. She does not speak but I am aware of her unasked questions, the tears in her eyes. How can I explain to such a simple soul that we have been cast out on the whim of the king? I doubt she even knows his name. Yet, to feed his empty coffers and salve his desperation for a son, our world is turned upside down. I cannot explain something I do not understand myself. God rot the king.

They say he is pleased with his new queen, who is meek where Anne was forthright. It is said she has embraced her role as stepmother to the king's daughters and has asked that they be allowed back to court. It is not long since they were royal princesses, but now Lady Mary and Lady Elizabeth are merely the king's bastards, as displaced and dispossessed as I. At least they have the benefit of a stepmother to protect them from the vagaries of the king.

Summer lingers on, the air remaining hot and sultry, although the leaves are turning and the nights are drawing in. We begin each day wrapped in our insufficient cloaks, yet by noon we have thrown them off and search around for shade when we rest upon the wayside.

The road is coated with dust; the ruts made during August rain have dried hard in the late summer sun. Frances' infirm foot is causing her pain. She limps along but tries her best to smile as I encourage her, telling her it is but a few steps more, just round the next bend. Soon, we have fallen behind the carts, where thick dust thrown up by the wheels smothers our faces and turns our habits grey. It lodges in my throat, my lips dry and crack, and the blister on my toe smarts like the devil.

When at last we spy a wayside inn and someone calls a halt, I sink gratefully into the long grass. I kick off my shoes and loosen the bonds that secure Andrew to my back. I lie down to look up at the sky that is blue and unblemished by cloud. I would give all I have to stay here and sleep, but the child is whimpering for his food and Frances' ankle needs tending. It is double the size it should be. I roll over and haul myself up again.

"Hush, Frances, do not weep. Let go my sleeve. Take Andrew while I will beg a ride for you on one of the carts for the rest of the way."

She blubbers into Andrew's hair while I hurry off in search of Sister Dorothea, whom I discover doling out rations to the hungry party.

"Sister Dorothea." I lower my head respectfully. "Sister Frances has injured her ankle and is in great pain. She cannot walk. Perhaps one of the other nuns would give up their seat in the cart for her?"

She sniffs and hands me a small loaf, a chunk of cheese.

"I will see to it," she nods curtly, not from unfriendliness but because she is overwhelmed with unaccustomed duties.

"Can I be of help, Sister?" I ask, in the hope that proving useful now will put me in her favour.

"No." She jerks her head in the direction of Andrew's wails. "See to the child before he deafens us all.

Here, take this." She offers me a skin of water. "Bathe Frances' ankle; it will soothe it but not heal."

I turn to go, almost bumping into Grace, who has come up unseen behind me. I cling to her arm.

"Grace, can you help? Sister Frances is injured and Andrew needs feeding. I cannot tend them both."

She nods sullenly.

While I spoon cold broth into Andrew's mouth, Grace lowers Frances' ankle into a bucket of cold water, her shattering cries at the shock attracting curious glances.

"What a horrible journey," I say by way of conversation. "The road is so hot and dusty."

"These things are sent to test us." She does not smile, does not meet my eye. Andrew refuses the next spoonful so I take the opportunity to poke some bread and cheese between my own lips.

"Have you eaten, Grace?" I ask, passing the bread to Sister Frances. "You are welcome to share with us."

"I have had sufficient." She looks away, across the group of bewildered travellers. "We shall be on the road again soon."

How it pains me to rise from the cool grass and resume the tortuous walk. My legs feel heavy and my eyes are sore and gritty. Andrew, overcome with heat and fatigue, soon sleeps again, and I try to keep my mind away from what awaits us. Instead, I focus on the repetitive tramp of our feet. Miles pass, miles of low-lying meadow, good pasture and thick wooded hills. We cross a stone arched bridge, where a fellow takes coin before we are allowed to cross.

As we reach a bend in the road, a shout goes up on the way ahead and we spy another small band of travellers. I crane my neck to the front of the cavalcade, and see that the strangers have stopped; probably as wary of robbers as we are. Our own steps falter and we wait while a figure detaches from the other party and lopes toward us. He is tall, slightly stooped, and wears a monk's habit. I release my breath before I am even aware I'm holding it. Holding his arms aloft, he moves slowly toward us, making it clear he means us no harm. He searches our faces to discover the sister in charge until he alights upon Dorothea sitting tall, with her whip held ostentatiously in her hand. I wonder if she'd dare to use it.

"What do you want?" Her voice is guarded, almost hostile.

"I mean no harm, Sister. We seek help. One of our brotherhood has fallen ill."

After considering a while, Sister Dorothea clambers from her seat and, keeping hold of her whip, follows the fellow toward the shade of an oak, beneath which his companions are gathered. I step forward to follow, and Grace joins me.

When we reach them, Sister Dorothea is leaning over an elderly monk who, from the hue of his cheek, has little time left on this earth.

The young monk blinks rapidly, pushing back his fringe from his sweating brow. "He was hale enough this morning but around noon he complained of tiredness and … and he collapsed soon afterwards."

Grace offers him a flask and he drinks deeply, smiling quickly in thanks. While Dorothea does what she can for the sick man, I stand awkwardly at Grace's side, unsure how to begin a conversation. Having seen few men in my life, I examine him closely when he isn't looking, noting the bristles on his chin, the broad set of his frame.

"Do you travel far?" he asks at last.

I open my eyes wide.

"We've travelled from Arden – two days journey for the likes of us."

"Did – was – has your priory also been closed?"

I hesitate before I make an answer, absorbing the stark misery in his face. He need not explain that his fate has been as sorry as ours. The lump in my throat grows harder as I nod. I swallow painfully.

"Yes, and our sisterhood dispersed."

"It's the same with us. It is happening everywhere, God rot him..."

"Amen."

It is Grace who has spoken and, startled by the venom in her voice, the monk and I both turn to look at her. She curls her lip. "We shouldn't stand for it. Margery is right. There are hundreds in our position. We should march on the capital and demand a return of our rights."

"I never said that. It wasn't what I meant!" I nudge Grace sharply in the ribs before turning back to the stranger. I shake my head in denial. "I would never say such a thing."

"But ... some houses are doing just that. In Lincolnshire, they are standing against it. They are demanding justice and not just religious folks either. I've heard tales of lay folk, gentlemen and nobles too, who deplore the king's actions and seek to turn him from this course. They believe he is misled by evil counsel and wish to put their case to him, show him the error he is making. Hundreds of years of devotion are being destroyed in an hour; hundreds of monks and nuns turned out; the sick and elderly with nowhere to turn to ... it is as if he hasn't thought the thing through..."

"Perhaps he doesn't care..."

I stop mid-sentence when I realise Sister Dorothea is closing the old man's eyes and praying over him, assigning his soul to God. The monk notices my distraction and turns, crying aloud before hurrying to the side of his friend. I am reminded of Sister Mary's passing and something inside me, that I had thought already broken, shatters a little more.

Wilberfoss Priory is vast compared to the crumbling modesty of Arden. We stumble through the gate, a weary, dusty band of travellers. While Andrew screams in my ear, I crane my neck at the soaring church tower, the opulent windows and, for the first time, understand that not every priory is like Arden.

I'd never quite understood the king's determination to claim the riches of the church, but now I see. This place must be wealthy indeed, and Wilberfoss is just one of many. Being so close to York, this foundation must benefit from the patronage of those eager to secure their place in Heaven. Generosity to the church is a sure way to erase earthly sin. I turn in a circle, my head tilted back, admiring the tracery of stonework embellishing the pinnacles that seem to almost pierce the heavens.

"It is so big!" I say, growing dizzy.

"And this is nothing compared to some of them. Rievaulx and Fountains are three or four times as big as this, for all their supposed Cistercian humility."

I turn toward the quiet voice and find the monk we had spoken to on the road. A flush of embarrassment creeps upon me. Unaccustomed to addressing strangers, let alone those of his sex, it takes a while for me to find my tongue.

"I've never been anywhere, never left Arden before."

As I speak its name, a longing for home washes over me. A yearning for the chaos of the kitchen; the stench of the barn; the solitude of the garden; the high empty moor; and the sighing winds of home…. Blinking rapidly to dispel the sorrow welling in my eyes, I turn away from him and focus my attention on the nun who has come out to greet us.

"Silence!" Her voice slices like a blade through the chatter. "At Wilberfoss, we pride ourselves on obedience, and our control of our tongues. Idle chatter is the result of idle minds. You will remember that while you are here."

Her announcement is greeted by shuffling feet and the exchange of rueful glances. Andrew begins to cry again and I jiggle him on my hip, but his snivelling draws the nun's attention. She raises her voice in an effort to speak over the din he is making. Many faces turn toward us and my cheeks begin to burn.

"Sister Eleanor will escort you to the refectory, where your names will be taken and further instruction given. Be so good as to conduct yourselves quietly and in a seemly manner."

She glares at me. Her mouth is lined and tight, her eyes burning with displeasure. As we move away, the monk catches my arm, forcing me to stop. Slowly, I look down at his fingers on my wrist. His nails are grimy from the road, and I notice how childlike my hand is next to his.

"We must say goodbye," he says. "I am to lodge here overnight before continuing to York in the morning. I am glad to have met you, Sister ... Sister ...?"

"Margery," I say. "I am just Margery."

"A novice?"

I shake my head and shrug my shoulders, realising I have no real status. I am nothing. "No. I am just a servant, I suppose."

"Oh, I had thought ... by your habit ..."

Frances tugs at my sleeve. I give an apologetic smile before heeding her.

"I wish you a safe journey," I call as he darts away across the compound. He lifts an arm in farewell before I turn to follow the others.

The vaulted roof of the refectory yawns above us. Our footsteps echo on the flagged floor and bounce off the high ceilings, turning our voices into clatter. I open my eyes at the rich tapestries, so bright in the gloomy hall. They depict the life of Christ, from his miraculous birth to his resurrection. I know the stories well but have never seen them brought to life so vividly before. Despite the nun's demand for silence, there is a babble of unmuted conversation as we anxiously wait in line. An unsmiling sister takes down our names and status.

Sister Dorothea gives her details first; she is then ushered to another corner where they hand her a pile of clothing and instruct her to leave by another door. Even Dorothea seems uncertain; her usual brisk manner is cowed and submissive. One by one, the nuns' names are recorded and, as the queue shortens, Frances begins to sniffle. I squeeze her hand, sensing she is dreading the moment they ask her name. She knows as well as I that her speech alone will mark her as an idiot. Grace is just before me. When they ask her name, she lifts her chin and speaks clearly, her cultured tone marking her as a gentlewoman. But it makes no difference. The nun frowns and runs the inky tip of her pen along the column.

"You are not on the list."

"Perhaps you have a separate list for novices. I have not yet taken my vows. I was due to do so when this … when we heard the priory was to be closed."

"There is but one list. If you are not on it, you cannot stay. Only those we have agreed to house are to be admitted. That is my instruction." She jerks her head at one of her fellow sisters, who steps forward to escort Grace away. I can contain myself no longer and, with my heart leaping in my chest, I push rudely forward.

"Where is she supposed to go? We were all part of Arden; provision should have been made for all of us."

She looks at me with a sour expression and puts down her pen, lacing her fingers as though she is about to pray.

"Am I to understand that your name will also not be on my list?"

I hoist Andrew higher on my hip.

"We will work as servants. We are strong and hard-working and require only food and shelter as payment."

"That is not in my instruction. You must go with the other girl. There is no place for you here."

"But the child! What is to become of us?"

"Yes. I see you have a child. Arden must have become very lax."

Her disdain is like a physical thing, it runs coldly over my body in the wake of her critical eyes. Fury rises within me like a swarm of bees and bursts impolitely from my lips.

"How dare you? I have a letter from our prioress! Is there no charity in this house? At Arden, we had none of the riches I see here, yet those in need were always welcomed, never turned away ..."

"This is not Arden, it is Wilberfoss. Now take your child and your simple friend and wait at the gate. It is possible you will be allowed to shelter here for one night, but in the morning, you must go."

"Go where?"

"That is not my concern."

Pursing her hirsute lips, she looks beyond me to the next in line and I am barged aside. I stumble into the cloister, hurry after Grace as she wanders, head down, toward the priory gate.

"Grace." My heart is hammering. "Where shall we go, what are we to do?"

Her small face is white and dirty, her eyes red and angry. She spits her next words as if everything is my fault, my doing.

"We shall have to join all the other vagrants on the road."

After a sleepless night, we are roused at dawn. A crust of bread is thrust into our hands before we are turned out onto the road. Grace stands a little apart from us but Frances clings to me, her cloying touch making me want to shake her off and run as fast as I can from the responsibility of caring for her, for the child ... for all of us. Andrew, his upper lip thick with snot, rubs his fist across his nose, smearing his cheeks. I stare at him for so long it begins to dry into a crust.

How has it come to this? Why have these innocents been thrust into my care when I am so ill equipped to protect them? Grace is walking stiffly away, her hands clenched into fists at her side.

"Grace!" I run after her, terrified of losing the only companion not solely reliant upon my strength. Her step does not falter but I catch up with her quite quickly, dragging the hapless Frances along with me. "Grace!" I cry her name again, grasp her arm and wrench her round to face me. I don't speak at once, as I try to catch my breath, panting like a dog that has lain too long in the sun. "We must stay together. The roads are perilous. We need each other. You must put your dislike of me aside, for all our sakes."

Her expression is devoid of emotion. She looks as if she scarcely knows me.

"The world does not centre on you, Margery. I do not dislike you, but I am ... lost."

"But we will find the way. You have us: Frances, Andrew and me. Together, we will survive. Let us seek shelter for today, away from the road, and consider our direction. There must be somewhere, some priory that will offer help ..."

"I doubt it. These days, there is much cruelty and very little charity left in the world. And all the religious houses are closing, there must be a thousand people like us, cast out, forgotten ... disregarded. If it was not a sin, I'd wish it all over, in an instant."

I stare at her aghast and hitch Andrew higher on my hip. He knuckles his eye and begins to whimper again, so to soothe him, I hook my hand through Grace's arm and force her to resume our path. Frances limps at my side and begins a monotonous moaning. I decide it is best to ignore Grace's last words and pretend she hasn't said it.

"Perhaps we can find a cottage or a holding, kind people who will offer us work. We could ask for food and a dry place to sleep by way of payment. Andrew is in need of milk ..."

My voice breaks as my attempt to be positive decays. It is so hard to keep going, so much easier to cast myself onto the roadside and give up ... stop fighting. But, as the sun tracks across the sky, we trudge onward, directionless. It seems like hours later when we come to a stop at a crossroads. Grace lets her pack drop to her feet and looks forlornly up and down the road.

"Which direction should we take?"

Grace shrugs; she doesn't care.

"Let us rest here a while."

I untie Andrew from my body and lay him in the lank yellow grass that flanks the road on either hand. My back feels close to breaking, my feet are rubbed raw, and my eyes are gritty with dust and weariness. Frances collapses beneath a tree, puts her head on her raised knees while Grace rummages through her pack.

"I have some bread left, a portion of cheese and not much water."

This is good. Grace is showing a need to survive. She offers Frances the skin. "Don't drink it all, Frances. Just take a small sip."

While she gulps it gratefully, I exchange looks with Grace.

"What way is York, do you think?"

"I don't know. Is that where we are going?"

I puff my cheeks, close my eyes and wish with all my heart we could return home to Arden. York is just a place I have heard of. I have no idea what may await us there. All I know is that it is not far from Wilberfoss, but I don't know in what direction it lies. I have never been there.

"That fellow we met yesterday said that many of his ilk were headed there. I don't know where else to go, what else we can do."

"Well, I don't care; whatever you decide."

The conversation lapses. We lie in the grass and doze for a while and, when we are rested, we pick a trail at random. As the hours and the miles pass, we begin to encounter other travellers, moving in the opposite direction. Some are traders, their carts laden with produce; some are landowners, their wealth marked by their carriages, their fine clothes and the servants that travel with them. But most people we encounter are like us, dispossessed, seeking a place of safety in this immense and shifting world.

As we pass a mixed band of men and women, some in monastic robes, others in laymen's garb, I gather my courage to ask direction of them.

"Which is the road to York?" I ask and they point ahead.

"That way," they say.

"Back the way we have come?" Overwhelmed with fatigue at the thought of retracing our steps, I close my eyes against it, swaying on my feet. A hand falls lightly on my arm.

"Come, child. You must travel with us. There is safety in numbers. You all look exhausted; here, let me relieve you of your burden."

Andrew squawks as he is lifted from my arms and I try to take him back.

"No, really; he is no burden."

But Frances has already taken the old man's arm and Grace has fallen into step beside him. She looks at me wearily over her shoulder, defeat in her eyes and, realising there is no choice, I go with them. Hoping against hope they are not a band of thieves.

We set up camp in a small copse. After three days of unseasonal, sweltering temperatures, the weather breaks unexpectedly. At first, we welcome the chill breeze after such an oppressive day, but when large raindrops begin to patter through the leaves, we draw up our shawls and hoods and huddle beneath a stand of oak. The old monk, whose name, I have learned, is Brother Michael, scowls at the sky.

"I knew we should have pressed on to the city." He fumbles in his pack. "Here, take this for the child."

He throws me a rough blanket, musty and none too clean, but I accept it gratefully and draw it over our heads like a makeshift tent. Andrew grabs at it, uncovering his head and wrinkling his nose as the rain wets him. It becomes a battle between us; as fast as I cover him, he drags it off again but, at the first crash of thunder, he goes very still and his eyes open wide. His terrified screams go on and on, shattering my nerves. I jog him up and down, holding him close, but he doesn't calm. He needs milk more than blankets.

"Come." Brother Michael propels me toward the shelter of the wagon, where Grace and some other women have wisely taken refuge. I scramble into the cramped space, Frances following behind, treading on people's toes and causing uproar.

"Sorry, I am so sorry," I apologise for her. She sits beside me, too close for comfort for it cannot be helped; there is little room to move. We can barely see each other's faces as we crouch in darkness, hoping the storm will be over as quickly as it came.

After a while, I become aware of the familiar aroma of the barnyard and I realise I'd seen the woman beside me earlier, driving a small flock of dark-fleeced sheep. The sweet nutty smell clings to her skirts. Wondering if she may have milk to spare, I smile at her and she grins back, gap-toothed and friendly.

"Where have you come from?" I ask.

"Yorkshire," she says. "I'm from Nunburnholme."

I glance at her muddy brown skirts.

"In Holy orders?"

She shakes her head, showing me the gaps in her teeth again.

"Oh no, I was a lay worker at the abbey. I worked on the grange. 'Tis all gone now." She shakes her head sadly.

"Gone?"

"Aye. The priory building stripped of anything worth more'n a pinch of barley, the lead taken, the bells melted down, and the treasure … well, I dare say that now lines the king's coffers. Or that of his dogsbody, Cromwell."

She spits the name as if it is a curse, but her bravado is shattered when she cowers at the flash of lightning and ducks her head from the crash of thunder that follows. The next sheet of lightning lights up Frances' face, revealing her gaping mouth, her cheeks drenched with tears and rain. She lets loose an unearthly yell and buries her face in my shoulder.

"Eeh, it's like the end of times," the woman cries, her words making Frances weep all the louder.

"All will be well, Frances." I try to comfort her, pulling a rueful face at my newfound friend. "We've never been out in weather like this before. We always had the comfort of the priory. We used to tell each other tales to keep our minds from it."

"I know a story." The woman fidgets on her bottom, seeking what comfort she can before she begins her tale. Her greasy cheeks shine in the ill light. "My story is about a house of nuns. It was a sisterhood of simple, good women who tilled the land and worked hard for the good of the community. They served the king and God for the benefit of all men, but one day, as they were quietly praying, men arrived from London Town; king's men with the stench of lechery and evil about them. They ravaged the nuns, abused the prioress, and if I were to repeat the evil things they accused the holy sisters of, my tongue would shrivel in my mouth."

This wasn't the sort of tale I'd hoped for, but it makes me wonder what truth there is in her words. There were few riches to be plundered at Arden but I wonder if the roof there has been destroyed, or if the dormitory where we slept has been despoiled. Perhaps Marigold has been butchered and eaten? Is the garden trampled now? Does Sister Mary rest in peace with the other members of our departed sisterhood, or have those devils disinterred and scattered their bones? I tear my mind from the horrible picture, place my lips on Andrew's hair and kiss him hard, closing my eyes and praying for all our souls.

I am not sure anyone is listening.

The sound of the rain increases and I peer out from beneath the wagon to watch it dance on the earth, quickly forming into puddles. Close by, a girl begins to snivel. Another follows suit and I wish my friend had found a happier way to distract us.

Andrew is wriggling, fractious at the tightness of my grip and, remembering there is a crust in my pocket, I put it in his hand. He sucks on it as if it will be his last meal. He has not sufficient teeth to chew it but it appeases him and that is good enough for now. The woman's voice slows and stalls and she looks around, belatedly realising the effect her storytelling is having, and she mercifully mitigates the ending.

"But God is ever on the side of righteousness. He wreaked vengeance on those devils and showed the king the error of his ways. The houses were all restored, every one of them, and all the chattels returned. Indeed, happiness soon returned to Nunburnholme."

"And every other religious house," I add, relieved that her tale-telling is done. I rest my head back against the body of the cart and close my eyes. When the next bolt of lightning sheets across the sky, I do not even jump.

As the thunder rolls away, the rain stops as suddenly as it began. We sit up straighter and look at each other, listening to the steady drip of rain falling from the branches. "Is it over?"

I poke my head from beneath the cart, looking up at the leaden sky. There is so much moisture dripping from the trees that it is as if the rain is still falling. We should shelter until it has stopped but I am cramped and uncomfortable so, with Andrew clinging like a monkey to my chest, I climb awkwardly out and straighten up, staggering at the lack of feeling in my legs and grabbing at Frances for support.

"My legs have gone numb." I stamp my feet, trying to bring back the feeling.

"Margery? Is that you?"

A monk steps from the gloom of the oak trees where the menfolk have been sheltering. His hair is plastered to his head, a shawl of damp darkening the shoulders of his habit. I open my eyes wider in recognition. His smile is wide, welcoming, and I notice he is missing a tooth. I cannot help but smile in return.

"What are you doing here? I imagined you'd all be settling in at Wilberfoss by now."

He touches my upper arm, urging me to stand aside to allow the women behind me the space to leave the shelter of the cart. The sun emerges, catching the raindrops, dazzling me and making me squint.

"They would not allow us to stay. Our names were not on the list so they sent us on our way, even though I have a letter from our prioress." My tone does not express the enormity of this disaster but I can see he understands. His mouth tightens, his chin jutting forward.

"It is an outrage." He ruffles his wet hair, the longer sections outside his overgrown tonsure standing up like a crown of thorns. "Something must be done. Yorkshire's roads teem with people like us – the dispossessed, the vulnerable. What do they think will become of us?"

"I don't believe they care..." I walk with him toward the fire, which is burning brighter now the flames no longer compete with the teeming rain. A strong stench of wet ashes reminds me of bonfires in the barnyard at Arden. Life was hard then but it was secure, and we were safe in the bosom of the Lord.

Someone hands me a cup. I look around for Janet, the woman with the sheep, but my attention is dragged back to his continuing conversation.

"Some of the men are saying there is much disquiet in York ... I am minded to go and join with them but ..."

"But what?"

"No matter. This morning while I was out foraging, I saw a barn ... quite empty and remote ... we could rest there tonight. It will be safer and considerably drier."

I am so tired that I don't know what to say. We are all in dire need of sleep and time to recuperate, and the tiny supply of food we carried with us from Arden has all but gone. I look about me at the sorry gathering. This morning we were tired and hungry and devoid of shelter, but now that night is drawing in, at least we have company. That is some small improvement.

"I need milk for the child, or grain to make into a mash. All he has had today is a little stale bread ... I must speak to that woman."

I walk rudely away and, smiling with more camaraderie than I really feel, I approach Janet to beg a little sustenance for Andrew.

The earthen floor of the barn is scattered with the mouldering remains of a harvest. One end is thick with ancient animal dung, the other drier and the thatch in better repair. We gather there; while the men search out wood to build a fire, the women spread out their damp outer clothing, hoping it will dry. I settle Frances as close to the makeshift hearth as I can, tell her to take off her shoes and ensure she dries her feet properly. Her ankle is swollen, the redness of yesterday turning blue. Were we at home, Sister Maude would have prepared her a salve of calendula and comfrey, but here there is nothing. All we can offer is a wet cloth to hold against it. Grace murmurs her sympathy and makes Frances comfortable, but that is all we can do.

"You have done well, Frances, to make so little complaint. The pain must be great." I kiss the top of her head and she burrows beneath her insufficient cover and attempts to sleep.

I have a skin of milk tucked into my belt and the promise of more tomorrow. I can now give Andrew the nourishment he has been lacking and pray that tonight, he will sleep the whole night through. Using her as support, I lean against Grace's back, tuck Andrew into the crook of my elbow and spoon the milk into his mouth, rueing each dribble that he wastes down his chin. While I am doing so, a shadow falls across us. "I thought this might come in useful." The monk holds a large basket beneath his arm.

My eyes widen. "Oh, for Andrew? Yes, it will. Thank you. Where did you get it?"

He squats beside me.

"Oh. I find that if you do favours, they are often returned."

Andrew's appetite is quickly sated. Soon, his eyelids begin to droop and he becomes less and less eager for each spoonful. Cradling him in one arm, I shake out his covering with the other and lay it in the basket before placing him gently inside. His face is filthy, plastered with dried snot, and his chin wet with dribbled milk, but I am so afraid of waking him that I daren't clean it. As I draw the wrap around him, he knuckles his eye, flooding my heart with love. At least he has eaten and will sleep the better for it. I stand up and turn to my benefactor.

"Thank you, Brother ... Oh, I do not recall your name."

"John. Lately known as Brother John, but since I am cast out I am putting off my robes and letting my tonsure grow. My days of prayer are done and from now on I will live as simply and as honestly as a man can in this tainted world."

"Amen."

Our eyes meet. His are soft and kind and, I hope, honest. Although there is nothing to laugh about, amusement stirs like tiny tickling fingers inside my belly.

"Come," he says. "I believe Brother Michael has a barrel of wine, probably not the best ever tasted but good enough to ward off the cold and ease us into sleep."

As night encroaches, we sit ringed about the fire, exchanging stories of how we came to be here. There is a common theme to each tale; monks and nuns, noviciates cast from their life of prayer; lay brothers and sisters who depended on a religious house for their livelihood; all thrown into penury.

"If this continues ... where will the sick people go? The monastic houses have always provided ease for their suffering; where will the destitute turn for a meal and a bed for the night?"

As they warm to the subject, their voices rise, speaking all at once, crying out against the injustice, and then one voice, louder than the others, speaks.

"It is the smaller houses they attack now and much of the hardship can be absorbed by the greater, but what will happen when they fall, too? Cromwell won't rest until he has destroyed our church entirely. It was one thing breaking with Rome, but this?" Brother Michael's rheumy eyes switch from face to face in the light of the fire. "This will change England forever. These actions will never be reversed."

In the long silence that follows, all I hear is the crackle of flame, the groaning of the barn timbers in the encroaching wind, and someone sobbing quietly in the vastness of the barn. But the stillness is broken at last.

"We must hope that the protest in Lincolnshire will have good effect. We must pray that they show the king the error of his ways."

I want to listen but I am growing sleepy after the rigours of the day. My lids are heavy, my head drooping until John leaps up from his place beside me, his sandaled feet kicking up dust from the floor. Rudely awoken, I sit up suddenly, pretending I had not been on the cusp of sleep. I surreptitiously wipe a trickle of drool from my lips. John addresses the gathering with vigour. I wonder where he finds the energy.

"Words will not win this ... this war. It is action we need; men and weapons. It is not just monastic folk like us who abhor it; the nobles speak against it also. Good northern lords who dislike the changes to religious practice as much as we. They are the people we need to speak to. We can do nothing alone. We need to urge the lords and landowners to act, for the good of all people in the realm."

A ragged cheer goes up. John ruffles his hair, looking down at his ragged clothes, his roughshod feet. "I feel I must do something, but who will listen to the likes of me?" As he realises the hopelessness of his task, his former enthusiasm dissipates. I link my arms around my raised knees.

"What is happening in Lincolnshire?"

He turns and speaks as if only to me, although the rest of the company listens intently to every word. With the attention of the barn upon me, I feel my face redden.

"When the king's officials arrived in Louth, the parish priest preached a sermon against the actions of the king's men. The populace was outraged and rose up in huge numbers, the commissioners fled and some of the local landowners joined the rebel cause. Nobody likes the changes. Even those who lacked the courage to join in did nothing to quell the riot."

I look about the barn; every face has now turned to John. Even Frances has woken up and is staring at him, her face alight, her mouth slightly open. She looks almost pretty. The men nod their heads, assessing the truth and judging the possibility of a similar thing happening here.

A young woman clothed in the soiled robes of a novice stands up and moves into the ring of firelight, her eyes shining, her fists clenched.

"If this happened everywhere ... throughout the realm, the king would have to stop. He would be forced to restore our houses. We could all go home!"

"There is more than a little hope." John stands up again and raises his hands. "Men are organising a rising, a march south to implore the king to reconsider. The following is growing by the day and I say we should join with them."

Brother Michael shakes his jowls regretfully. "A rout? A siege? That is not the Lord's way."

"As a last resort only. Their intentions are peaceful and they intend harm to no man, only to remove those of the king's men who mislead him with bad counsel. Only then, if this fails, will they fight and die if necessary for the good of God's church. I say we discover for ourselves what is happening and whether we can be a part of it."

I grab Frances' hand, jerk her toward me and suppress her cheer before she can make it. This is dangerous talk and it sounds like war to me. How did I, Margery of Arden, become involved in plotting a rebellion against the king's men?

That night, as everyone lies sleeping, my mind refuses to settle. Unable to quell the teeming thoughts in my head, I rise and creep to the door of the barn. Outside, the sky is dark; a high white moon tosses and turns in a feathery blanket of cloud. I lean against the wall and look up at the heavens that seem so close. What would God have me do? I have been raised to believe the king is God's representative on Earth and, if this is so, how can he be wrong? In resisting the king's will, are we not also resisting God's? I feel very small, far too weak and insignificant to carry the burdens placed upon me. Can I help put right the king's wrongs as well as lead Grace back from the misery she has fallen into? Can I protect and nurture her child, and Sister Frances too? I had thought these tasks were difficult enough, yet if I am to follow my new friends into York and help the pilgrims to defend God's church, it will all become harder. I bow my head, and whisper a prayer for guidance.

When I sense someone approaching, I open my eyes to see grubby sandaled feet, the mired hem of a dark robe.

"Brother John." I clear my throat, wiping away a renegade tear as he comes to stand beside me.

"Call me John. I told you, I am no longer 'brother'." He smiles gently, as if I were a small child. His eyes seem to see right into my mind. I look away.

"What were you thinking, Margery, when I came upon you just now?"

"I was praying for guidance ..."

"You are uncertain if our path is the correct one?"

"It isn't just that. If I were alone, I don't think I would hesitate, but ... I have Andrew and Frances to care for and they are vulnerable. Grace is ... delicate, too."

"They who march in unison protect one another. There is strength and safety in numbers."

It is the second time I have heard that sentiment recently. As I absorb his words, we move quietly away and seat ourselves on a fallen bough. John is older and wiser than me; perhaps he knows the answers to the questions jangling in my head.

"Do you think the king will listen to people like us? Do you think we can trust him to restore our houses and let us all go home? Will things really ever return to the way they were before?"

He pauses, tilting his head back to look at the drama of the sky.

"Who can say for certain? I hope so and I believe that if enough men wish for it ...."

"But aren't we the king's subjects and, as such, bidden to do as he instructs? Sometimes, we desire a thing so much that we become blind to reality. The dream blinkers us ... fools us, so that everything seems to be truth. When I was a child, I believed I was the lost daughter of a nobleman and that one day he would come back for me and I'd be reunited with my mother. I dreamed he would take me home so I could live out my life in comfort and happiness."

He sits up straighter and looks at me questioningly.

"You are of noble blood?"

I laugh and duck my chin to my chest.

"No. I was a foundling, abandoned at the priory door when I was a few days old, but a young girl has her dreams."

His finger brushes beneath my chin.

"You are pretty when you smile."

I drag my chin away, my cheeks burning as I reject the absurd notion that his words are in earnest.

"Don't toy with me, John. What I meant was, sometimes believing isn't enough. Facts are what matter.

Dreams and wishes are nothing ... unless you are a king, when dreams and wishes can be made real. I fear that this march you speak of will end in carnage."

"No, no, I don't think so. I heard today that already, here in Yorkshire, men sworn to our cause in Richmondshire, Mashamshire, Sedburgh and Nidderdale have mustered and are occupying Jervaulx Abbey. They've already restored Coverham – we outnumber the king's army. He will have no choice but to heed our demands. You must take heart, Margery."

I look down at our fingers that have somehow become joined. I dearly want his words to be true, desperately wish to share his conviction. Decisively, I withdraw my hand.

"What do you mean, 'the king's army' – do you think there will be a fight?"

"I hope not. I pray not, but we must see what awaits us in York."

As we make ready to leave the next morning, a man arrives and tumbles exhaustedly from his horse. He throws the reins to a child.

"Hold this for me and I'll give you a penny. Where is Brother Michael? Or John, can you direct me?"

I point a finger in the direction of the barn and, without a word of thanks, he lopes off, leaving me to wonder at his errand as I roll our bedding into a bundle.

"How far is it to York?"

I look up at Grace, who stands, hands on hips, beside me.

"John says half a day's ride, longer if we tarry, so you'd best have your pack ready."

"He likes you." She smiles slyly, making my temper prickle.

"Don't be ridiculous."

"I saw him try to hold your hand."

"Were you spying on us? He was merely trying to offer me comfort. I was upset. Yesterday was hard."

"Every day is hard."

She wrinkles her nose as I tear away Andrew's soiled clout and clean the shite from his buttocks.

"Pass me that clean linen, please." She does as I ask, watching as I tie it on him and scoop him from the ground. When he has stopped squalling, I prop him against our baggage so he can see and be entertained by the activity in the barn. Day by day, he becomes more difficult to amuse, demanding constant games and songs. Although I love him, his constant need of care is draining me. Grace looks away into the distance, narrowing her eyes the better to focus.

"My advice, Margery, is if you can get a man, do so. Life is easier with a partner, a helpmeet. It would be better for Andrew, too ..."

"And what would you know about that? You've birthed a bastard child alone; that's hardly a recommendation for matrimony, is it?"

At her injured expression, I soften, guilty of my callous retort, but my head is aching and I am weary to the bone. "I'm sorry, I didn't mean that, Grace. I am tired, and finding it hard just now. Brother John was being friendly, that is all. I am hiding nothing. There is no attraction, nothing at all between us."

"We shall see; it's early days yet," she says with the ghost of her former smile.

I open my mouth ready to make a sharp rebuke, but John and his companion emerge from the barn and I forget what I was going to say. As soon as she hears his voice, Frances runs to meet him and hangs off his arm. Paying little heed to her adulation, John heads straight toward us and, by the time he is before me, Grace's insinuations are making my cheeks burn. It seems we are all smitten by John.

Grace's inferences have found their mark and inwardly I begin to question his intent. There is nothing about me to attract a man but ... I've heard it said that men are impartial in their time of need. I shake my head and chase away these strange thoughts. Grace is mistaken. A fully-grown man would see nothing in a half-starved waif like me, but now she has spoken, I find I can't quite look him in the eye.

I fasten my gaze on the side of his head and notice the way the sun shines through his ears, turning them as red as an autumn leaf.

"My friend brings ill news," he says. "The Lincolnshire rebellion has fallen; collapsed under the king's promise of a pardon if they return peaceably to their homes."

"What homes? We have no homes to go to!"

John scowls, looking at the ground.

"It is disheartening. The rebel army was twice, maybe even thrice the size of the king's. Had they stood firm ..."

The messenger takes up the story. "As I understand it, the king threatened dire punishment if they did not disperse, and the royal army was only forty miles away. The gentry who were part of the rising lost courage and decided it was better to sue for pardon. There was a great falling out then between the common folk and the men who had agreed to lead them but, in the end, they were all persuaded to go home. Suffolk, who refused to negotiate with a mob, left them little choice but to back down. But I doubt there will be real peace, not until the king has honoured his promises. Time, as they say, will tell."

"So, that is that, then," I say, tying the bindings of my pack tighter than is necessary. I haul the load onto my shoulder. "What are we to do now? Sleep beneath a hedge until the priory reopens?"

My hands are trembling, my whole body convulsed with rage, but I don't know why I am so angry. John places a hand on my arm, the fabric of my robes suddenly so light I can feel the heat of his palm as if it lies directly against my skin. I suppress a shiver.

He frowns beneath his brows, his darting eyeballs illustrating the rapid process of his mind.

"I am not convinced the king will keep his word. I don't see how he can ignore so many dispossessed subjects. When he took the oath of kingship, did he not promise to protect even the meanest of his subjects? I think we should remain here for a day or two, and wait to see what happens..."

I watch John's inward battle with disillusion until he eventually emerges with something resembling hope. For his sake, I suppress the questions on my lips; we cannot remain here indefinitely. The owner of the barn will surely notice our presence soon and turn us off his land. Winter is coming; how long will our threadbare robes and moth-eaten blankets provide protection against the approaching cold? His sudden smile chases the rising tide of anger from my heart. His missing tooth draws my eye; the dimple in his left cheek far more beguiling than his rhetoric. John is an idealist, an optimist; his faith in God surpassed only by his self-belief.

Yet, over the weeks that follow, I am forced to wonder if it is my own pessimism that is at fault. No one else seems to share it. Slowly, our numbers grow; men, women and children fill the barn and we learn of other communities converging on York as if some event, some life-altering phenomenon, is to take place there. Our makeshift camp grows more comfortable as the men patch up the holes in the barn roof and walls, and fashion makeshift stools and tables. The people that were strangers to begin with become companions; women of ilk gather to gossip or pray, so, as the chill winter creeps steadily from the north, in the bosom of our newfound family I find it grows warmer instead of colder.

And, as if in answer to our prayers, the common folk of Yorkshire rise up in support to join the march and, before the end of October, our cause has become an unstoppable wave.

Robert Aske, a lawyer whom we learn has agitated for an end to dissolution, arrives and organises our raggle-taggle band of dissatisfied subjects into a formidable protest. Our numbers swell so much that on the day we finally enter the city of York, we are some ten thousand strong.

My companions and I are lost among this vast company, yet I feel vibrantly alive, proud to be part of something so much greater than myself.

As I stand with John, Frances and Grace in the crowd, Robert Aske is a great distance away, and I am so small I cannot see him as he speaks on the market cross; yet I hear him give voice to his rhetorical dream and his words fill me with the conviction that we shall be triumphant.

'For this pilgrimage we have taken is for the preservation of Christ's church, of this realm of England, the King our Sovereign Lord, the nobility and commons of the same, and of the intent to make petition to the King's Highness for the reformation of that which is amiss within this realm.'

His words are met with great cheers and before we disperse, he forbids any violence or destruction upon the city or its inhabitants. Within hours, we learn of the successful restoration of the nunnery of St Clement, and the Augustinian priory at Healaugh. There are those who distrust him, swear he has ever been a dissenter, a troublemaker, but to me, treading the same path as Robert Aske is akin to rubbing shoulders with the pope.

He has become the saviour of our hopes, the restorer of our dreams, and, for the first time, I harbour real faith that, one day, everything will come right and I will return to Arden.

I close my eyes and picture it. I forget the harshness of life at the priory and remember only the soft calling wind on the heath, the purity of the nuns' voices in the nave, the soft, nutty goodness of Marigold's teat, the warm camaraderie of the kitchens. Most of all, I recall the security of routine as we attended the same tasks, the same prayers, lived side by side with the same companions for day after day after day.

"Surely, you don't believe the king will do nothing to stop us." Grace's voice pulls me from my happy dream. She is doling out bowls of soup to a long queue of pilgrims. Her habit is worn and soiled, her face bears the fatigue of the road, the weeks of sleeping on hard earth, but she is beautiful still. I yawn and give myself a shake.

"John says our numbers far outweigh the king's armies. Despite the strength of our position, Master Aske still favours a peaceful outcome and has sent a – an envoy to request a meeting at Doncaster."

"And the king is just going to roll over and agree to his terms? That doesn't sound like any king I have ever heard of, least of all our present one. Just because we want a thing, doesn't mean it will happen."

A few weeks ago, I would have said the same, but recently, the fervour of my fellow pilgrims has convinced me that anything is possible.

"No one is speaking against the king; we merely demand the removal of his evil ministers. Cromwell is a base-born bully who has climbed far above his allotted station."

She raises her eyebrows, grimacing with derision.

"That sounds strange coming from you," she says as she serves the soup with greater fervour. She waves her ladle beneath my nose. "I just don't think the king will be pleased and although I agree wholeheartedly with the motivation for this protest, I have more fear of the king's vengeance."

I am so glad she is actually communicating with me that, at first, I don't mind the bleakness of her words.

"Does that mean … you won't march with us?"

"I don't know." She smiles woodenly at the next woman to hold forth a bowl for her to fill.

"But where would you … you wouldn't leave us?"

She pauses in her task to look at me, her face full of regret.

"I don't know. We will have to wait and see."

Like a bucket of icy water, Grace's defection douses the fire of rebellion in my heart. She may not treat me very kindly, but the thought of waking in the morning without her goes hard with me. Since she came to Arden, my life has changed. I have been enthralled by her elegant manners and strange ways of thinking and acting; she has been a beacon illuminating my ignorance. I've never lost hope that one day her recent ill humour will pass and she will be as she was before. If we part, that hope will be extinguished.

That night, I toss and turn beneath the scanty cover, sigh and blow in the darkness and long for the oblivion of sleep. In the end, when the first light of dawn is glimmering, I give up and roll from bed to creep outside. The camp is just beginning to stir; a woman blows on the embers of a fire while her child knuckles his eye and grizzles for sustenance. When I left him, Andrew was sleeping on Frances' sturdy bosom, and an hour's freedom from him is very welcome. As I tiptoe through the hunched shapes of the snoring pilgrims, I realise John's sleeping place is empty. But I know where he will be so I head for the Minster.

The cloisters are deserted when I pass through toward the postern door. I enter the nave and shiver in the chill darkness. The church is silent but, spying a candle burning in a side chapel, I creep closer and recognise John's bowed head. Unwilling to disturb his prayer, I try to keep warm, shifting impatiently from foot to foot as I wait for his devotion to end. If anyone will understand that me and Grace must not be parted and help me to persuade her to stay, it will be him. I peep around the corner, into the chapel.

The soles of his shoes are almost worn through; the hem of his robe is as ragged as my own. He does not sense my presence and, like a spy, I watch his unselfconscious conversation with God. He seems very troubled, although he gives little sign of being so during the daytime. I wonder what he prays for. Peace perhaps, or the required strength for the task ahead. Perhaps he mourns the weakening of his calling and seeks a way back into God's favour.

I suppose that once the king has seen sense and the religious houses are restored, we can all go home. How strange that will seem. I will miss them all. These people who were strangers a few weeks ago are like family now; it will pain me to part from them. Brother Michael, Janet the shepherdess, Sister Julia who sings so sweetly … John's prayer ends so suddenly that he has risen before I have time to creep away. He halts abruptly when he sees me, halfway between the door and the altar.

"Margery. Is anything wrong?" His feet are soundless on the tiled floor, his face full of concern, his fingers warm on my hand. A moment ago, I would have complained of sleeping badly because my anxiety for the world and all the bad in it had grown so vast that I was in danger of it swallowing me whole. But now, as the real reason for my insomnia becomes apparent, I find I cannot speak of it; not to him, not to anybody. I have no idea what answer to give him.

His features blur and merge one into the other as sorrow gathers on my lashes. I try to blink the moisture away so I might see clearly and tell him what I really need to say.

"Margery," he whispers, and his voice is so soft, so rhetorical, that when he slides a hand beneath my veil and cups my cheek, I do not pull away. Instead, I close my eyes and roll into the comfort of his body.

It takes a long time to unburden my soul of all the leaden pain it holds. He listens patiently to my sobbing story, shakes his head, murmurs my name, pushes against me to kiss my wet cheeks, my nose, my lips and, like an undernourished kitten, I discover I am suddenly starving and greedy for more.

19th October 1536

At first, when John realises my intention to join the pilgrims on their march to Pontefract, he objects.

"It is too dangerous, Margery," he says. "You would be better off waiting here with the child. I will return as soon as I can."

Grace looks up from the pot she is stirring.

"You can be sure I will be going with them. There is no option now but to fight this."

"And so will I!" I am both hurt and angry that he thinks me so feeble that I must stay behind.

"You must think of the child … and Frances." He takes my shoulders, pushing me gently out of Grace's earshot. "You are precious to me. I will feel better if you are here. Should things become violent …"

"Then we shall stay well back out of the way, but I don't see why they will need to use force against us when our protest is peaceful. Nobody has been injured yet. Besides, you have no jurisdiction over my movements."

I look down at my shaking hands, hating to be at odds with him. He is silent for so long that I am forced to look up again and I find that his face is pale, and pinched about the nose and mouth – I realise he is trying to subdue his rage. He pushes me roughly from him, and steps away.

"You are right. Being neither father nor husband, I cannot direct you. I spoke only out of concern. I would have thought you would be too exhausted from the road to want to travel further."

I can sense his disappointment in my mulish determination but I will not change my mind.

"No, John. I am quite recovered, and it is but one day's journey and time to rest before we travel aback again."

I look past him, over his shoulder, to where Grace is making no secret of her curiosity; every part of her is straining to overhear our words. Remembering our friendship, I take pity on him and rest my palm on the back of his hand.

"All will be well, John. I give you my word." He smiles tightly, turns on his heel and stalks away, going about his business as if I mean nothing at all to him. Perhaps I do not. Perhaps I am nothing more than the other camp followers.

By the time our party draws close to Pontefract Castle, the surrounding hills are already thick with pilgrims. Small groups have formed, fires have been lit and the women are busy producing makeshift nourishment for their menfolk. Farther off, the armies have set up camp; the soldiers clean their plate and sharpen their blades in case of conflict. Smoke wafts across the hillside to our place among the dispossessed monks and nuns, and the ordinary folk who are making a stand for the ways of the old church.

I'm surprised to see so many women and children. I'd imagined we would be among the few. It is a noisy yet cheery gathering. While young girls mind their siblings, their brothers dart and dive among the company, getting into mischief, singing songs that are so rude they make the pious among us blush.

I drop my pack, set Andrew on the ground and press a hand to my aching back. We covered many miles very quickly, and I am glad the journey is over. Trying not to think of the return walk to York, I shade my eyes and gaze up at the towers of Pontefract Castle, looming darkly against the scudding clouds. Those inside the thick stone walls are very secure, but it is not so for those outside. As untidy as a row of broken teeth, ramshackle bevies and shelters lean against the outer walls. They are deserted now; the blacksmith's fire is out and there is no sign of life, for all have retreated inside. The drawbridge is raised and the battlements bristle with men at arms. Yet despite their defensive stance, I am not afraid, for our peaceful band outnumbers them many times over and we will not be easily beaten.

"Impressive, is it not?"

Grace comes to stand beside me. She stares grimly at the fortress, her hands on her hips, her veil blowing in the buffeting breeze. "I rode here once with my father when I was a girl. It was hung with pennants then, ready for a day of jousting and celebration."

She rarely speaks of her life before Arden; in fact, apart from necessary communication, she hardly converses with me at all.

"What was your father like?" I ask, casually, as if I am not eaten up with curiosity about her childhood. She wraps her arms about her body, grasps her elbows and closes her eyes, remembering.

"A good man," she says in a sing-song voice. "As good a husband as my mother could have asked for, and as good a father as ever a girl had."

"Yet your brother is not a good man. Isn't that a little strange?"

As I kneel beside Andrew, she turns toward me, frowning.

"Brother? I don't have a brother."

"But you said he cast you out ... after your father and your betrothed died."

"I said cousin not brother. And no, he is *not* a good man. But there are many like him who will stop at nothing to secure their fut–"

Her words are severed by an uproar nearby. I crane my neck to see the cause of it and become aware that Frances has wandered off. Leaping to my feet, I snatch Andrew from the grass so suddenly that he begins to bawl.

"Frances! Where is Frances?"

And then I hear her voice, as deep and discordant as a cracked bell. "No. Stop it!"

I hear her panic, sense her confusion. With Andrew clasped to my chest, I push a way through the crowd, elbowing and shoving until I discover a group of half-grown boys. They have formed a circle around Frances, who is wailing as they shove her one from the other. She stumbles, arms outstretched, her mouth wide. They are laughing so loudly, so engrossed in their torment, that they do not hear me screaming at them to stop. I continue to yell into the chaos while Andrew, terrified by the fracas, screams shrilly in my ear. Then a voice, louder and more authoritative than my own, breaks through the din.

"Stop! Stop! Leave her alone! Leave her, I say!"

A horse pushes into the melee and the noise ebbs. The bullies subside and silence falls. Frances is on her knees in the circle of tormenters, expecting more to come. She is too afraid to move, yet afraid to stay. The man dismounts slowly, hands his reins to a servant and approaches Frances, placing a gentle hand on her head. "What is the meaning of this?" he asks quietly, his gaze switching from one miscreant to another. "Why do you plague this child?"

All eyes are on him. The guilty drop their chins; the innocent watch and wait. He bends down and places his hand beneath Frances' elbow, urging her to rise. She wipes snot and drool onto her sleeve and anxiously searches the crowd, seeking and finding me. I give myself a shake and step forward.

"Thank you, sir. We – I – Sister Frances and me, we are grateful to you for your kindness."

When she hears my voice, Frances wipes her tears away and relief spreads across her cheeks. She casts herself into my arms and I regard her rescuer over her head. He raises a warning finger.

"You must take better care of her. She is ... vulnerable."

"Yes, sir, I will. I didn't think to find unkindness among the pilgrims."

"Nor I, but I fear wickedness is everywhere. It is our job to seek it out and destroy it. What is your name, child?"

I look up at him, the breath catching in the back of my throat as I look properly at his face for the first time. He has just one eye. It shines out fearsomely, as piercing as the sun. The other socket is empty, withered and puckered with a scar running from it to the corner of his mouth. Suppressing a shudder, I look away.

"Margery."

"And what brings you here ... Margery?"

At first, I wonder what he means and I stutter and stammer before composing an answer. "After the king's men shut down our priory, my sisters and I travelled here from Arden. We seek justice from the king, as does everyone gathered here."

"And we shall get it. The evil men who sit on the king's council shall be punished, as will these miscreants today ... although perhaps not quite so harshly."

He smiles suddenly and I cannot help but give him mine in return. He bows his head and wishes me good day, as if I am a lady, his attention making me swell with pride before he turns to walk away. He has not been entirely swallowed by the crowd when I call after him.

"Thank you again, sir, for coming to our aid." He does not turn again but acknowledges my words by raising his hand in farewell.

"Come along, Frances." I slide my arm about her shoulder, hitch Andrew higher on my hip, and walk with them back to our hearth. Grace is just a little way behind me but I know better than to ask her to carry the child.

"How fortunate that man happened along," I say with relief. "I don't know how I would have fought them all off single-handed."

"You do know who that was?" She halts abruptly, so I stop too and turn around to look at her.

"No; do you?"

She laughs, pulling a disbelieving face.

"You've never heard of the great one-eyed Robert Aske? The man who has pledged his life to our cause; who swears to restore and protect the true church?"

"That was him? That was Robert Aske?" Incredulity robs my voice of power, making it issue in a rasp. Of course I have *heard* of Aske; his name has been on everyone's lips for months now. He is the reason we are all gathered here instead of perishing on the roadside. There are those who speak of him as a rogue and a bully but, to us, Robert Aske is our leader, sent by God to save us all.

As Grace moves away, I notice her body shaking with mirth, but I do not care. She can laugh all she likes, for the encounter has left me feeling as if God himself has reached down from Heaven and given me his blessing.

When darkness falls, we lie beneath the stars, the damp ground seeping into our bones, the air around us cramping our limbs. It is a wonder I sleep at all. With Andrew on my chest and Frances curled like an enormous dog behind my knees, I listen to the snores, the farts and the coughing of our fellow pilgrims. I don't know how any of them manage to sleep. It seems to me that each time I relax into slumber, a dog barks, or a child cries out in its sleep, startling me to wakefulness again. It is near dawn before I finally drift into uncomfortable dreams.

By noon the next day, a rumour spreads that Aske is preparing to go into the castle, where he will negotiate with Sir Thomas Darcy and his council.

"Is it safe to do so?" I ask when I learn of it. "What is to stop them from imprisoning Aske and turning him over to the king?"

Grace shields her eyes from the sun and squints toward the castle.

"I'm sure Aske has thought of that."

Janet, who has just come by with a skin of milk, playfully pinches Andrew's cheek and butts in on our conversation.

"Last night, when we gathered at the fire, the men were saying as how Master Aske has demanded a hostage to stand in lieu of his safety. A wise move, I'd say, in the circumstances ..."

"Perhaps Lord Darcy has more than a glimmering of sympathy for our cause. He can like the dismantling of the church no more than we."

"That's true. Rumour has it he'd join us if he weren't so afraid of the king's wrath."

All day we wait, passing the time in idle conversation about the turn of events, the possible outcome of the stand-off between king and church, and the forthcoming negotiation between Aske and Darcy.

"Where John?" Frances asks for the hundredth time. A little way off, a boy plays a merry tune on his pipe and a group of children form a square and begin to dance, hopping and skipping, light as fairies. When she sees them, Frances forgets to chafe for John's return and gets up to join in, lumbering behind them like a performing bear. As I watch them, I realise there's never been time in my life for such things. My existence has been one of toil, humility and servitude, although I never realised it at the time. I've never danced, not even on a feast day. I look down at my blistered feet, one toe protruding from my sandal like a malformed claw. Even if I had the time, I am sure I'd never school my body to move so daintily. Dancing isn't for the likes of me.

A peal of laughter breaks out and I see that Frances has fallen. I start to my feet, every instinct urging me to rush to her aid, but Janet holds me back, bidding me wait and watch. One small girl pauses in her dance and holds out a hand to haul Frances to her feet. Keeping their hands joined, they begin again, weaving in and out of the pilgrims, a dash of joy in the sombre crowd. These children are younger than the boys who taunted Frances; they accept her and are laughing with Frances, not at her.

Their gaiety relaxes me and I hum along, swaying back and forth, Andrew's head lolling in the crook of my arm. But my leisure is cut short when a murmur of anticipation runs through the crowd. I turn from the dancing children toward the castle.

The drawbridge slowly lowers and a group of men appear from the depths of the keep. It was such an important negotiation that I'd imagined it would take much longer. The crowd pushes forward, cramped together, watching and wondering. Narrowing my eyes the better to see, I recognise Robert Aske in the company of gentlemen, his tall, stooped frame ill clad beside the finery of the lords, and his beard unkempt.

"Which one do you think is Darcy?" I ask Grace, moving closer to her. She shrugs.

"The shorter one in the middle. And I can't be sure, but I think the others must be William Gascoigne, Robert Constable, and that one there ..." I follow the line of her pointing finger, "... I think he is perhaps the archbishop of York."

"How do you know so much?"

She shrugs again.

"I listen to the men as I serve their supper and, of course, I have met Lord Darcy and Sir William before…. They wouldn't recognise me now, of course."

I glance at her soiled clothing and doubt even her own mother would know her.

"What are they doing?"

She points to where the smiling Aske and Lord Darcy turn to the crowd and raise their joined hands. They are seemingly in accord.

"They have come to some agreement; that much is sure."

The murmur of the pilgrims rises in volume to a babble of speculation. Can Lord Darcy have so easily been persuaded of the justice of our cause? With men like him championing us, the king cannot fail to be swayed. Since more and more people have joined our ranks, landowners, tenant farmers, priests and scholars, it seems nothing will prevent our quest for justice. John estimates our numbers at almost forty thousand strong.

*

Christ crucified!
For thy wounds wide,
Us commons guide!
Which pilgrims be,
Through God's grace,
For to purchase
Old wealth and peace
Of the spirituality.

Although we are weary, we sing loudly as we move across the countryside. It is a new melody sprung from our endeavours to restore the old ways of the church. Grace tells me it was written by one of the monks from Sawley Abbey after Aske successfully restored their house. Now that we have hope, there is a new vigour about us. Lord Darcy and his ilk's pledge to join with us has bolstered our resolution. Everyone is now certain that success cannot be far away.

We move like a dark shadow across the hills, up and down the rolling slope toward the River Trent, where we are to make the crossing. Yet, as we draw near to Doncaster, Aske calls a halt and the news trickles down to us that the Duke of Norfolk has mustered on the banks of the River Don on behalf of the king. He is unwilling to fight us, though, and wishes to parley instead.

I am grateful for the chance to rest. We are all in dire need of it. The large blister on the side of Frances' foot is beginning to fester. If I can light a fire and heat some water, I can clean it properly before applying the salve I use on Andrew's sore buttocks. I settle her comfortably against the bole of a tree, and place Andrew on her lap. He squirms like an eel but, although her head lolls back on the bark pillow, her grip on him is tight. I look at her slack mouth, her bone-white face, the circles around her eyes. Poor Frances can have little understanding of this never-ending journey yet she rarely makes complaint. Above all else, I wish I had better means of caring for her.

With her usual competence, Grace sets about gathering wood for a fire, organising the youngsters among us to go in search of a river or a spring.

John sprawls on the damp earth and doesn't meet my eye as he answers my many questions. When I've dressed her wound, Frances moves to sit closer to him, plucking handfuls of grass and piling it playfully on his knee. For once, his tolerance fails and he shakes it off but, unperturbed by his irritability, she piles it on again, our conversation too deep for her to grasp.

"Norfolk is growing old. Of course he doesn't relish a fight, especially since we outnumber him. He will offer Aske the moon regardless of whether or not he can deliver it."

Grace looks up from her task.

"I remember my father saying Norfolk would do whatever it takes to remain in the king's good graces; that is why he has survived when so many have perished."

"So far…"

A ripple of laughter runs through us. Even though we are fit to drop with tiredness, we cling to humour, looking on the bright side. There are those among us whom I am sure would go to their deaths smiling in the face of it, believing in reprieve to the very last.

"Of course, Norfolk betrayed his own blood to save his own skin."

Grace's sudden announcement startles me. She clutches a ewer beneath her arm and stares into the flames. I replace the stopper on the pot of salve.

"Did he?"

She nods, a grimace of distaste passing across her features.

"He did. Anne Boleyn and her brother George are – were – his niece and nephew. He presided over their trial and did nothing to try to sway the king to leniency. He just stood by and watched as they were shamed and condemned to death … or so they say."

How does she know such things? I had not realised Grace was a champion of Anne Boleyn. Although the manner of her death was horrible, I have always had more pity for Queen Catherine, who was ousted from her place when the king took a new fancy. It was due to Anne that England broke from Rome in the first place – it opened the door a little wider to those who support Luther. Since it was reformers who initiated the closure of the monasteries, Anne was the catalyst of all our current troubles. I give myself a shake and refocus on the present. What has passed is passed. There's no point in dwelling on it.

"So much for kin," I say, raising my eyebrows and laughing. "Perhaps it is fortunate after all that I have none. Now, where shall we sleep tonight, do you think? There is still enough daylight to march on to the next town. I wonder what Aske will decide."

I have almost forgotten how it feels to live in the same place every day, to wake in the same bed, eat at the same table, pray in the same chapel ... in fact, I have almost forgotten how to pray. There are regular services but, most often, Andrew demands my care, or some other matter that cannot be ignored diverts me from attending. Or perhaps I am too guilty, too ashamed to present myself before God in my sinful state.

Me and John have not been together since that night at the Minster. I tell myself it is circumstance that keeps us apart, but I cannot shake the nagging fear that perhaps he used me, robbed me of my most precious ... my *only* virtue, for the sake of a moment's passing pleasure.

27th October 1536 – Marshgate Priory

While our leaders take up residence in Mashgate Priory, the rest of the pilgrims camp in the surrounding meadow, close to the river Don. As the name of the house suggests, the land is damp and full of small winged beasts that emerge after dark to bite us.

"I hate these things! They are like small vindictive devils." Grace claws at her arms and smacks her own leg in a vain attempt to kill at least one of them. We pile what greenery we can find onto the fire to smoke them away, but the fire then burns so slow and cold it ceases to warm us. We are forced to choose between dying from the cold and being eaten alive.

I wrap Andrew so tightly in his blanket that he screams with the frustration of not being able to move his arms. I am rummaging through my pack in search of something to soothe him with when I hear the sound of footsteps behind me.

"Here you are, sweetling; still warm from the teat."

I look up to find Janet holding out a skin of milk.

"Oh, thank you. What would we do without you? I shall never be able to repay your kindness."

I hug it to my chest while, with a deal of huffing and puffing, she kneels on the blanket to poke Andrew playfully in the midriff. To my chagrin, he ceases bawling immediately and gives her his sweetest smile.

"Of course you will. One day, when all this is over and the world is set to rights again." She smiles widely, a scrap of food stuck between her front teeth. "My sheep will be as glad as anyone when this pilgrimage is over. They snatch a bite here and there as we travel but I can tell that they yearn for their home pastures ... just as we all do. The milk yield is less than it used to be but ... don't you worry, pet, your babe will not go hungry, not as long as I can tempt a drop from their udders."

The word 'udder' evokes the memory of the satin soft pillow of Marigold's flank against my cheek. I think of Arden. The vibrant summer colour on the heath will now be fading to purple, umber and gold, and the wind will be blustering about the gables, the mud deepening in the byre. Will I ever return? I have travelled so far and am so besmirched in sin that it seems unlikely now. Perhaps God has forgotten me – forgotten all of us.

"Hey!" Janet gives me a gentle shake. "We've got to keep smiling, chicken, or there's no point in being born."

She hauls herself to her feet, the fusty aroma from beneath her petticoats wafting around us. As she turns to go, she pauses. "If you need anything, lass, just call for me. I'm not far away for a chat, or if you want me to take the young'n off your hands for an hour or two. I can see it's a heavy burden you're carrying."

I begin to thank her but, glancing at Andrew, I see he has somehow wriggled free from his blanket cocoon and is on his belly, reaching out to tug the hem of my gown. My eyes widen and my mouth falls open.

"Andrew! When did you learn to do that? You're so clever!" I fall to my knees and place him on his back again, tempting him to demonstrate his new mobility.

"Poor dab," Janet laughs. "After all that effort to get there, you go and put him back where he started!"

As she turns laughingly away, I scoop him up to anoint his dribbly cheek with kisses. Pride turns into happy tears, and I realise that perhaps my burden isn't so great after all.

Darkness falls, heavy and damp. We wrap ourselves in cloaks and blankets and huddle as close to the fire as we can. As always, although it is a mix of pain and pleasure to play, the old game of 'do you remember' begins again. Disembodied voices recall the old days, before the break from Rome when King Henry hadn't lost all hope of begetting an heir. Everyone talks of and longs for the days when he was hale and full of good fellowship and the whole of England was merry. Of course, I knew nothing of it, cloistered away at Arden, but I relish the memories the others relate.

"Perhaps our memory is flawed. Perhaps distance somehow softens the past and presents a prettier picture than the reality. Although I remember the discomforts of Arden, it seems to me that the nights were less cold then and I was certainly not so wretched..."

Someone throws a log on the fire, extinguishing the flames and plunging us briefly into deeper darkness. Another voice issues indignantly from the night.

"Our way of life continued unchanged for hundreds of years, it is no wonder we feel lost. The sense of continuity was comforting, the feast days and traditions of worship gave us purpose. Our days were divided by prayer, ordered and inevitable, like the months of the year, the days of the week. We were part of something greater than ourselves – something divine. Now there is nothing but heresy."

I tilt back my head to look at the heavens, but dark scudding clouds obscure the stars.

"What must God make of all this?"

A new voice answers, a male voice tinged with anger that initiates a completely new thread to the conversation.

"Of the conflict? Man has fought in His name since the days of Christ – and will always do so."

"Everything is so fractured now – laity and clergy alike are questioning things that have never been questioned before. This new religion–"

"That is behind it all. Cromwell leans on the king, like a serpent slowly pouring the poison of religious reform into his ears. *He* is the enemy. *Cromwell* is the one who must be stopped. Even the nobility are against him …"

"Is Cromwell not of the nobility too?" I ask in surprise.

"No!" Derisive male laughter blooms in the darkness and I blush, feeling foolish for having spoken and glad no one can see my face in this all-encompassing darkness. "He is of base origin and the penury of his early years has made him greedy for power and position. He sates his hunger for riches and authority by feasting on the flesh of the church."

A rustle of clothing testifies that more than one of us is hastily marking the sign of the cross. I whisper silent prayers.

"But he shall *not* prevail," the voice continues. "He shall be struck down and peace and piety will return to England once more."

"Amen." Grace's whisper hushes in my ear and, grateful for her presence, I sink against the comfort of her shoulder. For once, she does not pull away, and we both look down at the shadowed features of her slumbering son.

I am tired beyond tears, yet sleep evades me as usual. The momentous events that are emerging give me no rest, and my mind gallops out of control like a runaway mule. Tomorrow, talks will begin between our leaders and the Duke of Norfolk, whom I have learned is ruthlessly on the side of the king, come what may. As John has assured me, our greater number ensures Norfolk will do all he can to avoid a fight. John says the duke has little option but concede to our wishes, but I cannot believe our demands will be so easily won.

While our betters negotiate, and although our opinion means nothing, the rest of us break into dispute. Some pilgrims want to fight while the opportunity is in our hands, but others are obedient to Aske, who, remembering Norfolk as the victor at Flodden, refuses to countenance such a thing.

"Norfolk is a fair man. He may be persuaded to speak to the king on our behalf, show him our intentions are peaceable. In resorting to combat, we condemn ourselves as traitors."

"No, the time for peace has passed. We should stand against this injustice and fight – like Joshua at Jericho!"

John glares at the crowd, defying any to argue with him but, although I do not say so, I think he is wrong. When we originally set off, our mission was a peaceful one; persuasive rhetoric should be our weapon, not staves and stones.

For a day or two, John goes about with a scowl as deep as a well. He is anxious for action, his blood hot with the desire for vengeance upon Cromwell and his band of brutes. While we are settling for the night, I see him slide a dagger beneath his makeshift pillow, and during the day he has taken to carrying a stave – he calls it a walking stick but it could easily double as a weapon. The thought of fighting makes me shiver. No matter what crimes the king has committed, violence, even in God's name, is always wrong. I am sure of it.

When the decision to negotiate with Norfolk is taken, John stays behind, his dark expression casting gloom on us all, making every one of us doubt.

"No good will come of it, you mark my words. The king is beyond reason. Cromwell has whetted his appetite for wealth and he cares only for gold. Greed makes the king blind to the needs of his people. It is a trick. I do not believe they will honour any negotiation with us."

Andrew stirs in his basket. I pull his shawl high around his head and pat his back until he slumbers soundly again. When I look up, John is still staring sulkily into the fire.

"What do you think will happen … if the king agrees to our demands?"

He curls his lip in derision.

"He will not agree. I have no expectation of it."

"But if he did, what would happen to us? Where would we go?"

His face is grubby, a smear of soot on one cheek, his fingernails black at the edges. It is hard on the road to remember that cleanliness is next to godliness and we are all in a similar state.

"Back to our houses, I suppose. Those that have been damaged must be rebuilt, the treasures returned."

Even I can see that the king will not willingly agree to this. I had hoped John might mention settling in some village together, a modest home where we could raise Andrew and perhaps some children of our own. I do not press him. I link my arms about my raised knees and think of the long road to Arden and how much harder it will be to travel in winter.

"Why are you sighing?"

I look up, startled.

"I hadn't realised I was. I was just thinking ..."

"Of home?"

"How did you know?"

"We all think of home, of the future, but even if we are allowed to return, can it ever be the same?"

I think for a long moment.

"I'm not sure it can be. I don't think *I* can even be the same. Before I left Arden, I never knew there was so much ... so much *world* outside the cloister. I've met so many different people. I hadn't realised before that there was such a variety of faces or so many differing opinions, so many shades of right and wrong. Since leaving, I have seen cruelty and kindness in equal measure and I've learned so much about ... ordinary life, the life of a lay person. At Arden, it was unchanging; the people I saw, the chores I carried out, the prayers I heard, the places I frequented – to go back now might feel like ... imprisonment."

I cringe as I speak the word but he does not judge me. Instead, he laughs gently through his nose. I turn to him, my mouth stretched in surprise. "Am I not wicked to speak so?"

"The truth is never wicked. Honesty is a virtue." His sigh echoes my own. "In truth, Margery, you will be safer at Arden than out in the world. The security of numbers we have now with the pilgrims cannot last. We must disperse one day, go our separate ways ... and small parties are vulnerable to footpads and worse. If you are able, you should go home as quickly as you can."

His words are like a knife beneath my ribs.

"I thought, perhaps, if we were granted a pension, I could set up a modest home somewhere with Grace and Frances ... to raise Andrew ..."

"A pension? You really are naïve! After this is over, no matter what the outcome, we won't be rewarded for it. The king may allow us to return whence we came, but only to keep the roads free of beggars. That's why I say we must fight, but if we lose ... well, there is no rosy future for any of us."

Sometimes, I wish he would lie, care enough about me to try to soften his stark outlook. His pessimism is torturing me – I wish he would reach out and soften his words with a gentle touch, but instead he gets up in a flurry of dry fallen leaves and I find myself staring at his sandaled feet. His big toe is crooked and hairy, the nail long and broken. I wonder why I have come to care for him. Perhaps it is because he is the only one to have ever wanted me ... however briefly. I expect that since I let him have his way, he sees me as wanton, someone to be discarded like a soiled rag. I bite my bottom lip, willing myself not to beg, not to question, not to let him see my disappointment.

As I surreptitiously dry my tears, we are interrupted by the arrival of Grace. She comes crashing through the copse with her hand clenched tightly around Frances' wrist. Her face is white, her eyes huge and dark.

"What is it?" I scramble to my feet, my own worries forgotten. Frances shows no sign of upset but makes herself comfortable, sitting far closer to John than is seemly. Instead of pushing her away, he wraps her shawl more tightly around her. I suppress a pang of envy and turn my attention to Grace.

She is standing motionless at the fire, the light of the flames forming a nimbus around her, turning her into a statue of the Virgin. Her inner tension is evident from the set of her shoulders, the tautness of her neck. I move close beside her and slide my hands up her arms. "What is the matter?"

"I saw someone ..." She speaks slowly, as if unable to believe her own words. "Someone I used to know. Someone I thought to never see again."

I move closer.

"Who? Who did you see, Grace?"

She looks at me, her expression like that of a calf headed for slaughter.

"My cousin. I saw my cousin, William. He is in the company of Lord Darcy and it seems has become part of the pilgrimage."

"Your cousin? He is here? The one who stole your property and turned you from your home?"

"Yes. That is the one. He is here."

She steps into my arms, hungry for comfort, and I wonder how she will overcome this. Yet when she releases me at last, it is as if she has thrown off a cloak. Her face is lighter, the surliness vanished. "Margery," she says, "I feel as if I've been released from gaol. I suppose it was the shock of seeing him ..."

"But ... why does it make such a difference?"

"I don't know. Seeing him there in his fine get up, on his high horse about the injustices of the king, made me realise he is just a man, and not a very effective one either. I have faced greater threats than he these last months and, when this is done, I will find a way to seek justice for myself."

She smiles widely at the company. "We must organise supper," she says, her voice bright and positive. "And where is that boy with the pipe? Let's have some dancing and merriment. There is no need to be so dour."

Moving with purpose, she galvanises everyone into action. "John, skin and gut the rabbit you caught this afternoon. Frances, go gather kindling from the copse, please. Let's stoke up the fire a bit."

I watch her move with vigour, her movements no longer heavy, and discover a Grace I have never seen before. Perhaps I have never known the real Grace. Even when she first came to Arden, she was never like this. She has always been lethargic, resigned to her fate.

She looks down at her hands, turns them over and exclaims over the grime beneath her nails. Spying a bucket, she plunges her hands in and scrubs her fingers hard enough to make them bleed. This new Grace is determined enough to reclaim her rights; in fact, she seems determined enough to succeed at anything. Perhaps now, she will be strong enough to look upon her son. I take a step backwards.

"I must go and ask Janet for milk. Will you watch Andrew?"

"It will be better if you take him with you," she replies without turning around. "I know nothing of babies."

My heart plummets. She is not ready to acknowledge him; my role as surrogate mother is not over yet. With a sorry heart, I pluck Andrew from his sleeping place and leave her to her scrubbing.

When I return, she is singing a merry tune about a miller and a pig, but the sound does not fill me with the joy it should. This new-found positivity may well prove jading after a while. She may feel reinvigorated but we are still rebels, still at odds with our king. We are still homeless, still hungry, and far from home.

John returns with the skinned rabbit and Frances rushes to welcome him as if he has been away a week. He drapes an arm about her shoulder and passes the skinned carcass to Grace, who throws it in the pot with a handful of dried peas.

"Stocks are very low," she says, as if our meagre supply is usually vast. "But I expect this will all be over soon now that Aske has agreed negotiation with Norfolk."

"Has he?" I exchange glances with John. "When did you hear of this?"

She opens her eyes wide.

"Oh, didn't I tell you? I learned of it just before I saw William. I must have forgotten. I believe Aske and the other gentlemen met with Norfolk this morning."

She searches out a ladle and begins to stir the pot, seemingly oblivious to the importance of the turn of events. We now have hope. If the king's men have agreed to our terms and a pardon is to be issued, we can go home to Arden.

If not, we go to war.

I endure an anxious, almost sleepless night. A light rain falls, dampening our blankets and seeping into our bones. Frances, curled up behind me, sings a loud tuneless melody in which the only discernible word is 'John.' I am thankful that Andrew sleeps. As the sky begins to lighten, I watch his face materialise from the dark, noting the delicacy of his features, the likeness to Grace that increases the older he grows. When my child is born, will he look like me, or like John?

I remember Grace's great distended belly, her full blue-veined breasts when she carried Andrew. I prod curiously at my own body and find it as flat and bony as it ever was, but I have no idea how long it takes for a child to start to show.

It has been weeks since I gave myself to John and now, if he does not take me to wife, those short moments of sin may result in a lifetime of shame. But, since most people believe Andrew to be mine, people already look on me askance. Oh, so many worries plague me; I am overwhelmed by the bleakness of the future. I can think of it no more. Far too late to even contemplate sleeping, I hump deeper into the blankets and turn my face from the lightening sky, the sounds of people stirring in the pale morning.

Crim, Cram, and Rich,
With three "L" and the lich
As some men teach.
God them amend!
And that Aske may
Without delay
Here make a stay
And well to end!

Closing my eyes and willing sleep to come does not work and, eventually, Grace's voice singing the anthem of the pilgrims draws me from my sleeping place. Leaving Andrew tucked oblivious in the covers, I join her at the fire. She vigorously thrusts a burnt stick into the embers to restore the flames but, on hearing my step, she pauses and smiles over her shoulder.

"You're up early," she says. "We are the only ones abroad yet."

"Even Andrew hasn't stirred. There was a time when he woke every couple of hours. I am glad he sleeps the whole night now."

She makes no reply. My patience thins.

"Grace, you can't ignore him forever! If nothing else, he is part of our family. Soon, he will be walking, running around; will you continue to shun him then?"

Her expression turns mulish.

"It is painful to look on him."

"Force yourself, just once, to touch him, pick him up. See him for the child he is and forget the rigours of his birth."

"How can I *ever* forget that? It was like being tortured in the depths of hell. I can never look on him without recalling every detail, every twist of the knife!"

A memory of that night creeps into my mind: the praying nuns, the incompetent administration of Frances, Grace's screams as she fell victim to our collective ignorance. I see again Andrew's limp body, his corpse-like face, his bloodless lips. Fear twists my heart. What will it be like for me, giving birth on the road? At least Grace had the luxury of a roof over her head, a soft mattress to lie upon, a brazier to take the chill from the room. I may well have to give birth in a ditch and, if I die, what will happen to Andrew? What will happen to my child? What will happen to Frances?

My head teems with unanswered questions as problems pile up, one upon the other. Turning suddenly on my heel, I stride away through the camp, leaving Grace to tend her own hurts while I worry about mine.

After all our hardship, all our efforts, Aske and Norfolk come to peaceful terms. Two of our leaders, Sir Ralph Ellerker and Robert Bowes, agree to ride south with Norfolk to lay our petition before the king.

Speculation abounds among us.

"There is nothing to stop the king from just throwing them in the Tower and having done with it. They may be riding into a trap while we troop peacefully home."

"Or they could betray us, turn their coats and denounce us all."

"I've long suspected Ellerker's loyalty to us. In the beginning, didn't he refuse to join us? And before he came over to us, he went out of his way to defend Hull for the king."

Nobody is confident that things will go well in London, and an air of insecurity, of distrust, seeps through the pilgrim camp. Our leaders wear worried frowns and frequently we hear tales of argument and dissent between them. There is just one thing we are all united on and that is the cause of our Mother church: a cause that must not be lost.

2nd November 1536

After they ride away to petition the king, the pilgrims remain behind. We are aimless, our loss of purpose giving way to petty squabbles, fights among the menfolk, and dissent among the children. As the days progress, it grows colder, and the young and old begin to sicken. Frances, ever afflicted with chilblains in cold weather, snivels miserably by the fire. I take Grace to one side. "We cannot stay here. We must seek shelter."

"Well, many of our party have returned to their houses. Do you think we should travel back to Arden?"

As I think of it, nestled in the frost-rimed heath, a wave of longing washes over me, but I push it away.

"The prioress isn't there, and neither are our other sisters. For all we know, it is overrun with locals, or destroyed at Cromwell's hands."

"We won't know if we don't find out for ourselves. How long did it take to journey here? Could we be back by Christmas?"

"Back to what? A cold hearth, a raided store cupboard, and an empty barnyard? It would be foolish to consider it. Grace, we must not listen to our hearts, we must use our heads. I will speak to John ..."

She rolls her blanket into a bundle.

"Is he your master now? Why don't you just marry and be done with it?"

I do not reply but my cheeks grow hot and a lump forms in my throat. She stops what she is doing and sits back on her heels. "He hasn't asked you, has he? Is he your sweetheart? With all your quiet conversations and covert hand-holding, I thought that was the case."

I shake my head wordlessly. Lately, John has spoken only of the rebellion, the lack of food, ways to keep the cold at bay. He is courteous and friendly but there has been no tenderness, not since that night.

She stands up, regarding me with her hands clenched on her hips, her stare so intense I cannot look away. "If his feelings for you have changed, it is just as well you didn't give yourself to him."

My heart breaks. I can ignore it no longer. I am a fallen woman. My life is ruined. I fall to my knees, covering my face with my hands. Within moments, I feel her beside me, her fingers in my hair, her arm about my neck. "Oh, Margery, you didn't, tell me you didn't?"

Her sorrow sounds as acute as mine. She rocks me in her arms, crooning comforting murmurs until my weeping lessens enough for me to breathe again.

"Why didn't you tell me?" She offers a soiled kerchief but I refuse it and search instead for a clean spot on my petticoat. I blow my nose hard.

"How could I?"

My voice sounds thick and nasal. She nestles closer, her arms strong and firm about my shoulders.

"You can tell me anything, you know that. Do you … have you … will there be a child?"

I stare bleakly at the vast grey sky.

"I think so." My tears gather again, and drop upon my cheek. "How will I care for two infants when I can scarcely feed myself?"

"We will find a way. I will ensure it."

Voices break into our conversation and I hide my face as John and Frances enter the clearing. John bears a small sack of grain and a couple of turnips. With difficultly, he loosens Frances' grip on his hand and holds them aloft as if he carries a king's ransom. Belatedly, he recognises my upset.

"What's the matter, Margery? Are you ill?"

Grace releases me, rises to her feet and, taking John by the arm, drags him away but not out of earshot. Frances pouts and follows them but I am too full of care to call her back. Instead, I turn away and bury my head in shame as Grace's voice echoes through the wood.

"I had thought better of you, sir," she snaps. "Margery is a good honest girl, an innocent! How dare you defile her with your evil ways? You will do good by her and her child or, by Heaven, I will report you to the Archbishop."

I cannot look.

John sputters a denial.

"What do you mean? What child? I never touched her!"

I peep from the crook of my arm, disbelieving my own ears. Grace's fury increases; I can see it in her bunched fists and red cheeks.

"Margery would not lie!"

A short silence follows while my heart thumps in my ears. John clears his throat, shuffles his feet and speaks again, quietly and precisely.

"Then, perhaps she is mistaken."

Grace sticks out her chin.

"Did you lie with her?"

"No!"

His outrage is convincing. Glimpsing Frances' uncomprehending confusion, I wipe my streaming tears. Grace turns toward me.

"Then ... Margery?"

I stand up and force my trembling knees to take me towards them. I can't bear to look at John so I direct my gaze a little to the left and wish I were a thousand miles away. Through dry lips, I speak of my shame.

"That night in the Minster ..."

He makes a sound, something between a laugh and a cough; a sound of disbelief, of relief.

"That was a kiss, Margery! Ill advised perhaps, but you are not *defiled*. It takes more than a kiss to sully a woman, or to make a child!"

"Does it?" I turn questioning eyes on Grace, wondering what more there could possibly be between man and woman than that glorious kiss. She smiles suddenly, her face suffused with love and laughter.

"Yes, Margery, it takes so much more than a kiss."

They are smiling, they are *laughing* at me. Shame burns my ears, overwhelming the relief that I am not to be a mother in the spring. I don't know if I should laugh or cry so, instead, I turn and run from the humiliation of my own ignorance.

"Margery!" John calls after me but I keep running, do not look back.

"Leave her," I hear Grace say. "She just needs time."

I stay away until dusk. I weep and rage in turn as I wrestle with humiliation. I imagine them scorning my lack of education, the story passed around among the other pilgrims, turning me into a laughing stock. I have been away for hours and miss Andrew, fret that he is missing me and may be neglected in my absence.

Will they remember to change his linen, mix his grain as he likes it, make sure his milk has not soured? In the end, duty drives me back. I dry my eyes, brush the dirt from my skirts and, with my chin as high as I can lift it, I march back to camp.

It takes all my resolve to walk up and pluck Andrew from his blanket, feel his bottom for dampness. To me, he seems a little pale, a little dishevelled and somehow melancholy, as if he has missed me.

Grace is stirring gruel in a pot over the fire. She looks up with a smile.

"There you are. We are travelling back to York in the morning."

"York?" My voice is husky from weeping. I clear my throat before speaking again. "Why?"

"Now that Norfolk has ridden south with our petition, it makes sense to seek shelter. It is so much colder now winter is upon us."

Andrew makes a grab for my nose, his palm sticky with dribble, and I capture his hand in mine and blow raspberries on his fingers. He laughs, his mouth agape, his two tiny bottom teeth gleaming white. I kiss his head, close my eyes and inhale the healing loveliness of him.

December 1536 – York

The road to York holds no joy for me. I am weary of trudging about the countryside and long for the unchanging days of Arden. To think I once found the thought of the outside world fascinating. I would give anything to live those dull, predictable days again. Yet it is well that we have returned to the small comfort of York, for the roads have grown treacherous in the increasing cold. Even when crossing the market square my ankles turn on the frozen mud, so I am forced to take small steps, hobbling like a crone.

I have taken to leaving Andrew with Frances at the hearthside while I venture out to find a few scraps of food. She is heavy with a head cold and I know Andrew will soon be likewise, yet I struggle to find the nourishment they need. I never imagined the world could be as cold or as hard as this.

In the Minster, Archbishop Lee preaches of the virtues of obedience and we shiver as we listen stone-hearted in the bone-chilling nave. It is too late for obedience. We cannot change what we have done, we can only wait and hope, and pray for the king's mercy.

Nobody imagined we'd have to wait so long for the pardon; most of us thought we'd be safe home by Christmas, but winter has settled on us hard and still there is no news. The hills beyond the city are white, the skies black and heavy with further snow to come. While the rich folk feast at their warm firesides, the dispossessed perish in the deserted streets. Each day, the Minster fills with people seeking the pity of the church, and the paltry heat of the braziers.

When darkness falls, the cold increases, and our thin blankets do nothing to warm us. We huddle together with Andrew between me and Frances, while Grace clings to my back; but still we shiver.

"Where John?" Frances asks at every fifth heartbeat, and soon I am so weary of the question that I block out her voice. During the darkest, most miserable part of the night, I fear for our survival. I would not be surprised to wake to find Andrew stiff in my arms, or Frances covered in a blanket of frost.

When John seeks us out in the morning, Frances is still sleeping, and we are able to question him without interruption. I see straight away that something has changed. Keeping my eyes turned from him, I nudge Grace to alert her to his presence.

"You have news," she says, moving toward him. "Has the king made up his mind?"

John shakes his head.

"Nay, but he has invited Aske to court for Christmas."

Grace exchanges glances with me. I shrug my shoulders, at a loss to understand what this might mean. What are we to do while our leader enjoys the high life? How shall we survive while he grows fat at the king's expense?

I sigh and frown, wishing – not for the first time – that I'd never come. I should have left the fate of the country in the hands of other, stronger folk. Why did I not wait for the king's men to leave Arden and find a way to creep back inside? I cling to the old ways.

"What will Aske going to court serve? Why – what – do you think he has a chance of changing the king's mind?" Grace kneels at the hearth, poking the small flame with a burnt stick.

"I don't know. I expect they will discuss terms … conversation is often more productive than letters passed back and forth."

Discussing terms while dining on roast swan and honeyed wafers! It makes me uneasy and I am grateful when Grace asks the question I long to voice.

"Can we trust the king? Can we be sure there is not some … other plan?"

While my belly rolls at the thought of the king's dinner, Grace scowls at John, who holds out his palms toward the fire.

"You can't be sure of anything when it comes to the king. We can only hope that Aske has the skill to help him see the error of his ways."

And then what? I ask myself. What will become of us all? I want to go home. I want things to be as they were before. I want to hear the rough tongue of Sister Dorothea, feel the lash of the prioress' girdle on my palm, the damp dark comfort of the dormitory, the stench of the barnyard, the freedom of the fragrant springtime hills.

Frustration bursts from me in a cry. I bury my face in my hands, forcing back the urge to scream. There is nothing to be done but wait; shouting into the wind won't help at all.

Trapped in winter's frozen fingers, we wait a few weeks longer until, eventually, word filters to us that not just Yorkshire but the whole of England is covered in ice. In London, King Henry and Queen Jane travel on horseback from Whitehall to Greenwich, beside the frozen River Thames. I have no way of knowing how far that is but those around me exclaim over it, so I imagine it is distant.

We also learn that the king has made Aske the gift of a crimson coat, and I expect everyone at court is clad in furs and velvets. Here, on the pilgrimage, we wear the same threadbare habits we've been wearing for months. I expect the king's daughters are well nourished and warm, not like my Andrew, who has become a skeletal starveling. We should never have left Arden ... we should have stayed at home.

I have forgotten our forced eviction, the forlorn expectation of being taken in by the nuns at Wilberfoss. I have forgotten that, then, I believed the world to be a kind place, the sort of place where the desires of women like me mattered.

Waiting ... waiting ... waiting. Tempers grow short and friendships are broken, but we cleave to one another, back to back against the brutality of the world. Leaving Andrew and Frances under the watchful eye of Janet, we venture out to look for work; a few hours service in exchange for a loaf. Some of the women among us creep to the darker side of town to offer men the comfort of their bodies in exchange for a penny or two, but I would sooner perish of cold and hunger than stoop to that.

When we approach the market square, a party of horseman is cutting its way through the crowd. We turn toward the sound of hooves, see a few ragged men raise their fists, muttering curses as they are forced to move from the path of the gentlemen as they ride by. Grace grabs my arm, forcing me to stop.

"Look," she says, with a wicked narrowed stare. "There he is."

"Who?" I scan the crowd for a familiar face.

"Him," she spits. "My *dear* Cousin William."

I follow her gaze to a tall fellow who has just dismounted from his horse. He is good to look upon, his expression is open and seemingly honest; his clothes are of good cloth and his mount bears a fine ornate saddle. To me, he looks like a great lord, a prince even, and there is no outward clue to the evil that lurks within him. But Sister Dorothea always said that you can never tell where the devil chooses to make his lodging.

Cousin William passes the reins to a groom and sprints up the steps to the Minster. I had imagined an older man; someone jowly, balding and stout. This man is in his prime and, from his looks, you'd never guess the darkness of his soul. At the top of the steps, he turns and calls some instruction to his page. Grace holds her breath, ducking her chin into her shoulder as his eyes run over us, but he does not falter. No doubt he sees only two down-at-heel nuns, not the pretty cousin he robbed and ill-used.

As we watch, he rubs his hands together and draws his thick cloak tighter across his chest. I wonder that he can feel the cold through so many layers of woollen garments. People like him know nothing of hardship; their world is so different to ours. He cannot imagine the pain of chilblains, the rolling discomfort of an empty belly, or the misery of watching the child you love grow weak from want of nourishment.

"I wonder if he ever thinks of you or if he gives any thought to your fate now the priory has closed? He clearly knows all about it or he'd not be part of the rising."

"I daresay he forgot about me the moment I was dropped at the priory door. He is intent only upon what he can gain. I hope he perishes of the pox."

"You might get your wish. With a face like that, the whores will be after him."

Grace throws back her head.

"Hark at you, so worldly-wise!" She slides her arm through mine and, lifting our already mired skirts from the filth of the street, we continue on our way.

It is the hungriest festive season I have ever endured. At Arden, there would be a goodly table with pies and pastries and sometimes a goose provided from the prioress' purse. What I miss most is the sense of family, the sense of belonging. Here at York, we are among strangers and, although our pockets are bare, we constantly look over our shoulders, fearful of pickpockets.

Somehow, although the youngest and oldest among us sicken, Andrew avoids the fever. He is hungry, ever fractious, always wailing for food. Now that he has sufficient teeth, I pass most of my paltry serving to him, but the satisfaction of seeing his hunger sated does nothing at all for my own ravenous, rolling belly. I notice a growing weakness in my limbs, a breathlessness when I walk, and I know I am slowly starving. So when John appears an hour after supper with a brace of skinned hares, my reticence melts away. I smile widely, forgetting my shame and looking directly into his eyes, but the moment they meet, the memory of that kiss I had mistaken for so much more intrudes. I whip my face away before he can speak to me.

For a while, everyone is busy preparing for the meal, our mouths watering, teased by the aroma of roasting meat. I am so desperate for it I would eat it raw.

It has barely cooked enough to eat when we fall upon it, burning our fingers and tongues but, once our initial appetite is sated, we slow down, taking time to savour it. Who knows when we will enjoy another such meal?

"I wonder when we will have news of Aske," I say, not for the first time. "Perhaps he is having such a high time at court that he has forgotten us."

Frances leans against John's arm. Every so often, he pops a strip of meat into her mouth and she swallows it, barely chewing. Grace wipes grease from her lips with the back of her hand and tears another strip from the hare's carcass.

"Aske is not the sort to forget. He knows he must tread carefully. I expect he is slowly courting the king, explaining our cause, helping him see it from our position. We cannot expect to hear word before the Feast of Fools is over."

"Feast of Fools? What is that?"

She rinses her mouth and wipes her fingers.

"The Feast of Fools is a special day at court when life turns topsy-turvy. The king gives up his throne to the Lord of Misrule, who is usually one of the royal fools, and everyone at court has to follow his orders. As you can imagine, he leads them all on a merry dance and the king can do nothing but play along."

I frown, failing miserably to imagine a lowly fool ordering the king to bring him wine, or sit on a stool at his feet. Surely, Grace must have misunderstood. If our pilgrimage has taught me anything, it is that the king greatly dislikes to be mocked, and I cannot imagine him accepting instruction from those beneath him.

I try to picture Robert Aske, that large lowering one-eyed man, enjoying such unruly courtly games, and the memory of his face reminds me of his honesty. He will not forget we are starving, he knows our struggle to exist. His mission is to turn the mind of the king from destroying our Holy Church. He will not forget that, not for one moment. If I had any, I would lay down coin against him countenancing such frivolity while his followers suffer penury.

Each moment leads to the next, slowly adding up to an hour, that hour expanding to a day, that day to a week, that week to a month. In January, it snows again, wetter this time, the damp penetrating the thick walls of the Minster and the thin coverings on our backs. I grow so hungry that my teeth become loose and my skin breaks out into sores. When I wash the shite from

Andrew's body, the bones of his knees are like knuckles, his ribs like hoops on a broken barrel. I am not sure how much longer we can go on.

Dissent is so rife among us that faith in Aske begins to falter. Dispossessed monks gather in groups to mutter against the king, against his men, and even accuse our leader of having forsaken us for the pleasures of Greenwich.

"Home." Frances huddles inside her ragged habit and repeats the word over and over. I try to explain that Arden is no more, and that our sisters are scattered, but she cannot understand. She looks at me with her strange almond-shaped eyes and repeats the word. "Home. Home."

Her once-hefty body is now wasted, the habit that once fitted too snugly about her round belly now hangs empty. If I do not find us proper lodgings somewhere soon, I know we shall all perish. I see the confusion in her eyes and my heart turns over at the peril I have led her into. I take her into my arms and she weeps hot tears on my shoulder.

A great shout goes up from a group of men playing at dice. They roll about the floor like curs arguing over a bone, and I draw my charges away to a spot closer to the door. We are safer away from the rough drinking men, but the draught blows more fiercely here.

I tuck Andrew beneath my arm, wrap my blanket snugly around him and try to ease him to sleep. *Please God,* I pray, *please help us. Please send a resolution. Let me go home once more.*

January 1537

I must have dropped into a blissful slumber for, when the door is thrown open, I jerk awake. My head is heavy, my mind confused as I focus blearily through the gloom. A man is waving his arms, shouting something. I shake my head, forcing myself to make sense of his jumbled words.

"The East Riding has risen in defiance of the king!"

The company erupts in a babble of voices, questioning, exclaiming, a few of them cheering. Rudely awakened by the sudden din, Andrew begins to bawl and I sweep him into my arms, put my lips against his head.

The voices of the angry men clash like swords.

"It's about time; how long are we supposed to wait? I say we should join them ..."

"No. We must be patient. Aske says the king is considering our requests. He has already promised a parliament in the north, a visit from the king himself. Once he sees—"

The voice of reason is cut short, its caution drowning in the rising tide of anger. I watch their excitement grow, their conviction that we must seek another way for the restoration of the church. They have tried the peaceful path and now, having lost hope in Aske, they want to resort to rebellion. With fear washing in my belly, I jiggle Andrew on my hip, pressing my lips to his clammy forehead as our unity fragments. Men are shoving their scanty possessions into packs, kissing their weeping women, abandoning their starving children and embarking on a God-forsaken mission.

What will become of us without our men? Who will hunt? Who will protect us? But surely, they will not all go – a few will remain behind. John! I search the hubbub, pushing and shoving through the crowd until I locate him standing alone in the shadow of the wall. I stop, unsure now that I have found him of what I am going to say ... and then he sees me and smiles, his mouth stretching, his missing tooth drawing my attention. Remembered attraction twists in my gut and heat rushes to my cheeks. Removing the straw he has been chewing, he throws it to the floor and reaches out to take my arm, drawing me and Andrew to the safety of a chapel.

"Margery."

"John. What will happen now? What should we do?"

He is silent, his eyes narrowing, his brow lined with thought.

"I think I will join with them, but you, Margery, you should return to Arden …"

"But …"

He holds up his hands, ordering me to be silent, and I subside, waiting for his words.

"I know Arden is closed, but there must be somewhere nearby, some neighbour who showed you kindness. You belong there, Margery, not here amidst this … violence. You must get Andrew and Frances to safety … Grace will help you."

"But what about you? This rebellion … it is ill advised. The king will not show mercy twice … wait until Robert–"

He cuts me short again. "Aske has failed, Margery. I am certain he is more of a hostage than a guest at court. The king seeks to drive a wedge between us and the nobles. He knows he is powerless against so great an army as ours, so he stoops to duplicity to divide us. Nothing is beneath him."

An overwhelming wave of exhaustion washes over me. I lean against the wall, slide to the floor and sit in a heap. I can fight no more. I will do as John says. I will go home to Arden. Although there is nothing there and the kindly neighbours of John's imagining do not exist, I shall return and see what future can be made there. I will not be sorry to leave York, for it has shown me nothing but suffering.

He squats at my side, places a hand on my cheek, and I wonder if he is going to kiss me again, but instead, he smiles gently, stirring my heart.

"Get yourselves away from here. I will come to you afterwards ... if I am able."

By the time my eyes are dry of tears he has left, his robes sweeping a cloud of dust from the floor. Dragging a hand across my cheeks, I struggle to my feet, while Andrew clings like a cleaver to my torso. *Cleavers*: little sticky green balls that cling to my skirts when I'm working in the garden. The thought of the garden is like the taste of honey – sweet and warm and revitalising. I will go home. I will go home to Arden this very day.

In a matter of hours, Grace, Frances and me are among the disbanded pilgrims travelling the road out of York. Some intend to join the fight, some are fleeing from it, but none of us is happy. We are defeated, hungry and disillusioned with our grand cause, which, in the beginning, promised so much.

Occasionally on our journey, we are passed by horsemen; they gallop past, cloaks flying, leaving us to curse at the spattering mud kicked up by their horses. I wish I had a horse or an ass to speed us on our way. Sister Mary told me a story once of a winged fairy creature that could fly away from danger. I wish I were she, or had a magical candle that could burn away the years, taking me backward in time. If only all this were a dream and in the morning I could wake and find myself safe in my narrow cot at Arden, with Sister Dorothea scolding me for being late for Mass. I clench my jaw and place one foot before the other, head down, making for home.

February 1537

While we can, we pilgrims journey together, but soon it will be time for us to turn from the main road and take the less travelled way that leads to Arden. Food is even scarcer now. Janet's sheep have dwindled to just three and, with little access to pasture, their milk is drying up. She travels ahead of us on the road and I draw comfort from the scattering of droppings underfoot that inform me a remnant of the flock still lives.

When it is time to halt for a while, I will share my small loaf with her and, from the kindness of her heart, she will spare me a little warm nutty milk, which is the only thing keeping Andrew alive. I just pray we reach Arden before it turns rancid, and that God will provide some other way of feeding him.

There is no joviality among us now. News comes daily of a new rising, fresh vengeance of the king's men upon the rebels, and we all fear we will be next – even though we want no part in the violence.

"Where John?"

I ignore Frances and link arms with Grace.

"How long before the road to Arden diverts?"

"I don't know, Grace. In many ways, I am loath to part from the company – we've been together for so long and without Janet and her flock … what will Andrew do?"

Grace bites her lip and shakes her head as if she has greater worries.

"We must head north as quickly as we can; we have to distance ourselves from this."

Noting her wrinkled forehead, I grasp her sleeve and pull her back.

"What aren't you telling me?"

Strands of fair hair have escaped the confines of her veil; she drags it back and turns into the wind as she replaces it. She pauses while Frances stomps past before putting her head close to mine and speaking fearfully into my ear.

"Norfolk has reached Westmorland and raised the king's banner. He is determined to make a stand against us and put down the uprising. Even though we have no part in it, if we are captured ... the punishment will be–"

A great cry goes up and we both turn to find Frances sprawled in the dirt. We run to help her to her feet. While Grace does her best to brush the mud from Frances' skirts, I pick stones from the palms of her hands, her miserable cries grating on my nerves, drowning the soothing sounds I make.

"We must move on." Grace glances along the road. The gap between us and our companions is widening. Behind, a party of boisterous youths is catching up with us. As they draw parallel, they take note of Frances' bedraggled state and pause in their journey to add to her torment.

One of them darts behind and lifts the back of her habit, revealing her dirty legs. Frances whips around and lashes out with her fist, by chance catching one fellow beneath the jaw. Once, such a blow would have floored him and even now, he puts up a hand and looks at it as if expecting blood.

"She struck me!" he cries, indignation blossoming pink upon his cheeks. "The idiot struck me!"

His friends collapse into laughter, clutching at one another's robes, but the injured boy does not see the joke. With his face full of menace, he leaps forward and punches Frances hard on the shoulder. I hear the crack of bone. Grace forces herself between our friend and her assailant and I do likewise.

"Leave her alone. Go."

We stand side by side, our chins raised, our eyes fixed on his snivelling features. Beneath my habit, my knees are shaking as hard as if I have the plague. We have no weapon to use against him and although I cast about for some way of fending him off, there is nothing to hand. And then, as if she has spoken into my ear, I hear Sister Dorothea's voice. I make myself as tall as I can. My tongue moves and words issue from it that are not my own.

"The Lord sees all our sins," I declare, fixing him with my narrowed eyes. He scowls and glances from me to Grace, who clasps her hands in the manner of the prioress.

"But He is forgiving to those who truly seek repentance."

He spits on the ground, missing her skirt by a shade before he backs away. When he is at a sufficient distance, he shouts an obscenity about idiots and what should be done with them.

As they scamper off, we exhale in relief. "Thank goodness," Grace laughs. "There must still be some semblance of godliness beneath the grime that smothers us."

She attempts to brush dried mud from her garments, sending up a cloud of dust, but gives up, knowing there is little point. We will soon be mired head to toe again.

"Come along, we must hurry to make up lost time or we will make no progress today. Andrew will soon be wailing for his dinner and we will be forced to stop again."

With a hand to her injured shoulder, Frances weeps loudly, her face smeared with tears and snot. "Where John? Where John?" she wails, her voice keeping monotonous time with our steps. In the end, unable to bear any more, Grace turns on her.

"He has gone, Frances. Do you hear me? Gone. Ridden off with the other fools to face probable death. Now hold your tongue and walk."

I can see from her expression that she regrets her words before she has finished speaking, but the damage is done. Frances refuses to be appeased, and refuses Grace's profuse apology. She stamps along behind us, her chin on her chest, tears trickling down the side of her nose. I hoist Andrew higher on my hip and we travel in silence for what remains of the daylight.

Although I try to distract her and make her smile again, Frances will not look at me. We halt at dusk and make camp at the side of the road, but she refuses to help Grace gather wood for the fire. She sits apart from us, her back against a tree, her knees drawn up to her chin and her blanket swathed so high that we cannot see her face.

"Let her sulk," Grace says. "She will forget about it soon. Wait and see; come morning, she will be her usual self."

I hope so, I think, as I prepare a makeshift bed.

We sleep early, worn out by the rigours of the day, and wake in a cold blue light that promises nothing but misery for the journey ahead. Andrew starts to wail the moment he wakes, his piercing cries jagging on my nerves. In a useless attempt to keep him warm, I drape the blanket over us as I attempt to feed him but, like a beggar in the night, the penetrating cold seeks a way in, finding every nook. In the early morning gloom, Andrew's pinched white face, crusted nose and chapped lips reproach me for the mistakes I have made. Perhaps it would have been better to stay in York, where at least there was a roof above our heads.

While I am packing up, Grace returns from making herself comfortable in the nearby wood.

"Where is Frances?" she asks with a nod at her empty sleeping place.

"Did you not see her? I thought she'd gone with you."

Grace shakes her head, the bones of her skull stark beneath her white skin. Then she rummages though our things.

"Her pack is gone."

I scramble to my feet.

"Gone? Are you sure?"

I twist my neck this way and that, searching for a sign of her well-loved figure, her wide, smiling face.

"Perhaps she is with Janet ..."

But Janet is camped nearby. I can see her wide hips as she squats to milk her remaining sheep. Frances is not with her.

"Janet!" I call, and she turns her head, waves a cheery hand. "Have you seen Frances this morning?"

Her smile fades. She shakes her head and my stomach rolls sickeningly.

"Nay, chicken, I haven't. Has she wandered off?"

"She is probably not far away."

Janet stands up, bucket in hand, and catches sight of one of the camp boys.

"Hey, Ned – have you seen young Frances this morning?"

The boy shakes his head.

"Go in search of her and if you bring her back, I will give you a cup of milk."

Further persuasion unnecessary, he ducks off through the trees, calling her name, but some instinct tells me she will not answer.

My fingers fumble with Andrew's linen. I wrap him tightly in his blanket and summon Grace to help secure him to my back. Grabbing my pack, I kick cold ashes over the fire.

"Wait!" Grace hurries after me, forcing me to stop. "What if she returns and we're not here? What will she do then?"

I think rapidly. Grace is right. One of us must remain behind.

"You wait here then. I will travel on ahead. I must find her ..."

"Where will you look? Will you stay on the road or turn off for Arden? She will not know the way home. How will you know which road she has taken?"

I frown, shaking my head as I try to stem rising panic. I dash away tears.

"I don't think she's gone home. I think she has gone in search of John." My words are swallowed by grief

144

and worry. I close my eyes, clenching my jaw tightly. Grace's fingers encircle my wrist.

"Oh Margery, I hope you are wrong. She will never catch them up; John and the other men left long ago. If she ... or you, are caught up in the fighting ..."

There is no need for her to speak of the great danger we will both face. Our gazes lock as we silently acknowledge the truth. I nod wordlessly but can see no other choice. I have to find her. I can't allow a simple girl like Frances to wander the countryside unattended.

"It makes no difference. I have to go."

She draws me into her embrace, her ribs clashing against mine, and when we draw apart, she starts to fumble with the knots that bind Andrew to me.

"What are you doing?"

"You cannot take the child into danger. He will be safer with me."

"But ..."

"I will care for him properly, Margery. He is my son, after all..."

Once, I would have given anything to hear her admit that, yet now he is everything to me and I do not want to let him go. Somehow, our souls have become entwined; his misfortunes will always be mine. With breaking heart, I allow her to take him from me. He knuckles his eye, puts his thumb in his mouth and frowns at the grief I am struggling to conceal. I stroke his head, the fine hair clogged with grime.

"Stay with Janet, Grace, at all costs. Andrew needs the milk and ... sing him the pilgrims' song. He likes that; it seems to help him sleep."

With a ragged breath, I turn on my heel and walk swiftly away, setting off on my own into a world turned mad. I do not allow myself to look back.

It does not take long for the sounds of the camp to dwindle, leaving me isolated – alone, as I have never been before. The road stretches dauntingly before me. I miss the weight of Andrew on my back, the simple conversation of my friends. I am dwarfed by the giant trees that flank the road; the woodland is dark and intimidating, hiding God knows what. I feel it pressing down on me, a thousand eyes watching as I pass, each bush, each bend in the road concealing a villain. As I trudge doggedly on, I realise how insignificant I am. With all the prayers the good Lord receives, why should he pay heed to mine? But still I beseech him. Please, let me find Frances around the next corner. Let her be safe. Help Grace care for Andrew. Let them be hale and hearty when I return. Watch over John and those who fight against the wishes of the king.

Each word of every prayer marks time with the steady progress of my feet. My heart quails at what may lie ahead and I long to turn back to the safety of the other pilgrims but, reminding myself of Frances' vulnerability, her innocence, her ... I force myself onward. One step follows another; one more bend in the road; a wayside bothy; a river to ford; a hamlet. Night will soon fall and I realise I haven't eaten since dawn. I hesitate outside a tumbledown holding where a thin spiral of smoke seeps from a ragged thatched roof.

The dwelling could be full of thieves, or it could be a place of God. As I linger outside, trying to make up my mind, an elderly fellow emerges from the yard. He looks me up and down and tucks the jug he carries beneath his arm.

"Can I 'elp 'ee, lass?" he bellows.

I return the stare, assessing the goodness of his heart, until he tucks his hand behind his filthy ear and bends it forward. "Speak up though, won't 'ee; I'm a mite deaf."

He grins, gap-toothed, the lines of his face imbedded with the filth of years, but I sense a friend.

"I need shelter for the night but I have no coin. Is there a barn or a–"

He steps forward and, instinctively, I draw back, reassessing him, unsure of his intent.

"I'll not hurt 'ee, lass. My good wife would ne'er forgive I were I t' send a nun to sleep wi' the goats."

I allow him to take my elbow and guide me beneath the lintel. Warmth assaults my frozen skin as a woman, as wide as a church door, turns from the cooking fire to greet us, ladle in hand.

"Hello, who 'ave we here, my dear?"

I have never been so relieved in my life. Kindness hovers around her like a nimbus. She puts down her spoon and bustles forward, tossing questions at me without waiting for my answer. Quickly, I am drawn into the firelit circle and plied with incurious questions and food in such quantity that I wonder if I can manage it.

Too close to the fire but too tired to move, my cheeks sting as they begin to thaw. The old man, whom I discover is named Jed, dumps my cloak and pack in a corner. His wife, Joan, thrusts a bowl of hot broth into my hands. I look at it. More food than I have eaten in one sitting for months. Unexpectedly, my stomach turns at the prospect and I am unsure if I can swallow it. I pick up the spoon and let my tongue decide. A thousand flavours burst upon my palate and my belly rolls, my throat tightens …

"Ye must take it slow, child. Let thy gut become used to it. I warrant 'tis a while since 'ee ate."

"It has been long since my hunger was fully sated …"

"Sometimes takes a while. Thee might find 'ee can only manage a spoon or two at first."

She ladles out two more bowls, handing one to Jed who squats at my knee, slurping and smacking his lips.

"Have 'ee travelled far, lass? Did they shut down your house?"

I nod sadly. "Yes. I am from Arden, close to Hawnby."

She shakes her head, the name unfamiliar to her, and waits for me to continue.

"My companions and I joined the pilgrims. I've been as far as York, to Pontefract ... everywhere." As I relate my adventure, I am astounded at how widely I have travelled.

"Where are they at now, thy friends?"

"Back on the road a way. We ... I ... lost someone in my charge. She is vulnerable ..."

"Vulnerable?" She falters over the word and I hesitate, searching my tired mind for a substitute.

"She is simple ... has difficulties. People ... bad people, make fun of her and seek to do her harm."

"Nay." She places both hands above her substantial stomach and shakes her head. "They never do. Folks can be so cruel."

I put down the bowl and stand up, take two steps toward her.

"Have you seen a girl passing by? She is this tall ..." I hold my hand at the approximate height of Frances, "in a habit like mine, with a – a ragged cloak."

Joan shakes her head regretfully.

"I wish I had, child. JED ..." she raises her voice. "JED, didst thou see a girl passing, not quite right int' head?" She whirls her fingers in a circle at her temple while Jed gapes at her, absorbing the possible meaning of her words.

"I see a cart earlier, a band of rebel monks, I'd say by t' looks of 'em. A gurl were sittin' ont' back showin' her knees ... she could be a nun by her cloes."

"T' roads are full o' nuns these days." Joan shakes her head.

I put down my bowl.

"A nun. What way were they headed?"

"Eh?"

"What way were they going?" It goes against all my training to shout but I am anxious for his reply.

"East. I doubt they'll get far, the poor beast drawin' t' cart looked set t' drop any minute."

It *must* be her. I go to the door, look out at the deep blue sky, the bitter bright stars, and know I cannot travel tonight. I must wait until dawn.

I need all the sleep I can get but my mind will not rest. Jed snores in his pallet on the other side of the hearth, competing with every creak and groan of the roof timbers. I start at the cry of some animal as it falls victim to an owl or a fox. I should thank God for the provision of these kind people who have offered the safety of their hearth and roof, but I do not feel blessed. I am steeped in shame at my own foolishness that has led to this. Huddled in my cloak beside the dying fire, I try to count my blessings. I am warm while my friends are cold; fed while my friends are starving; safe while my friends are at the mercy of the world. But I would give years of my life to be with them now, to have Andrew slumbering softly on my chest. Each time my limbs relax and my mind begins to slide into sleep, an image bursts in my mind of Frances at the mercy of a gang of strangers. I jerk awake and clamber from my blanket to pray and beg God to keep her in his sight.

It is only a few months since I left the security of Arden and in that time I have travelled far, learned much from countless people. I have mingled with rich and poor, the unlearned and the wise. I have seen great kindness but also great cruelty. I have known suffering and been overwhelmed at the way those in need share what little they have with their friends. I was fortunate indeed to find Jed and Joan. I focus on their goodness and hope Frances also finds herself among such kindly folk.

I take my leave of them as early as the light allows, hitch my pack onto my shoulder and set up as rapid a pace as I can sustain. As the hours stretch toward noon, I pass other groups of travellers, which reminds me how foolish it is to travel alone, especially for a woman. I search each band of pilgrims carefully, looking for the familiar ragged cloak, the broad shoulders and the wide smile of Frances.

"Have you seen a young woman, a nun, travelling with a band of monks?" I ask of them, but each time I meet with blank expressions, the slow shake of a head.

I join such a band of travellers while I break my fast. I still have the small loaf and corner of hard cheese that Joan insisted I carry with me. I share it gladly with my companions, my small contribution adding to their meagre fare. As we eat together, I tell them of my quest to find Frances.

"You must hurry, lass. If she is captured by the king's men ... they're not likely to show mercy ... not this time."

"The Duke of Norfolk?"

"Aye, that's him. The gentry are abandoning Bigod's camp in droves."

"Bigod? Who is he?"

"He's the one behind this latest uprising. He's no faith in Aske and has taken matters into his own hands."

The people around me begin to argue; some are for the old ways, others for a compromise. Most of them just want an end to it, the right to live their lives as they have always done.

"I heard Bigod's plan was to take Norfolk prisoner and hold him hostage to the king's agreement to our demands."

"I can't see the king doin' that. He'd as soon lose Norfolk than face."

Again, the babble of voices swamps me. I chew the last vestiges of my scanty meal and stare into the distance. I no longer care what the king decides. I just want peace. I want to be reunited with my friends and left alone to live life the way God intended. Whatever that means.

When the meal is over, I bid them farewell.

"You should travel with us, lass," they say, but I shake my head. There are old men and children among them and I must travel as swiftly as I can.

The afternoon is one of watery sunshine, with intervals of fine freezing rain that soaks my habit to the knees and masks my cheeks with moisture. I am freezing, my limbs heavy and stiff. It is almost nightfall before I spy the tall spires and roofs of a town ahead. I am unsure which town it is but I know the gates will already be closed for the night. I look around for a place to rest. In the dusk, the lights of a small hamlet straggle up the hill, the road through it shining pale in the moonlight.

And then I notice the flicker of a fire in a small copse beside the road. I halt and listen, unsure whether to approach or travel quietly by. No doubt these people are also awaiting entry to the town in the morning. I smell roasting meat – rabbit, I think – and there is a murmur of laughter that piques my loneliness. I have just decided to make myself known to them when somebody starts singing. And then a voice, louder than the other, joins in: Frances' voice!

Without further thought, I plunge headlong from the path and into the ring of firelight. The company leap to its feet; I hear the rasp of metal as weapons are drawn. Someone thrusts me harshly against a tree, the bark rough through my habit, and a blade wavers just below my chin. I drop my pack with a cry and raise my hands in supplication.

"I mean no harm," I plead. "I carry no weapon."

"A woman!" The man lowers his sword and the company relaxes. Some turn disinterestedly back to the fire but enough remain to discomfort me.

"Margery!" Frances barges through the ring of men and springs forward into my arms. I draw her close, breathing in the musty scent of her robes, stroking her unwashed hair. She is safe; she is breathing; she is here.

"Margery my friend," she tells them, signalling the monk to sheath his sword. "Margery my *sister*."

The band of raggedy monks warily withdraw their weapons, one or two give me greeting while the others turn away, satisfied I pose no threat. I stroke Frances' filthy face.

"What were you thinking of to leave us, Frances? We have been so worried and I have travelled far to find you."

"I want John." She wipes a tear from her cheek. "I find him."

"It is not safe, Frances. John will return after–" I halt mid-sentence. After what? After the battle? After the victory? What if there is no victory, what if there is only defeat? I finish my sentence lamely. "Afterwards, when it is all done."

Belatedly, I turn to the monks. "I must thank you for taking care of my sister. She is ..."

"We know what she is, Sister Margery. We found her travelling alone ... it is not safe for anyone to travel unaccompanied, let alone the likes of her, yet it seems you too ignore the danger."

They stand in a ring of judgement.

"My concern was to find her, take her home."

"Home?" Frances looks up, her face alight with hope. "Arden?"

"Yes," I say. "Home to Arden." There is, after all, nowhere else to go.

It is good to sleep with the warmth of Frances' back behind me and suffer the assault of her snores; snores I once complained of. All I need is Andrew on my chest and Grace slumbering nearby and I will be content. Tomorrow, I think, as I drift off, tomorrow we will travel back, meet them on the road and break our ties with the pilgrims and all will be well again. Perhaps we can prise one of Janet's sheep from her and take it with us. Perhaps things will be well after all. Peace falls. We slumber.

A scream rips the darkness. I scramble from my sleeping place, blindly groping for Andrew before I remember he is not with me. Frances clutches at me, her breath hot and putrid in my face.

"What?" I cast about, squinting through the gloom. Horses! Many of them! I grab Frances' wrist.

"Run, Frances, as fast as you can."

We run, heads down through the darkness, away from the cries of our dying friends and the sickening thud of their falling bodies.

Ducking through a garden gate, I cast about for a hay store or a tangle of bushes that might conceal us. Grabbing her wrist, I pull Frances into a briar patch, the thorns snagging and tearing at our robes and limbs. As we crouch in the dark, she trembles, wiping her wet cheeks on my sleeve. I can just distinguish her bone-white face and the stark terror in her eyes, and I am sickened with guilt that I have led her to this. Her life is now forfeit to my mistaken conviction that simple folk can make a difference.

I grope for God in the faithless void of my mind, begging that the king's men grow tired of the hunt and ride away, back to their warm hearths, their laden tables, and their fragrant, sinful wives. Frances' teeth begin to rattle, her breath faltering as her courage dwindles. I give her a gentle shake and put a warning finger against her lips, beseeching her to be silent, to be brave for just a little longer.

As the stealthy hooves draw closer to our hiding place, we hold our breath, sinking deeper into the undergrowth when he halts just a little way above our heads. The dank aroma of rotting vegetation rises; the tang of frost tickles my nose and pinches my toes. Frances trembles so violently it is indistinguishable from the juddering of my own body. I fumble for prayer, nausea washing over me as I fail to recall a single one.

There's a creak of harness as the rider shifts in his saddle. I cannot see him but when the horse snorts, in my mind's eye his breath mists the darkness, rising wraith-like in the night. I can feel the rake of the man's gaze as he searches, seeking out our hiding place. My lungs strain fit to burst, my chest is aching, and I am ready to relinquish my freedom for just one blessed breath. The horse stirs, turns and moves away, and we fill our lungs with fresh damp air. We clutch hands as the vague hope of escape returns.

Then noise erupts with a harsh yelp. A hound is loosed and, with a furious growl, it crashes through the hedge. As I fall backward, I glimpse a lolling tongue, and yellow eyes stare briefly into mine; cold, murderous eyes. Frances' scream shatters the night as the jaws clamp down upon her wrist.

"Let go! Let go!" I strike out with my bare feet, feeling the crack of bony ribs beneath a silken coat. The hound yelps but holds on fast, screaming aloud as I kick out again, hammering his head with my heels. The air fills with a confusion of hooves, screaming women, and triumphant male laughter as they lay hands upon us. As they drag me to my feet, Frances gives a loud unintelligible sound that breaks my heart.

"Please," I beg, as my hands are wrenched behind me and roughly held. "We are nuns from Arden. My sister has done nothing. Take me but ... let Sister Frances go – she ... she doesn't understand."

A white dagger of agony flashes though my skull as my captor clouts me around the ear. My head rings and my vision blurs. Through a fog of pain, I realise they are hauling Frances from the ground, dragging us both rudely forward.

"Hold them," the man on the horse orders, and their grip tightens as he slides from his saddle, hawks and spits on the ragged skirts of my habit before slowly unfurling a rope from his belt.

The knots are tight about my wrists; my hands are numb. I cry out as the horse jolts forward and, tethered to the saddle, all we can do is follow him. Agonisingly, we retrace our route back the way we have come, through the hamlets and homesteads that earlier offered us shelter.

Our cause is lost. Our peaceful mission to bring England back to the true church has failed; doomed by the promises of a false king. In the lightening dawn, the slack-limbed, sightless bodies of those who aided us sway as we pass by. The voiceless, lifeless men, women and children who dared to share our questioning of the king's wisdom gape blindly at our passing.

Me and Frances will join them soon; our useless lives cut short, our fruitless existence ended in ignominy.

My throat grows tight. How have we come to this?

At first, I fear he will sling a rope over the next low-hanging bough and end our suffering here and now, but instead he forces us uphill. When dawn is almost breaking, he calls a halt at a church, where tombstones loom drunkenly from the morning mist and the frosted grass crunches beneath our feet. At the church door, he leaps from the saddle and unties the rope, dragging us, weeping and fighting, into the nave. Beneath the rood, a blaze of candles burns and, as we are dragged past, I whisper a frantic prayer that is broken short by a rough hand on my shoulder.

The earth disappears from beneath my feet and we fall, our limbs barking against stone steps, our heads crashing on the flagstone floor of the crypt. The darkness is so intense that I cannot see Frances; I can only hear the dry rasping terror of her breath. I grope toward her in the dark.

We cling to one another, panic making my heart falter and my blood pounding like a drum in my ears. She trembles in my arms, the hoarse bark of her voice calling on God.

"Oh Frances, I think I have led you into hell."

A rustle of straw and a shadow looms close; a voice breaks through the darkness.

"Hell would be hotter, so I am told."

Frances breaks away from me, reaching out, casting about unseeing, calling his name. "John! John!"

It cannot be him; this cannot be real! But this is no spirit – he is real. He is flesh and blood. His hands are on my arms, on my face, his lips on mine before he pulls me into the haven of his arms.

"Margery," he says. "It *is* you, and Frances too? Where are Grace and the child?"

"Oh John." I cling to his foetid robes and bury my head in his chest, tears of terrified joy stealing my voice, making it rasp. "You are not dead."

My hands confirm this, my fingers running over the hard bones of his torso. He winces and pulls away when I touch his ribs.

"You are injured?"

"They gave me a beating. It would have been better if I'd surrendered with dignity but ... by Christ, I am filled with fury. Did they harm you?"

I do not even flinch at his blasphemy.

"Only a little. At least we are alive."

"For now," he says, dampening my delight.

My eyes slowly adjust to the darkness and soon I can discern Frances clinging to him, her cheek against his upper arm. Oblivious to what may befall us next, she is blissful to be with John again. I clutch at my rapidly dissolving joy.

"I thought I'd never see you again," I say, my voice raw with emotion. I reach for his cheek, cupping it in my palm, and when he shrugs my hand away, his sheepish smile softens the blow of rejection.

"We are not alone, Margery."

He clears his throat, his gaze scanning the room, and I slowly come to realise that the outer reaches of the crypt are peopled with fellow prisoners. I hear a murmur of greeting, a few groans from the ailing. My mouth falls open.

"How long have you been here?"

"Just a day or two, but we are the lucky ones. When the king's men hunted us down, some were hanged where they were captured, we passed their corpses on the road; men, women and ... and children too."

"Oh dear, dear God. I pray Grace has the sense to take Andrew far from here. She must not come looking ..."

In my mind's eye, I see her travelling, head down against the driving rain, Andrew tucked within the comfort of her cloak. Where will she go? What will become of them?

"You must not think of that. You must worry only for yourself and Frances."

I had not realised I'd spoken aloud. I look down and notice our fingers are still entwined; reluctantly, I withdraw my hand.

"Come," he says, "there is scant comfort but rest your bones with me." He escorts us to a place of dubious cleanliness near the wall. My mouth is parched, my belly rumbling for want of food. I try not to think about it but Frances moans and gripes of her need.

"They will feed us soon, Frances." Hopeful that she will not recognise my lie, I pull her head to my shoulder and gently pat her until her sobs lessen. Once I am certain she has fallen asleep, I ply John with questions I'd not want Frances to hear.

"What will happen to us, John? Are we to hang?"

He moves, the straw rustling beneath him.

"I do not know. Perhaps; or maybe they will prefer to prolong our suffering, let us witness the devastation our actions have brought down upon our fellows."

"We did nothing but follow. We only wanted the king to understand–"

"*You* did nothing but follow. I, and most of our fellow prisoners here, stood with Bigod against the king's men. We obstructed Norfolk; we spoke out against the king's rule, chose the church over the monarchy – that will not pass unpunished."

"So, we have no hope."

I have never seen a man hanged although I've passed many a gibbet on the road, averting my eyes from the feasting crows. How will I find the strength to die a noble death, if there can be any nobility in a felon's penalty? I imagine the thick rope being looped about my neck, a baying crowd drowning out the specious prayers spouted by a traitorous priest. Will I remember that God is merciful, that His forgiveness outweighs that of the king? Will I be strong enough to face it, or will I die like a screaming lunatic, fighting for blessed life until my final breath?

John's arm snakes around my shoulders and I relax against him, resting my cheek on his chest. His breath is warm on my skin and I do not mind the foulness of it for he is alive, and human, and a friend once more.

"We were foolish to quarrel," I say. "We wasted so much time … time we will never have again."

"I was trying to protect you. I wanted so much more but feared … things would come to this. I didn't want to die and leave you shamed…. It was not easy to shun you."

"I wouldn't have minded …" Beneath the cover of darkness, I reach for his chin and pull his lips down to meet mine. We are silent for a long while, finding pleasure, a respite from our looming death.

Days pass. Days in which we lose track of time. We become accustomed to the pang of hunger, the absence of sunlight, the stench from the overflowing bucket in the corner, the rank taste of the water they allow us to drink. Life becomes a ritual of sleeping, waking, pacing the floor, and trying to reassure Frances, although even she must realise by now that all hope is lost. We take of each other what we can, while we can, but it is not much, and it is not enough … never enough.

Frances is fretful with a fever. Although I cannot see it, her shoulder, injured when the boys attacked her, is hot to the touch, and the dog bite on her wrist is weeping and beginning to smell. I have nothing with which to tend her. Thankfully, she falls into a restless sleep, her unconscious whimpers and mutterings breaking into my prayers. While the men speak in whispers, plotting, arguing, still looking for a method of escape, I plead with God harder than I ever have in my life. But I don't think He is listening.

Even at Arden, periods of devotion were broken up by tending the animals, working in the physic garden, and periods of contemplation in the chapter house. Now, during the hours I am not cradled in John's arms, all I do is pray, and fret, and pray again. I pray for all of us. I pray for England.

The door is thrown open, a shaft of daylight impaling the dark. We wince from it, putting up our hands to shade our eyes, blinking stupidly as a rough fellow in a leather jerkin takes two steps into the crypt, squinting in the gloom. He is followed by two companions who wave their weapons in our faces, shove at the men, pluck Frances from sleep and herd us like sheep toward the door. We cower from their swords and staves, and try to resist their roughness, but our limbs have grown so stiff from our incarceration that we cannot move swiftly. A fist in my lower back sends me sprawling into the filth.

"For God's sake, man, take your pitiful vengeance out on a man. Leave the women alone."

I struggle to rise. "I am not hurt, John ..." but I am too late. The gaoler clouts him behind the ear with the hilt of his sword and he sprawls to the ground, a great gout of blood splashing across my robes.

I scramble toward him, calling his name, but my gaolers haul me upright and propel me through the door. Blinded and dazed, I stagger to Frances, whose mouth is open, her wails drawing our captors' anger. One of them holds his stave to the side of her head, snarling at her to shut up. I spring forward and muffle her sobs with my hand.

"Quiet, Frances! Please, you must be quiet, for all our sakes!" Her sobs smothered, the gaoler spits at us before he backs away.

We huddle in a crowd, knowing the time has come. We are going to die. We do not even fight against it. I fumble for a final prayer, too afraid to close my eyes. I turn my head this way and that as I beseech God to be merciful and make our end swift and painless.

The gaoler strolls to the fore, his narrow gaze raking over us as he passes, as if we are lower than the wretched. All we have done is fight for our church, our home, our way of life. Who are these people who stand by and watch as it falls? They must surely have crawled here straight from hell. He is speaking. I blink, trying to clear my head, to see clearly, straining my ears to catch his words although I know I will not like them.

At first, just one or two phrases filter through to me. *Men … in his mercy … king … penalty … death.* Behind me, someone gasps; another falls to his knees and begins to pray. Men whose names I do not know but whose confinement I have shared begin to weep. Another is praying loudly for God's intervention but his prayers are cut off by one of our captors' boots.

We are going to die.

My mind wrestles with the truth of this. I must strive to be brave. Try to seek the strength of will to allow them to deprive me of breath, to stand firm and silent while they tie the noose about my neck and choke the life from me … but what about Frances? How can I persuade her to do the same? She will fight them. She will wrestle and weep and lash out until they lose patience and slay her as they would a beast in the slaughterhouse.

"John!" Frances' voice cuts through my musing. She points across the precinct and I turn to see them dragging John from the crypt. His head lolls lifelessly, his feet dragging, a trail of scarlet drops behind him. They throw him to the ground and the crack of his skull as it connects with the stone is a blade to my heart. He does not move and I realise he is dead. Drained of emotion, I wish I were, too.

John is lucky. Death is a release and God has been merciful, sparing him the horror of the noose. I thank Him for that, glad John will be spared the misery of watching me die. But it is hard to face death alone.

One by one, they take the men and force them to stand upon a platform beneath a triangular wooden frame. *The hanging tree,* I realise, the phrase suddenly making sense. I have heard it spoken of in grisly tales around the pilgrims' campfire, but the reality of it has always escaped me. I never thought to find myself here.

Frances slumps against my shoulder. When the trap falls and the first man swings, I turn her face into my breast so she will not witness it. But I force myself to watch and stand dry-eyed as, one by one, the life is wrung from their bodies. They are brave; martyrs to our cause. Can God really wish this to be so?

Only the women are left now. For the first time, I see their faces in daylight. Two of the women are middle-aged and there is a girl who can be no older than twelve. Next to them in line come me and Frances. Each one of us longs to flee yet we stand there, at the mercy of God and our gaolers, and wait for death. I wonder who will be taken first, or if we shall all be killed at once.

A man steps forward, roughly grabs a handful of the young girl's hair and drags her from the yard. We all cry out against him until a blade is thrust rudely against my spine, forcing me to be silent. Grabbing Frances' arm, I do as I am bid and follow them away from the hanging tree.

Terrified by this new violence, the women wail. The young girl screams but Frances, traumatised beyond tears, only whimpers. There is a sheen of sweat on her forehead and she bites her lower lip so hard that is it bleached white. As they drag us from the churchyard, I cast my eye back to take one last look at John's prone figure. "God bless you," I whisper as I am driven out of sight.

We are forced past the deserted village green, where the houses are closed, the shutters sealed. They urge us on beneath the swinging sign of the bush outside the deserted tavern, past the blacksmith's shop which is locked and barred. At the green pond, the ducks cease dabbling in the mud to cackle at our passing.

"Where are you taking us?" one of the women dares to ask, but we are given no answer. They march us on, staggering and stumbling, to the edge of the village. Where the river crosses the track, they force us to splash through the ford and order us to halt on the opposite side. We stand in a miserable huddle, waiting for the first blow, wondering which of us will be the first to die.

Behind us, the stricken village is silent; before us, the rutted road stretches emptily toward the umber moor. Perhaps some strange local custom demands that women should be killed beyond the parish perimeters. One of the men approaches; we cower away.

When he begins to fumble with her bonds, a woman struggles. He clouts her about the head and, after that, none of us dares to resist.

We stand very still as our bonds are loosened, our hands freed. Warily, I rub my wrists, but we do not run. Instead, we cluster like silly sheep, cowed to our captors' will. At least death will end the tortuous waiting. The gaoler reaches behind him and draws forth a whip that cracks the air as he brings it down upon us. It tears the fabric of my habit, cuts into my shoulder, and I scream as I never have before. As it falls again, we flee from it, our feet slipping and turning on the rutted road. With Frances' hand in mine, we run as fast as we can, away from the village, as afraid of freedom as we were of death.

We flee despite our injuries, our fever, our twisted ankles and our undernourished bodies. We run until the village is far behind us. Finally, when we realise they are not in pursuit and we really are free, our pace slows. We halt, bend over exhausted, fighting to catch our breath before looking one to the other in disbelief.

"I thought we were going to die…"

The girl lowers her chin to her chest and begins to sob; one of the women offers comfort while the other squats at the side of the road to relieve her bladder, a trail of dark pee pooling on the ground. I put a hand to Frances' forehead.

"She has a fever," I say to no one in particular. "We need a place of shelter." I scan the horizon for signs of habitation but there is nothing, not even a barn. All we can do is limp onward and hope that shelter and some kind of sustenance awaits us around the next bend.

Although we hunger and thirst, we exchange names as we shuffle along, uphill and down again, through heath and woodland. The girl is called Bessie.

"It's Elizabeth, really, after the princess," she says with a grimace. I remember the jubilation at the princess' birth, the determination not to be disappointed that she was not a boy, an heir for the Tudor throne. On the day she was born, nobody would have imagined that England would ever come to this; the queen murdered, the church fallen, the divided country in turmoil and ruled over by a despised king.

"My name is Agnes, and this is Ellen," the older woman confides. "I heard your ... girl ... call you Margery."

"Yes, and this is Frances. I am worried; the wound where the gaoler's dog bit her is festering."

"Dog bites can be right nasty..."

I show her Frances' wrist and we frown at the deep gash close to the bone, the empurpled angry marks that now stretch toward the elbow.

"Eeh, I don't like the looks o' that." She peers into Frances' face. "Does her face always look like that?"

"She is not usually so flushed..." As I reply, I realise she's referring to Frances' almond-shaped eyes, the flatness of her cheek. I draw myself in, offended on my friend's behalf. "She is a good soul, a good friend." I stick my chin out defensively.

"Nay, don't take on, lass. My sister birthed an idiot too but he didn't live beyond four year, to his father's great relief."

I realise Frances' good fortune to have been taken in at Arden. She could be a rich man's daughter and, if so, better to live as a nun than shut away from the eyes of men. I've heard it said some people like Frances are kept in an attic, or done to death before their first year. I do not know her story, or how she came to take the veil, but I am certain a more loyal woman never walked the earth. I do not answer. Instead, I link my arm through Frances'.

"We must search for a brook. We all need water and if I can bathe Frances' wrist, it might help reduce the fever."

Although it is not yet dark, it seems hours later when I spy the sagging roof of a barn at the side of the road and hear the gleeful babble of a stream. We stop and scan the surroundings, looking for foes. "There's a house in the hollow; a mill by the look of it!"

We follow the line of Agnes' finger.

"There's no smoke from the chimney, happen 'tis deserted." Ellen sighs. "I will go and see; you come with me, Agnes."

I lift the bar on the barn door, push it open and step inside. The air is full of dust, stripes of daylight illuminating the shadows within. It is dry and sheltered from the keen wind, and the aroma of summer leads me to discover that one end is piled high with sweet meadow hay. For the first time in more than a moon, we shall sleep soundly ... if we can find food to fill our bellies.

"Look for something to carry water," I instruct Bessie, "look behind that partition. It may be where they keep their tools." My fingers are already busy untying the knots that secure Frances' cloak. As soon as it is free, she sinks down into the hay and I tuck both her cloak and mine around her. She smiles at me through her fever but I am uncertain if she knows who I am.

She is very hot and flushed, and her skin is slick with sweat. Her eyes are unfocussed, and her breath tainted. At the base of her neck, a blue vein pulses, a sign that often accompanies fever. If only I could lay my hands on the goodly store of medicines we kept at Arden – a dose of St John's Wort or Salix might do the trick but, in the depths of winter, there is nothing growing and it will be months before the willow tree puts forth flowers and leaves.

"Bessie, did you find anything?" I call across the barn and, a few moments later, she pokes her head out from behind the partition.

"I did, Margery! I found something right useful indeed…"

Frances fidgets restlessly, whimpering, tears seeping onto her cheek. I place my hand on her hair.

"Don't cry, Frances. All will be well …" But she doesn't seem to hear.

A familiar sound from the other side of the barn halts my sentence and I look across to see Bessie leading a cow toward me. It lows again, mournfully complaining of an udder in need of milking. My mouth falls open in surprise.

"Will this do, Margery? I think her great tits be in need of easing." She squats down and squeezes the beast's udder. The cow lows again. "Aye, she's fit to burst."

I hurry forward, my heart lighter, for a cow is a gift indeed. We have water nearby and now the benefit of milk, which to starving people is almost as good as a hearty meal.

"We still need a bucket."

"There's one in there and a stool, but by the size of her teats no one's been by to milk her for a while."

"Fetch it, fetch it, then, girl!"

I lower myself onto the stool, resting my face against the smooth flank. I cannot help but think of Marigold. I close my eyes. The scent and sound of her nutty goodness squirting into the bucket evokes sweet memories of Arden. We'd thought we were hungry then, but the plain fare we enjoyed would be as welcome to me now as a royal feast. At first, the milk doesn't come easily, and I know from experience that despite her discomfort, the cow is holding it back from a stranger's hand. I stroke and gently squeeze, hum the lullaby I used to sing to Andrew, and soon I feel her relax beneath my touch. Milk begins to flow and as her udder is eased, I feel the tension seep from her body. Before I know it, the pail is half-full. It is all I can do not to drink straight from it.

The sound of Ellen and Agnes' voices enters the barn before they appear. They are excited, agitated, pleased as they bustle through the door. They stop short in surprise at seeing the cow.

"Where did you find that?" Agnes cries. "We'll have milk tonight to go with this, 'twill be a proper feast! We found the house all right but no one was home."

Ellen holds aloft a half-eaten loaf; Agnes carries a cheese and a flagon of ale. Slowly, I stand up.

"We can't just take their food; it is theft."

"The loaf is a few days old and the ashes in the hearth were cold, they might not return. It'd be a shame to see good food go to waste."

"Where would they go? Why would they leave and not take their cow; she's worth a mint o' money…?"

Bessie looks from me to Agnes, subsiding when she realises what is suddenly obvious to us all. Our spirits fall. The people who lived here must also have been taken by the king's men. Perhaps they offered aid to the pilgrims, or even joined the protest.

"God bless them," I murmur, making the sign of the cross, and the women bow their heads and pray with me.

When I dribble milk between Frances' parched lips, she tosses her head, throws out an arm and almost upsets the bucket. I try not to overwhelm her with nourishment but surely, the goodness will rouse her. Surely, given the strength, she will heal. Her tongue emerges to lick up the drops, and it searches feebly for more. I repeat the process but after what seems like hours, she has still taken less than half a cup. Between swallows, she fidgets and jabbers a string of nonsense. Sometimes, she laughs aloud, speaks to people I cannot see, and I look around me in alarm, afraid the barn is home to demons.

I had thought the milk would fight the fever but instead she grows rapidly worse. Her skin burns hotter and her sense of reality slips farther away. She converses with the dead; with Sister Mary, with John, and sometimes I think she is speaking with God himself. Sometimes, her words gush forth in an unintelligible torrent and then she pauses, as if listening for an answer, which fills me with terror. I cross myself and voice my prayer louder to overcome her rampant, bedevilled tongue.

I squat at her side, demanding that God should spare her, even as I wring my hands in hopelessness. My head is lowered as I beseech Heaven, when a sudden blast of hot breath falls on the back of my neck. Screaming aloud, I fall backwards, groping in the hay for something I may use as a weapon to fight off my attacker. A pair of large, black eyes blinks at me and a huge purple tongue flicks across a pink muzzle. I close my eyes, almost laughing in relief when I realise it is not a devil after all but the cow, somehow broken free of her ties.

My laughter is harsh, humourless, making me fear my own sanity. I glance across to where the other women are gathered but find that, having eaten their fill, they have all fallen asleep. Bessie is curled beneath Ellen's arm, Agnes a little way off, her skirts ridden above her sore arthritic knees. I am left with only the company of the beast to comfort Frances in her suffering. The cow noses the hay, tossing it into a small pile before dragging some into her mouth and chewing contentedly. She blows hard, spattering yellow dribble. Frances opens her eyes and blinks at the cow. After a moment, she reaches out to touch its nose and breaks into a smile.

"Marigold!" she sighs, and the joy in her voice breaks my heart. She thinks she has come home.

My face crumples, my head falling into my hands. If only it were so.

"Marigold" is the last word I ever hear from Frances' lips. During the darkest hour of the night, she takes a deep, shuddering sigh and forgets to breathe again.

"Come on, lass, y' must rouse yersel'. Moping won't bring 'er back." Ellen tugs at my hand but I close my mind against the necessity of moving on.

I cannot stir myself and so the other women take on the duties that should be mine. Discovering a spade and a mattock in the back of the barn, Agnes and Ellen dig a grave, and Bessie fashions a marker out of a fallen branch. They wash Frances' body and wrap her in her mildewed cloak, then drag me to the graveside for the reading of prayers.

Frances now lies beneath the sod, in unconsecrated ground when, if there were any justice in this world, she would lie within a golden shrine. I am in a joyless, frigid place.

I am not sure how I can go on. There is nobody to need me now. John is gone, Frances is gone, and Grace and Andrew are ... God knows where. Frances has been with me for my whole life; a helpmeet, a support and the closest thing to family I will ever have. The thought of never hearing her heavy laughter, or her earth-shattering snores, or her tuneless voice again is unbearable. I want to lie down in the hay and follow where she has gone. But it is a sin even to think it.

Ellen tugs my hand again and reluctantly I rise to my feet. Agnes puts her arms around me.

"I've filled our packs with what victuals I could find at the cottage," she says. It is still theft but I no longer care. What point is there in a sinless life when we are punished anyway? And in the cruellest ways.

"What about the cow?" Bessie loops her arm around the beast's neck. "We can't leave her here; she'll suffer without daily milking. If we take her, we will have nourishment on t' journey."

She is right, of course, but cows are sedentary creatures, not given to travel.

"She might die on the way," I say by way of feeble protest, but Bessie's mind is made up.

"She'll die anyway if we leave her here. I say we take her with us, give her a chance, any road."

"Very well," I say, lacking the energy to fight. "But you must care for her. I – I – people in my care don't seem to thrive and I doubt it's any different for beasts ..."

"Oh lass. Don't think like that! You always do your very utmost and that's all any of us can do."

I have no real notion as to the direction we are taking but the cheerless morning sun rises behind us, so I calculate we are moving west. We eat the last of the cheese quite quickly, but a little milk in the morning sustains us until the day's end, when Agnes makes a pottage with some dried beans before we settle for the night. We are eating better now than we have for months, but this doesn't cheer me. All I can think is that if we'd had food sooner, I might have saved Frances. Had I shown her better care, she wouldn't have fallen ill.

We follow the paths less travelled, avoiding towns and villages for fear of the authorities. A few times, we see other vagrants on the way ahead but, as keen as we to avoid trouble, they disappear from view before we draw close. I scan the ditches either side of the trail for fear of attack, for although we carry no coin, the cow, that Bessie has named Primrose, is a valuable beast.

"Where are we going?" Bessie asks.

"Up this road," Agnes answers.

"Yes, but how far? I have a hole in the sole of my shoe and I am so tired ..."

"Better tired than dead," Agnes responds, "which is what you'd be if fortune hadn't smiled on us."

"I wonder why they didn't hang us ..."

I have been so keen to put as much distance between us and our gaolers as I could that I'd not really considered it. "They hanged so many pilgrims; why not us?"

"Best not wonder the whys and wherefores of life. Best t' just take one step after another, each day as it comes, and hope that something better lies around the next bend. Bad fortune cannot last forever."

"You just said we'd had good fortune when they didn't hang us," Bessie exclaims.

"Aye, well, madam, you mind your cheek before I paddle your behind with my palm."

Bessie subsides into a sulk and tugs at Primrose's rope as she tries to snatch a mouthful of green grass that has somehow managed to thrive beneath a winter hedge.

One thing we overlooked in travelling with a cow was the scarcity of grazing. We can't carry hay with us and now that she has no access to it, her milk is waning fast. I decide that if we should pass a worthy-looking holding, we should leave Primrose with them in exchange for a meal and a few nights in a dry barn, but I don't speak of it to Bessie, whose protests will be loud and long. I cannot wait for the journey to end. I want to stop. I want to belong somewhere again.

Sleeping beneath a hedge at night is misery indeed. When the sun begins its downward journey, we begin to look for shelter. There are wayside inns aplenty but not for the likes of us, who travel with no coin.

"Perhaps there is a priory that will take us in."

"But the small ones are all closed now and the big ones will likely turn us away. They say the bigger the abbey, the smaller the vocation. It's all about money

171

these days …" Agnes spits on the ground, rubs her nose and peers into the distance. "There's folk on t' road ahead; look."

We squint into the watery sunshine. The approaching party have seen us too, and they pause as if uncertain whether to fight or flee. "What shall we do?" Agnes turns to me. Keeping my eye on the strangers, I shake my head.

"I don't know. They've seen us, let's wait and see what they decide."

We stand in a ring around Primrose. Bessie drapes her arms protectively across the beast's back.

"I recall the day when you could travel the byways in safety," Ellen sighs.

Agnes snorts derisively.

"Women alone have never travelled in safety, not in my time."

In my head, I hear Sister Dorothea, as clear as a bell. I repeat her words, even down to the tone of voice.

"We are not alone. God is always with us."

The women turn to me, brows raised at my newfound conviction and somehow, now that the words are spoken, I begin to believe them. Raising my hand, I call a greeting to the group of travellers and, slowly, they start to move toward us. Agnes creeps close to my side, placing a reassuring hand on my shoulder.

"Oh by 'eck, I hope this'll not land us in more trouble, lass."

As they come closer, we see it is a mixed party of men, women and children and we relax; thieves do not often travel with their families. When we can discern each other's faces, they halt and we make mutual assessment of one another.

"Greetings," their leader says at last. "We have met few women travelling alone on the road. Where are you going?"

He is of middling stature, his hair thinning, the bones of his skull visible. A small boy clutches at his cloak. At his side, a woman, some years younger than her companion, stares curiously at us.

"We were cast out of our priory," I say, deciding to be careful with the truth. There is no need for them to know we are pilgrims and only recently united on our journey. "We search for another house prepared to take us in."

"You must be careful. The king's men continue to seek out dissent; we passed a hanging tree a little way back." He spits on the ground. "Women were among the bodies and a boy, no older than this one."

He places a loving hand on the boy's hair and my throat closes in fear that a similar fate may have befallen Grace and Andrew.

"These are sorry days," I say, my voice issuing hoarsely. "Would you join us for supper? We have milk." I address the last words to the child, his answering smile breaking my heart. Where is Andrew? Has Grace kept him safe?

While they mutter among themselves, deciding whether or not to accept the invitation, Agnes pulls a face at my generosity. "We could be about to sit down and sup with the devil," she says as she swings the pack from her shoulder.

"We need to know what road we are on, what lies ahead. They may even have encountered Grace on their way."

"It'd be a right strange chance if they have." She stalks off to the wayside and spreads her cloak on the ground. As Bessie makes ready to ease Primrose's udder, our guests join us. They stand in an uncertain semi-circle until, with a sweep of my arm, I invite them closer.

"We have little but are pleased to share it with you."

I usher the women forward, take the boy's hand and introduce him to Primrose, who turns her head to sniff incuriously at his jerkin. He laughs as he pulls away, half-delighted, half-terrified, but quickly returns with an outstretched hand.

"Careful, son, some beasts can be nasty."

I turn to find his mother hovering hawk-like behind us. She lays a warning hand on his shoulder.

"Don't worry," I smile. "Primrose is very gentle."

She pulls a face. "I were worried by a cow when I were a girl. It scared the life outta me. I've never forgotten."

"My name is Margery." I stretch out my hand.

"I am Clara, and this is Adam."

"Come," I say. "Meet the others."

She follows me to the small fire that Ellen has set. The man I presume to be her husband has settled beside it. As he speaks, he swipes at the wisps of smoke around his head.

"England isn't the same without the monasteries. We made our living working their farms. I was a lay brother at Bridlington but our prior was taken for trial. We fled before the king's men could wreak their vengeance on us but ... I don't know where we should go. Perhaps I were rash ... we are likely to starve on the road very soon. What about you? Where are you going?"

I shrug my shoulders. Where *am* I going? There is only one place on earth that I have ever called home.

"Back to Arden," I reply before thinking it through. "It is the only place I know, the only place I can go."

"Is it far?"

"I don't know. It took a long while to get here but we took a roundabout route. I have no idea in what direction it lies. I understand it is some miles north of York."

"York is that way," Clara says, pointing back the way they have come, "about two days' journey, I think. It's hard to say if we're safer keeping to the busier road; there is an older path but ..."

Two days, and then the long haul back to Arden. It sounds daunting but what option do we have? I pull myself upright and force a smile.

"Well, that is where we must go. You are welcome to join us."

"What? Back the way we've come?" The woman's voice is full of dismay but her companion, Milo, puts a hand on her arm.

"We have little choice, Clara. Perhaps we should consider travelling with them. At least it is a destination. At least once we arrive, there will be an end to it. The road is no place for the boy."

I put up a hand and halt his speech.

"I must warn you, I have no idea what is there. It might be a ruin, it might be deserted, so don't go imagining a warm welcome ... but I don't know what else to suggest."

"'Tis a sorry pass this country has come to. I never thought I'd see the day I'd lack a roof over me head at night. You've heard about Aske, I suppose ..."

My head jerks up. "Aske? No; what about him?"

He curls his lip. "The king ..." he spits the word, "is livid at the latest uprising and took his ire out on Aske, even though he'd no part in it. He were still at court when t' fresh bout o' trouble started."

The king's vengeance has been harsh. There is not a village or town north of Sheffield that has escaped retribution. Men, women and children were punished; if they couldn't find a hanging tree, they strung them up along the roadside to rot like fruit left for the wasps to feast upon. The law decrees that treasonous gentry are too good for hanging so they are sent for execution instead. Fine powerful lords that a few months ago led our pilgrimage have been herded up, and now the king's gaols are overflowing. Robert Aske, that wild and honest man, is the scapegoat – we know he will bear the worst of the punishment, for he named himself our leader.

"What will they do to him?" I find I cannot swallow; the crust I am chewing turns to ashes in my mouth. Clara pulls a face.

"We all know 'twill be death. We can only pray 'twill be a merciful one."

Is there such a thing? If the king executes Aske for his crime against the crown, will that not make him a martyr to our cause? Is martyrdom a fair exchange for a violent death? It isn't a price I'd be willing to pay.

May 1537

We journey slowly, the boy and the cow he has befriended necessitating regular stops, and our weakened state hampering my inner sense of urgency. Often, we are forced to conceal ourselves from approaching horsemen; our terror of the king's men untempered by time. Most nights, we sleep in a copse or ruined barn; sometimes we are lucky and meet people who are sympathetic to our plight. They endow us with food from their scanty stores or let us share the warmth of their hearth for a night or two.

All of us are ailing, either from a cold in the head, or the rigours of the journey. I trudge, despondently placing one foot before the other, always pushing, always focusing on the thought of home; and of Grace and Andrew, who may await me there.

When we reach the fork in the road that bypasses York in the direction of Arden, I expect to take leave of Milo and Clara. I had thought they'd not welcomed my offer to come to Arden, but to my surprise, they ask permission to travel with us.

"There's nought waiting fer us in York," they say, "and your tales of Arden are so fine. Can we come wi' ye after all?"

Milo scuffs the dirt with the toe of his broken-down boot and I want to hug him. I glance at Bessie and Agnes, who nod vigorously.

"The more the merrier, I say," Ellen beams, hitching her pack higher.

"I don't know what we shall find at Arden. It is probably a ruin by now or perhaps it's already been gifted to one of the king's favourites."

We have learned of the king's seeming generosity in offering abbey lands to his favourites. It is a way of binding men to him, holding them fast in his debt to ensure they never support the reinstatement of the monasteries. Even the devout can be bought by the precious gift of land.

Agnes puts her arm around my shoulder.

"Well, lass," she says. "If we get there and find a ruin, mayhap we can make it habitable. You said it's out of the way o' the road; we might go unnoticed for years. And if we find a parcel of fancy folk livin' there, well, we will just have to turn round and seek another route."

I can think of no answer so I smile and shrug and we travel onward. This road is quieter; there are fewer horsemen now and our fear lessens. Close to sunset, we pause to ask directions of a cottar. He leans on his rickety gate and points up the track. "Hawnby is that way but I couldn't say how far."

"Have you encountered a young woman carrying an infant in the last few weeks?"

He scratches his head.

"I can't say I 'ave, lass, but I don't spend all my time standin' at t' gate. She might a slipped by when I weren't watchin'."

The last part of the journey seems the longest of all. Each bend in the road, each hill we climb that doesn't reveal the wet gleam of Arden's rooftops is a torture. When it is time to rest, I am reluctant to stop. I eat my food too quickly, with my eye pinned on the horizon as if hoping Arden will magically appear.

Yet as we draw closer and I begin to recognise the contours of the land, the cluster of trees on the crest of a hill, a tumble of rocks just below, I begin to fear what I will find. I know it will be changed. I know my sisters will not be there to greet me. There will be destruction, an absence of the life I once knew. Arden will be silent and spoilt, peopled only by ghosts ... but still my feet force me onward.

"We are almost there," I cry. "Only a mile or so more." My companions frown at the bleak, empty moorland. To them, it must seem as if we are entering a wilderness, but to me it is like Heaven. Around us, the heathland is burgeoning with growth, the scent of the thyme and heather is heavy on the air, and the wayside teems with birds busy with their young. I increase my pace, turn the last bend in the winding road and spy the gatehouse in the distance.

It looks just the same! It looks just the same! I come to a sudden stop, my companions clustering round me.

"It looks deserted," Agnes sniffs, her breath rasping in my ear.

"It has always seemed so. Arden is a quiet place. People have little cause to come here. That is why the one track leading to it goes no further."

I move on, quickly outstripping them, eventually breaking into a run. My ankles turn on the dried, muddy footprints of livestock that passed this way a long time ago. I pause at the gate and look up to where the admittance bell in the shambling tower should hang, but the bell of Arden is silenced now. I place my palm upon the fabric of the building and peer through the grille. I have seldom entered by this route but Sister Mary told me it was here that I was found, a thousand lifetimes ago.

I think about the woman who birthed me, whether my father still lives, whether he ever even knew of me. With countless memories of my childhood teeming in my mind, I tentatively lift the latch, expecting the gate to be locked and barred. It opens. Slowly, the inner yard comes into view.

I hover on the threshold, peeking at the overgrown courtyard, an abandoned barrow with a broken wheel, its contents spilled across the ground. It is deserted, as I had known it would be…. I step inside.

I have been gone for less than a year, but the weeds have grown tall; dead white nettles straggle across the path, new shoots burgeoning from beneath. Lifting my skirts, I pick my way through them and follow the worn flagstones that lead to the cloister door. The unoiled gate shrieks as I push against it, startling a flock of birds that fly up in a fluttering whir of wings. The prioress' beloved doves, I note, and the thought of eggs and pie makes my mouth water.

The cloister garden is rampant, weeds jostling with the roses and columbine. How well I remember the sisters here, reading or contemplating while I crawled about uprooting dandelions from the dirt. I glimpse the roof of the chapel; part of it has fallen in, perhaps by human hand, and some of the tiles have tumbled into the cloister. I find a way through the debris and into the church, where my sadness increases.

The nave that once rang with our tuneless voices is silent now, a great hole in the roof open to the sky, the floor beneath my feet strewn with leaves and thatch. It was never a grand church, never so fine as the ones I've seen upon my journeys but … it was *my* church. My mind conjures the sisters of Arden, grouped in the quire, their chins and voices raised in praise of God. I remember the prioress, so cold, so detached from us as she oversaw our devotions; Sister Dorothea, frowning at my discordant efforts to match their high notes; Sister Mary smiling indulgently over the top of her prayer book – and I recall Frances, her face lit up, bellowing her song with unrivalled joy. Now, there is only brooding silence.

I must get out of here.

Stumbling over the littered floor, I hurry toward the dormitory, past the infirmary where, among the weeds, the physic garden still abounds with herbs. Forcing my mind to a practical path, I feverishly gather chamomile and ginger, ransoms and feverfew to boost our exhausted bodies. In the vegetable patch, I spy wild lettuce, self-seeded beets, onions. A hen flutters onto a wall and looks at me indignantly before pecking at a worm.

Eggs! Arden will feed us. Here, we can grow strong again. Perhaps, given time, we can rebuild it. Perhaps the king's men will forget it, so far from the concourse of men, where forging a life is so hard.

The grass in the churchyard is springy underfoot. I look across the humps and bumps of the graves and make my way carefully between them. Four hundred years of Arden's community lie here: prioresses, sisters, and servants, but I do not linger. I pass them by, my feet leading me to the perimeter wall, to the place where we laid Sister Mary.

There should be nothing but a hump in the grass, perhaps a sprawl of brambles. I look at the neat rectangle of rich brown earth and my heart misses a beat. Someone has left a small bouquet of columbine.

"Grace?"

I whisper her name, turning my head, searching for other signs that someone has been here.

As I make my way to the kitchens, I feel hidden eyes upon me. I scan the empty windows, the broken doors, turning circles, hoping for a glimpse of Grace. I do not think to question why she might be hiding. I find the others clustered in the yard, standing close together. Agnes' mouth hangs wide.

"It's a proper mess, lass. I wasn't expecting this."

"We can clear it," I say, pushing my sleeves to my elbows. "Bessie, take Primrose to the byre ... it is that way. You might find some old hay or something remaining, or you can tether her in the meadow beyond."

As she leads the cow away, I try not to remember Marigold ... or Frances. I pick up a piece of timber. "Clear the path of debris and stack the wood in the kitchen, we can burn it. It will be chilly come evening."

"We've only just arrived. Can't we rest a while before we labour?"

"There's no time like the present," I say, my brisk tone echoing the phrase I heard so many times from the sisters. "Once we've a fire, we can prepare something hot for supper. I saw onions in the garden. They are old and gone to seed, but still edible. And there is a hen on the loose, she will have eggs hidden away somewhere."

"There's pigeons too." Milo cranes his neck to the tower where the doves are roosting.

As we work, I keep shivering, sure that someone is watching me. Every so often, I stop and look up, hoping to see Grace hurrying toward me with Andrew held tightly on her hip, but they do not appear. Perhaps it wasn't Grace who left the flowers ... but who else could it be?

Despite the toil of the day, when night falls I do not sleep. The beds in the dormitory have been righted but most of the mattresses are torn and sodden, and the roof above us is open to the sky. We salvage what we can, pushing the beds together at one end, and huddle beneath blankets – one by one, my companions relax into slumber, their snores offering some small comfort in the dark. I have slept here almost every night of my life and I should find security in that, yet all I sense is the absence of the holy sisters. My old life has gone, irrevocably destroyed and, where once I knew for certain what each new day would bring, now the future is blank and I am fearful of it.

<u>June 1537</u>

Yet slowly, some semblance of order returns to Arden. The paths are cleared, the rooms set to rights and, with Milo's help, we have even managed to partially repair the roof at one end of the dormitory. As the sun rises earlier and earlier each morning, I don't have time to take pleasure in the promise of warmer days and nights; instead, I fret that even as midsummer approaches, winter will not be far behind. How we will survive it, I cannot begin to imagine.

I had thought that returning to Arden would see an end to my worries, but after the initial relief has passed, I realise I was very wrong. Our feet and legs may be glad of a respite from walking, but our bellies still growl with hunger, and at night we still shiver beneath thin blankets. We need more food, thicker bedding, and the timbers we are burning will not last forever.

My inadequate shoulders droop beneath the responsibility of caring for everyone. Barring the children, I am the youngest member of the party, so why do they turn to me? I didn't ask to be their leader. Their constant questions tumble in my head, the insurmountable problems making me want to scream.

"Margery, Milo's tooth is aching, what should I do?"

"Margery, the cow's eye is sore and running, do you know how to treat it?"

"Margery, my belly is empty, what is for supper?"

"Margery, the sole of my shoe is worn through, who will mend it?"

"Margery, there are small black flies all over the broad beans, what shall I do?"

I can stand their incessant harping voices no longer. Throwing down the petticoat I've been mending, I spring from my seat, tripping over the leg of a stool as I run from the room. Ignoring Agnes' anxious voice calling after me, I head for the cloister and sink to my knees beside the broken water fountain.

Since we cleared away the rubble, the chamomile lawn has begun to regrow, the scent of it heavy in the evening air. I trail my fingers through it, the aroma evoking a thousand memories from before. Tilting back my head, I see stars emerging; the same stars that have shone down on Arden forever. I look about; the dark shapes of the buildings against the night sky are familiar, the sounds of the night are as they have always been. Yet nothing is the same. I am home, yet everything is different. I am exiled.

The place I longed to return to wasn't Arden at all. My longing wasn't for the here and now, it was for the Arden of yesterday, another time – an unreachable place of happiness and contentment; the years of my childhood. Now I am grown, there is only stress and sorrow at Arden. My head feels heavy, my neck droops and a tear drips onto my hand. I can be strong no longer. I am just Margery.

As much as I long for it, I am not allowed the luxury of wallowing in my misery. The next morning, before I have so much as washed my face or said my prayers, the problems begin again. I encounter Ellen just outside the church; she tugs at my sleeve and draws me to the shadow of the wall.

"Margery, I don't like t' bother you but … 'tis the second time this week …"

I breathe deeply, close my eyes, and ask the question, although I am in no rush for her answer.

"What now, Ellen?"

"I discovered a clutch of eggs, too many to carry, so I went t' fetch the basket to gather them in, but when I returned there were some missing ... it was the same two days since. I counted five," she holds up splayed fingers. "But when I got back, there were only three. Someone is stealing them."

I put my hand to my head.

"Surely not ... perhaps the hen is eating them. They sometimes do ..."

"Nay. That were my first thought but there's no broken shell, no mess in the nest. It must be one of us ..."

"Who would do such a thing? Who would sate their own hunger knowing the rest of us will go without?"

She shrugs, unwilling to voice her suspicion, while my own mind races. One of the children, perhaps? Or perhaps a fox visited during the night. I cling to this hope.

"A fox, perhaps?"

"Nay. I were gone for less time than it takes t' turn around an' no fox'd take just two."

I think for a moment, far out of my depth for problems like this. If one of us is a thief, then even if I discover their identity I am ill equipped, too softhearted, to punish them. I am beginning to understand why the prioress always wore such a sour expression; she, at least, was raised with expectations of authority. I am just a servant forced to play a part. I swallow, and grope for some semblance of authority.

"Say nothing to the others. Tomorrow morning, you and I will watch and wait. If the thief strikes again, we will have them, but ... how we will act upon it, I have no idea."

With a rueful smile, she squeezes my arm and, with a heavy heart, I pass into the church to unburden myself to God, although lately I have begun to wonder if He is no longer listening.

As we work through our day, I sense a heaviness in the air. I find myself watching and wondering about everyone, suspicion poisoning our former amity. I am cutting a carrot into paper-thin slices for the pottage when Bessie comes in and places a bucket of milk on the table.

"Primrose's yield is down," she says. "Perhaps she would do better off the tether; we should mend the broken fence in the meadow so she can graze at will."

"Yes. See to that, Bessie; get Milo or Agnes to help you."

"Agnes is working in the garden. She'll not thank me for dragging her away."

"Well, ask Clara then!" I know Clara has taken Adam to the stream in an attempt to catch a few fish for supper. The struggle of finding enough ingredients to put together a meal each day has fallen to her. I put down the knife.

"I'm sorry, Bessie. Forgive me. I will help you. When I've found Milo, we will join you in the meadow."

She hurries away but I follow more slowly, a nagging ache in my lower back. As I cross the yard, as if my thoughts are on a tether, my mind returns to Grace and Andrew. He will have grown now; he might even be starting to walk or to make a few sounds that pass as words. In the time we've been parted, he will have altered so much ... I wonder if he will even remember me. I try to envision his face, but it is indistinct – I cannot even count how long it is since we were parted. If I cannot recall the details of his face, there is no doubt he will have forgotten mine.

As I approach the barnyard, a figure rushes around the corner and runs full tilt into me, robbing me of breath and almost knocking me from my feet. He is no taller than I and a weakling by the way he fights. I scream

Milo's name and cling to the sleeves of my attacker's jacket, hanging on with all my strength to prevent their escape. It can only be minutes but it seems an age later when Milo comes puffing to my rescue.

"Gotcha!" He grabs the miscreant by the scruff of the neck and gives the boy a shake – a handful of beans falls from his pocket. No doubt this is the culprit that stole our eggs. I frown, and take a closer look.

"L-Luke? Is that you? Where – what – where did you come from?"

"You know him?"

Milo relaxes his grip, but not enough to let the boy escape. Barely recognisable as our former stable boy, Luke scowls at me, dragging his cuff across his snotty nose.

"I bin 'ere all the time."

I cast my mind back to the final days, when the king's men drove us out, but I cannot recollect Luke and Mark being present. Guilt swamps me that not once, either during or since the dissolution of our house, have I given them a moment's thought.

"And your bro– your friend ... w-where is he? Is Mark with you?"

The boy refuses to answer. He regards me sullenly, as if I am the enemy, as if it were me who destroyed the only security he'd ever known. In an attempt at compassion, I try to smile, but my cheeks are frozen and I expect my expression is wooden. Devoid of every emotion but guilt and shame, I take a breath and try to speak kindly.

"Why did you steal our eggs, Luke? Why did you not just come forward and tell us you were here? We would have welcomed you into our community."

"You'd have worked us t' death, like the other lot did. And they were our eggs before you came back ... Mark and me were faring well until you chased us out."

He is right. When we arrived, we just assumed Arden was vacant.

"Where is Mark now?" I gaze across the adjacent moorland. "Is he hiding? Is he watching us? Signal him to come and we will wash you both, mend your clothes and feed you."

While he stands undecided, Clara returns. She holds up a goodly catch of trout. "We've been lucky this morning, we'll eat well tonight ..." She stops when she notices the stranger among us. "Oh ... we've company." Her smile is puzzled but not unwelcoming. At first, I think the look of longing that rises in Luke's eyes is for the promise of Clara's motherly welcome, but following the line of his vision, I realise it is the fish that he craves.

Several hours later, the trout are cooked and Luke has joined us in the kitchen. His belly is full and Clara has scrubbed him so thoroughly that his face shines like a pewter plate. The women cluck and fuss around him, sneaking morsels from their own meagre plates to supplement his meal. Adam stands with his thumb in his mouth, watching and listening as Luke relates the tale of the day the king's men came.

"We saw 'em comin' and snuck away. We watched from t' hills an' saw you lot leave, and when you'd gone we saw the king's men drag the thatch from the roofs and smash the church winders. They stole the bell and the plate, even the stuff from the kitchens, and what they couldn't carry on their carts, they broke and scat about the yard. They even took Marigold an' most o' t' hens."

"Why didn't you come with us? You must have been so afraid ... so alone."

His eyes widen as he shakes his head slowly from side to side.

"We didn't know where you were goin'. We only know Arden, we'd no mind t' move from here. We were doin' all right until you came back."

I look at his thin wrists, his hollowed cheeks and know he is lying, but he is safe now. I try not to think of the increase in hardship with two extra mouths to feed.

Darkness is falling when a noise outside severs the thread of conversation. I snuff the candle while Milo creeps to the door and peers through a crack in the woodwork. Nobody breathes until, straightening up, Milo grins at us over his shoulder. The hinges groan and the bottom of the door scrapes across the flagstones to reveal a filthy boy.

Clara pushes back her stool and relights the candle.

"Eeh, Bessie, heat some more water. You come inside, lad, and we'll find you a bite t' eat. Look at the state o' your 'ands. Bessie, throw us that flannel, I'll give t' lad a lick and a promise."

Hours later, I help Clara make up a bed for the boys in the dormitory. Mark lies back and closes his eyes straight away, but Luke pulls his thin blanket to his chin and smiles his thanks. They seem smaller somehow, more vulnerable, as if Clara's flannel has washed away their bravado. Compassion twists my heart.

"It must've been hard for you, living here all alone, yet you managed well. You must be stronger than you look and ..." I hesitate as a lump rises, cutting off my voice. I clear my throat, blinking away the sudden mist from my eyes. "... you even found time to leave flowers for Sister Mary."

Luke scrambles to sit upright again, blinking in the flickering light of my candle.

"That weren't us, missus. It were t' other nun ... the one with the bairn."

My heart skips and dances.

"Grace? You mean Grace *was* here? She *did* come back! Where is she now? Where has she gone?"

I feel I have been walking the roads of England forever, yet I cannot remain at Arden while Grace and Andrew may be in danger. Now that I know what the outside world holds, it is harder than ever to leave. I bid my friends goodbye with promises to return as soon as I can.

"If y' don't find 'er soon, y' must come straight back," they say, and I nod my promises.

It is quiet while I travel the byways, but as soon as I join the main thoroughfare to York, I start to encounter other travellers; merchants and pedlars, journeymen and beggars. As before, whenever a party approaches from the opposite direction, I search for a woman and child, although I can scarcely picture Grace's face. I will know her when I see her, I tell myself.

One foot in front of the other, another yard, another bend in the road, another bridge, another hamlet – until the towers of York rise from the misty blue horizon. My weary steps quicken and my heart pulses, kindled by the realisation that the journey is almost over and I can find Grace and take her home.

The crowd of travellers thickens as I near the gates of the town. The walls loom over my head and, in the crush, I sense a heaviness. There are no smiles, no greetings, no laughter, not even the customary pushing and shoving to be first through the portal. I push back my hood and, catching sight of something, my heart leaps, my steps falter. Shading my eyes from the sun, I peer to the top of the town walls, where the heads of executed rebels stare blindly back at me. Contorted faces, frozen in the moment of death, vacant eye sockets, wild and filthy hair heavy with tar. As I look, a kite swoops down to peck viciously at the remains. My knees give out and I almost fall, but a strong hand grabs my upper arm, hauling me upright.

"Don't look, miss, just keep movin', an' it might be best t' keep your eyes on the ground once we're inside, for there's worse t' come."

Somehow, with his assistance, I manage to stagger on, carried forward by the momentum of those around me. They may not be taking me where I want to go but, with my guts swimming sickeningly, I follow regardless of where they lead.

When I was here before, just a few months ago, we had hope. The pilgrims were filled with conviction that our unity would force the king to alter the path he had taken. We believed our way of life would be restored, that one day we would be allowed to continue as we had before.

But now that hope has vanished. It ended with the first hangings; it died with John and Frances. I see now that there is no rosy future, and the best we can wish for is survival. The only hope remaining is to find Grace and Andrew, and perhaps salvage some small spark of joy and move with it into the darkness that is the future.

I allow the crowd to pass on without me, slumping in the shade of a wall to take refreshment from the skin of water I have carried from Arden. My feet are sore, my legs as heavy as lead, and the aroma of roasting mutton makes my empty belly growl. Yet I have survived the journey alone. I am here, I have walked to York; yet I have no idea what I will do next.

I lean against the wall to watch the teeming populace, and my sense of achievement dribbles away. There is little hope of finding anyone in such a crowd. A woman alone is always vulnerable, so I try to blend into my surroundings, tucking myself away into an unobtrusive spot from which I can watch and scan every face.

I sit there for most of the morning. As the sun moves across the sky, the throng increases, the dirt and the stench of the unwashed – of which I am one – becomes overwhelming. The path toward the castle is the busiest of all. As I scan the crowd, I dare not look away, and soon my eyes grow gritty from watching without blinking for too long. There are so many people that I cease to see them; each nose, each face merges into a heaving blur so, at first, I do not notice when a woman with a child in her arms passes by. She is already almost out of sight before I realise. Gathering up my belongings, I scramble to my feet and hurry after her.

"Excuse me. Please let me pass," I cry as I push and shove my way uphill. Some let me by without demur, but others scowl and grumble; one fellow pushes me roughly on the shoulder for my insolence. I scowl at him and duck beneath his arm, hastening after the woman who is now but two or three steps ahead. I want to cry out to her but, afraid she will melt away, my tongue will not make a sound.

I increase my pace. When the narrow street opens out into the castle compound, I am just behind her. I am sure it is her; the set of her head, the way she moves, her height, her build, *everything* screams that I have found her at last. And then the child in her arms turns his head and my heart explodes. I cry out loud. "Andrew!"

To him, I am just another face in the crowd and he looks right through me, a bubble of dribble on his chin. I see he has more teeth than when I saw him last and his dirty hair is thicker now, a cluster of greasy curls on his forehead. I reach out and place my hand on her arm.

"Grace!"

She turns. My smile falters and becomes fixed. *Oh, Grace.*

She is altered. It is as if years and not months have passed since I saw her last. Her skin is yellowed, her eyes sunken and ringed with lines. She might be thirty years old. She doesn't seem to know me.

"Grace, it is me; Margery. I – I am so glad to have found you..."

My happiness is not reciprocated. Her frown deepens; her lips move but make no sound. Without speaking, she passes Andrew into my arms, shakes her head and looks around for somewhere to sit. I follow her to a flight of stone steps, where she collapses like a sack of old rags. There is no semblance of the bright young girl I once loved.

"Have you been sick?" I settle beside her. Andrew squirms to be released but I hang on to him, longing but unable to take the time to express the joy of having him back. Something is very, very wrong.

"Yes, I've been sick. Some vomiting ailment that has left me weak ... it is rife among the poor but there are others in a worse plight than I."

"I never dreamed I would find you so quickly. I only arrived this morning. Are you well enough to travel back with me?"

She has not yet smiled or shown the least pleasure in our reunion. She looks bleakly across the castle square.

"I'll not leave him."

"Leave who? Andrew will come with us ..."

"Not Andrew ... Aske. *Robert Aske*. See where our efforts have led?"

She nods toward the castle mound and, for the first time, I drag my eyes from the tragedy of her face to properly absorb my surroundings.

I have been so focussed on finding her that I'd not noticed the sombre crowd gathered beneath the walls of the keep. Some are kneeling while some stand; the murmur of their combined prayers ebbs and flows as they focus on one object. I follow their line of vision to the towering walls of the castle, and horror scuttles like insects across my skin when I notice the figure of a man hanging in chains.

His robes have been torn away, displaying the marks of violence upon his body. He is filthy, his limbs smeared with his own blood, yet, as bruised and battered as he is, I know I am looking on all that remains of Robert Aske. With bile rising in the back of my throat, I stagger to my feet, but I force the sickness down. Making the sign of the cross, I call down a blessing.

"Do you think God cares?" Grace snarls. "Didn't we pray for His help from the moment it all began? Didn't we pray for the king's return to grace? Haven't I prayed every day since he was taken? God didn't listen when there was time to save him; why should He listen now?"

"Oh Grace, sometimes the Lord's plan is hard for us to understand. In time, it will make more sense ..."

She turns on me, spittle on her lips.

"This will NEVER make sense to me. Aske is a good man, an honest, religious man whose loyalty to the king NEVER wavered. Not once did he seek to undermine his rule, he merely wanted to show him the error of his ways ..." Her voice breaks. I place my hand over hers and squeeze gently.

"At least his suffering is over now. Take comfort from that."

Her head jerks up and her eyes bore into mine. Eyes full of anguish and pain – oh, such pain!

"Oh no, they are not, Margery. You do not understand. Aske's suffering is very far from over. Do you not see? Look at him! He still lives: do you not see?"

My head turns stiffly, unwillingly, but I force myself to look again upon the ravaged body. Grace must be mistaken. No king would be so inhuman as to inflict that much suffering upon a man. Aske is very still but, as I watch, his head moves just a little, and the chains that hold him clank as he squirms feebly against his fate. His weak groans evoke further prayers from the crowd – disciples, I see now, who are sharing his suffering.

Grace lowers her head, her words so quiet I can scarcely hear them.

"That is why I cannot leave. Until he has gone from this world, all of us gathered here will bear witness to his death. When he has gone, we will take word of it; spread the reality of what has happened across the country, across the world. Every man and woman must know the true nature of the king of England."

I have never watched a man die so slowly; not even peaceably in his bed. Those of us who hold vigil during those last hours of Aske's life feel each moment of his suffering, inhale with him each tortured rasping breath. Beyond thirst, beyond hunger, his existence is reduced only to suffering. Each time he lapses into unconsciousness, the cruel changing wind sets his broken body swaying and the chains bite deeper into his flesh. When Aske cries out, we all weep with him.

We pray for the Lord to take him, pray for it to be over, and when he is silent at last, we thank God for ending his torment, and ours.

A week later, Robert's body still hangs from the tower but it is certain now that his soul has passed. They do not take him down; they do not provide a decent burial. Some men whisper that they intend to leave him there for the crows to pick, but surely not ... surely not!

Misery presses down upon us, as heavy and dark as a storm cloud. I want to leave York but Grace is lethargic, lacking the will for anything. While I resume charge of Andrew, all she can do is droop in a corner.

"I shall never pray again," she says and, already fearful for her mind, I now fear for her soul too. I pray for both of us, beg God to help her understand ... but my own faith is faltering. How can this have happened? Why does He heap sorrow upon sorrow?

I burrow my face in Andrew's neck, inhaling his sweet milky scent, thankful that I have him, at least. He seems to remember me now and his innocent smiles help me begin to heal. It is impossible not to smile when he pulls at my nose, or tugs my veil, and when I ask for them, he bestows big wet kisses on my mouth that make my heart swell with love. I envy his innocence, his ignorance of the wicked world; he knows nothing yet of the miseries therein and asks only for food in his belly and somewhere soft to sleep. His simple needs distract me and are soothing to my troubled soul.

In an attempt to rouse Grace from wretchedness, I tell her about my friends at Arden, the start we've made on rebuilding, the life we've rekindled there. For the first time, she breaks from her misery to hurl stones at the brittle dream I've tried to make real.

"They won't let you stay. Once your presence is discovered you will be turned out again and all your work will be for nothing."

Anger stirs, dark and defensive. "At least we are trying," I retort, more sharply than I intended. "At least we aren't so steeped in darkness we can't believe that the morning will come. At least we are fighting. We have to think of tomorrow and what can be done to make our lives better."

She is silent for a while, trembling as she fights to contain her feelings but, tugging the veil from her head, she turns upon me. Her shorn hair makes her eyes seem larger, her cheekbones more prominent than before. Her lip curls with scorn.

"If the last months have shown me anything, it is the horrors that the future conceals. At least the past is honest, at least it doesn't offer hope – hope that will be dashed from our hands the moment we think happiness is ours."

We stare at one another, as far from friends as we have ever been. What happened to those brave girls on the moor? When did we stop believing that life was a problem that would right itself? We have to rediscover some trace of optimism.

"You cannot think like that." I lift Andrew in my arms and he kicks and wriggles like a weaner. "This child, your son, is the future. If you have lost the will to fight for yourself, you must somehow find the will to fight for him."

"And what do you think his future might be? Do you think he will die from hunger, or pestilence? If he reaches manhood, perhaps he will fall foul of the king and die horribly by the rope. Or perhaps he may be maimed and forced to live the life of a beggar instead."

I kick my stool away and begin to pace the floor, the child now tucked on my hip. I force my anger away and speak calmly, scraping the depths of my being for a positive reply.

"Or perhaps he may prosper. Perhaps he will become a great man, a soldier or a philosopher; perhaps he will … benefit from some great fortune and use it to the good of all!"

"You are ridiculous. Only the devil prospers … although … speaking of demons, my cousin is to die for his part in the rising."

Surprised from my campaign, I stop pacing.

"Cousin William? How do you know?"

She shrugs her shoulders.

"I saw him taken, he is held within the castle keep."

"Are you sure he is to die?"

"Why wouldn't he? The king is determined to make an example of those who stood against him. It is just as he deserves."

"Yet … he is your kin. Your only kin."

She shrugs again, the mulish expression creeping back across her face. My mind races. So much death, so much suffering. If William is Grace's only kin then, in all likelihood, he too has none and will go to his death without a single soul to mourn him.

"We should visit him."

"Visit him? Are you mad? Why should I do that?"

"Because nobody, whatever their crime, deserves to die alone. Not even him…"

"You know nothing of it. He is cruel. Look what he did to me! It is his greed, his fault alone that led me here …"

"And all of us, every single person on this Earth, have made mistakes. Forgiveness costs nothing but the relinquishment of pride, and pride is the greatest sin of all. You should cast it off."

She sniffs and folds her arms.

"Hark at your platitudes. You sound like Sister Dorothea."

"Who, beneath her stern exterior, was a wise and gentle woman. I am glad to be likened to her."

Andrew begins to cry. I bounce him, stroke his cheek and smile falsely, to prove our raised voices are nothing but chaff in the wind. "You should remember, Grace: Sister Mary always said that forgiveness benefited the forgiver more than the forgiven. If you show William clemency, you will feel better, I know it."

She fidgets, shuffles her feet and looks away from me.

"Even if I were to agree, there's not much chance that they will allow it. Look at me, I am a renegade nun dressed in rags; why should they allow me access to a condemned gentleman?"

Yet, for whatever reason, they do.

It takes a lot of persuasion, but eventually she agrees to go. I am not sure why I urge her to do so but, a few days later, we approach the prison precinct. The gaolers smirk at us when they see us coming and one of them blocks our way, his arms stretched across the doorway, his body odour as ripe as a stable.

"Seems Crum was right about your lot; two nuns and a bairn? I wonder which of you is 'mother' and which fortunate monk he calls 'father'."

Grace, steely-faced at their poor, sick joke, waits for them to cease their cackle and allow us passage into the gaol. Relishing his small power, the man is reluctant to let us off so lightly. He spits on the ground, just missing his own shoe, and sneers into my ear.

"Best take care. Once you are in there, they might lock you up an' all. All you ex-nuns are no more'n rebels. Don't think you fool us."

I smile coldly into his murky brown eyes. He looks away first and jerks his head, indicating to his fellow to show us the way. The deeper we are taken into the gaol, the darker it grows, and the more unbearable the scent of human suffering. Andrew, unnerved by the stench and the penetrating darkness, whimpers and clutches tighter to my neck. The warren of passages narrows as we go until the gaoler ducks beneath a lintel and fumbles with his bunch of keys. The hinges squeal, straw rustles, and a form takes shape in the pale shaft of light that issues from a grille set high in the wall.

"No funny business." The gaoler wags a finger at the prisoner and retreats to the door, party to every word we speak.

There's a rattle of chains as the prisoner moves closer; a tall shadowy presence, his features obscured by the ill light.

"What the devil?" He stares blankly at us. "I've made my confession; I need no truck with the likes of you."

"Do you not know me, William?"

He stiffens, turns toward us again and peers into Grace's eyes. Of course he does not recognise her. The last time they met, she was plump and pretty, clothed in silk – a prize for any man. He examines her gaunt, grey visage, takes in her nun's garb that is now fit only for a beggar.

"No; I don't know you."

She takes a step nearer, thrusts her face so close to his that he draws back, wary of her intention. His gaze flickers to me and back to Grace again.

"Why should I?"

"I am your cousin, the one whose inheritance you stole, the one you assigned to a life of penury at Arden. I'll warrant you never thought to see me again."

"Grace?" With a sceptical expression, he searches for a glimmer of likeness. His voice, when he speaks again, is full of doubt. "You look nothing like her."

He turns his eyes back to me. "And who's this? Queen Jane, I suppose, carrying the next king of England."

His laughter is humourless. Backing away from her, he drags his fingers across his cheeks, his nails dirt-rimmed and broken. It is clear he has been here for some time.

"I can prove who I am." Grace speaks again, drawing his attention from me. "I have papers from Arden that prove my birth and the legitimacy of my son …"

I gasp aloud at such a lie. She has never made secret of the fact that she was sent to us in shameful stealth. Tension crackles in the air between them.

"Your son?"

Doubt flickers. He struggles to maintain his nonchalance. "Much good that will do him. His inheritance is gone and our family name is now besmirched in dishonour." His voice is bleak. Grace steps closer, following as he retreats into a corner, his back against the dripping wall.

"You care about that, don't you, William? It bothers you that your name will be defiled forever, the bloodline ended. You hate to think of one of the king's favourites lording it at Selsby Hall in your place ... *our* place."

He rubs the end of his nose, sniffing unattractively.

"It won't matter once I'm gone."

Grace glances at me, moistens her lips and takes a deep breath.

"Your life is forfeit, William, there is nothing to be done about that, but the name ... *our* name, can be salvaged."

He gives another short bark of laughter, quite devoid of mirth.

"And how will you do that; go and convince the king that we're loyal after all? Go away, Grace, leave me to die in peace." He turns to face the wall, his head lowered.

"No. I won't do that." She speaks to the back of his head. "You once offered me marriage ..."

I gasp again. This is news indeed. The realisation strikes me that she has not made me party to the entirety of her plan.

"And I wouldn't have you because I was still grieving for Edward. Had I known then what I do today, I might have answered differently, but I was a child, full of bravado. I thought it noble to refuse a reasonable offer of marriage for the sake of a dead man. I was wrong. I had no right to deny Andrew the chance of a gentle life, with a father figure to raise him to his rightful place in society."

William snorts and tilts his head back as he turns to look at her along the length of his nose. His lip curls.

"And how you've suffered for your pride. Look at you; a cast out nun with a bastard child. If Cromwell knew about you, he'd be hauling your shame through the streets in support of his argument."

"Perhaps not. I have my marriage papers in my possession. There was no sin in my union with Andrew's father. We were pledged to one another before witnesses.

Had the sickness not come and father and Edward had not perished, you'd never have entered my life. I'd be home with my husband, raising our son."

His shoulders droop. He lowers his head and discards his haughty manner.

"If you'd taken me, I would have cared for you, Grace, did you know that? I'd have tried to be a good husband."

She swallows, flickers her eyes to Heaven, and I remember the tales she told me of his drinking and womanising.

"Maybe so, but I didn't give you the chance. What I'm offering now ..." she places her hand on his arm "... is the chance to put things right for Andrew. We will speak only good of you ... in public, at any rate. We will lay your body in a place of honour in the family vault. Just help me get Selsby Hall back and we in return shall pray for your soul for all eternity."

"Why would I do that?"

I know her well enough to recognise how desperately she is holding on to her patience. She lowers her lids and speaks so quietly that I have to lean closer to hear.

"Since you sent me away, William, if I've learned one thing it is that no matter how it goes against the grain, doing the right thing is the only option. If you want to die with honour, then I am offering you the chance to undo your sin against me. Confess in writing that you stole my inheritance and I may be able to persuade the authorities of the injustice of depriving Andrew, who is innocent of any crime, of his rights. Selsby Hall may yet remain in the family, for all time."

We wait so long for an answer that the gaoler pokes his head into the room. "Are yer finished?"

Without taking her eyes from William's lowered head, Grace waves him away. Moments tick by, the lantern flickers, and someone passes the grille in the wall, momentarily blocking the only source of light and air. At last, he turns around, slowly takes her hand and places his lips upon it. I do not miss the hint of triumph in her expression as she looks down upon his tarnished head.

He calls for paper and ink, which the gaoler brings reluctantly, banging it rudely on the table. William takes up the quill and stares at Grace for such a long time that the nib dries and he is forced to dip it again before beginning to write.

October 1537 – Arden

Three months have passed since we turned away from the broken body of Robert Aske and began our journey back to Arden. The pilgrims are silenced now; the survivors have crept away to mourn the perished. The king and his ministers do their worst and, one by one, the great abbeys tumble. The king's coffers now bulge with stolen wealth. On the way home, we learned that Queen Jane had fulfilled her promise and borne a son; an heir to the throne that we all hope will soothe the king's rage and divert his mind from destruction and death. Yet soon after, we heard the queen did not survive her childbed but perished a few days later, leaving behind a motherless prince. None of us doubts that her place in Henry's bed will not long remain vacant.

When they see us approaching, Milo and Clara and the others run out to greet us. Milo takes my pack and guides us inside. The arms of Arden welcome me and I am glad to be back in the fold.

"So, this is Grace and little Andrew ..." Clare opens her arms and takes him from me, prodding his belly, making him smile.

"We've heard all about you, Grace. Margery speaks o' little else." Agnes ushers her into a chair while

Ellen brings oatcakes and a flagon of water. Grace smiles her thanks but says very little, stretching out her feet to the hearth and examining each face as they regale us with their news.

Although there was time on the road to ask her about the lies she told William, I shied away from it. I've never doubted her honesty before but I watch her now as she interacts with the other women. She is detached, shy perhaps, or maybe just exhausted from the journey. When Clara questions her as to what happened in York, she evades the only harsh answer she can give and leaves it to me.

"Aske is dead," I tell them, and silence falls among us as we each think of him and the sacrifice he has made. It is Clara who breaks the chill by getting up to stir the broth, and she offers Andrew a crust on which to chew. The conversation returns to the expectations of the kitchen garden, the clutch of eggs found beneath a bush, promising an increase in our flock in this untimely season.

As usual at Arden, we retire when darkness falls. We will be up at first light and the long winter evenings are too chilly for comfort. We cannot even apply ourselves to mending and sewing when the light fades. Not that it is much warmer in the dormitory, for all Milo's attempts to repair the roof. The cold night air falls heavily upon us, hastening our preparations for bed. Glad of his warmth, I tuck Andrew against my belly and curl around him, my chin resting on his head. I close my eyes, the events of the day drifting across my mind. I have Grace and Andrew back yet, dear to me as she is, Grace is still an enigma, mysterious even after all the months of knowing her. Why did she lie about her betrothed? Or was it a lie? Perhaps she was telling the truth. It is so hard to know.

The matter will not rest and I wait all the next day for the opportunity to quiz her on the matter. It is toward the end of the afternoon when I finally find myself alone with her. I speak before I can persuade myself out of it.

"Grace; those things you told William ... about Andrew's father ... were they true?"

My cheeks burn. I wish I hadn't spoken, but there is nothing I can do about it, the words are out now. They seem to float in the air between us. Her face registers surprise that she hurriedly disguises, and then she laughs, the sound brittle and unconvincing as she continues to evade me.

"What things?"

"You said you were wed to him."

"Did I? I don't think I said that. I said I had papers proving our union was valid – I never mentioned–"

"You said you'd taken vows before God."

"Did I? I think you must be mistaken."

"I distinctly remember you using the word 'legitimate'."

She sighs and I see my persistence has made her cross.

"There are many forms of truth, Margery," she says at last. "How truthful was Queen Catherine when she swore on oath that she had not lain with her first husband, the king's brother? How true were the accusations of incest and treason made against Queen Anne? How true were the allegations of fornication and corruption made against the monasteries? We, all of us, use false words to achieve our desires ... our needs. If I twisted the truth a little in my son's favour, then ... that sin is not mine alone. I will pay for it come Judgement Day. As we will all pay for our sins."

"So, you weren't married? Andrew is a bastard."

She takes a deep breath and I can see her clinging to the last vestiges of her patience.

"Edward and me were pledged to marry, before witnesses. That used to be enough. I did not give myself lightly. I am no *whore*."

I flinch at the word. "I never suggested tha–"

She emits a growl of anger. "Had fate not intervened, we would have been wed. We'd have lived happily at Selsby Hall and none of this would have happened. Surely, even God will forgive me a small perjury for the sake of my son ... for the sake of all of us?"

"All of us?"

"Yes, all of us! Selsby Hall is – is – Oh, you can't imagine it, Margery. It is as unlike Arden as a church from a – a – a brothel. It is warm and safe with plenty of food, so much that nobody ever goes hungry, not even the servants."

It sounds like paradise. She plumps down on the stone wall, rising again as soon as the cold penetrates the thin layers of her clothing. "I – I hate it here. I always have. I wanted to take you away, take all of you to Selsby and share it all with you but ... well, it will never happen. I am sure William's letter must have reached the lawyers by now. I suppose we are doomed to stay here."

"Don't say doomed." I take her hand, smiling with a degree of certainty I do not feel. "We have overcome so much. If we keep faith, God will see us through. His plan for us is difficult to see, but from his seat in Heaven ..." I look up at the wide open sky "... our way is clearly marked. The future is not ours to know but ... trust in Him and it will all come right."

"Oh *Margery*! You know nothing! You can't imagine that there is anything in the world beyond hardship and hunger, but there is so much more!"

"If God–"

"Shut up! God is ... deaf, blind to our suffering; either that or He cares nothing at all for us."

"I have to believe He has a plan."

She snatches back her hand and casts a look of contempt upon me before she storms away.

At Arden, the summer is coming to an end. The stores are replete with beans and Clara has a goodly stock of honey, but winter will still be cold and hard for all of us. I am in the garden, sifting through sodden plants, garnering the last few seeds to save for next year's sowing. Nearby, Adam and Andrew are chasing one another on the mead; every so often, Andrew loses his balance and falls headlong into the wet grass but he makes no fuss. He clambers to his feet and, with a smile as wide as Yorkshire, toddles on again. The sound of his laughter brings a smile to my face, and I am almost content, almost happy.

Bessie and Ellen are squabbling over some insignificant matter in the meadow, and Clara is clanging pans in the kitchen. Grace is nowhere around, and I have no doubt she has gone out on the heath again, walking unaccompanied as she does every day. She never lets the opportunity pass to escape to the hills, but what she does there, or what compulsion drives her, I do not know. When I finally pluck the courage to ask her, she snaps at me.

"I go there to think and walk, that is all."

I could remind her of the selfishness of leaving the chores to the other women, but I daren't do so and in the end, I cease to ask at all. There are even days when I cease to wonder.

I stand up, place my hand to the small of my back and look at the stark outline of Arden against the scudding clouds. The church roof is still in ruins, the chapter house and most of the dormitory are still open to the sky. Yet I see none of that. Instead, I see it as it once was; small, humble and somewhat ramshackle, but home. The sweetest place of all.

The empty bell tower, the thick moss on the roof, the tall arched windows are open to the frigid Yorkshire air, and if I close my eyes, I can hear their voices. Sister Dorothea, high pitched and tuneful; Sister Mary, cracked and husky ... and Frances, like a wolf crying discordantly at the moon.

Sometimes, I imagine I hear their footsteps, the rustle of the prioress' forbidden silk petticoat, Sister Juliana singing as she stirs the kitchen pot. I am at Arden yet I am not at Arden. This is not *home* as I imagined it would be. Home is an unreachable place; it lies in the past, along a road that can only be travelled in the mind. Arden Priory is a ruin, and my family have long gone. Sister Frances has taken her place in Heaven and all that remains on Earth of the woman who raised me is a dark mound in the churchyard. As for John ... I have forgotten exactly what he looked like.

Adam shouts something, dragging me from my maudlin musing. I see Luke hurrying through the garden. His eyes are large, fearful.

"Horseman are coming," he says, pointing back the way he has come.

"Who is it?" I pick up my basket and drag Andrew from his game. "Come along, Adam, come with me."

Who can it be? Who would have business here at Arden? I have no illusion that it will be a friendly visit, no expectation of welcome news. Despite the nine people who live with me, I feel suddenly alone, and very isolated. Before I approach the gatehouse, I turn to Luke. "Grace is out on the moor. Go and find her; bring her back as quickly as you can."

For once, he does not complain, he does not argue, he does not suggest I send Mark in his place. He scoots through the gate and I pause for a moment, watching his fair head bobbing through the meadow before straightening my shoulders and approaching the priory gate.

"Take the children and go inside," I tell the women and, without argument, they hurry to do my bidding. I exchange anxious glances with Milo as we wait to greet the strangers. As I turn away, I notice Mark peering around the corner of the kitchen wall. With a jerk of my head, I silently order him away and he disappears. I wish Grace was with me but I stand as upright as I can, folding my hands inside my sleeves and raising my chin. I will look this new trouble in the eye, even if it kills me.

Slowly, the sound of hooves grows closer. The horses halt at the gate. I hear the creak of the saddle as someone dismounts, the jangle of harness, a murmur of voices, and then the wooden gates judder as someone thumps them, demanding admittance.

"See who it is, Milo." My voice issues in a squeak and I clear my throat, tensing my shoulders and gripping my hands so tightly that my fingers turn white. With a grimace, Milo pulls back the grille.

"A gentleman," he says, "by the looks of him."

I nod, indicating he should let them in, and he opens the postern gate. It groans on unoiled hinges to reveal two riders; a gentleman as Milo has said, and his servant. He is well turned out, his clothes clean and of a good cut. The stranger strides into the precinct and takes off his hat to gaze about the compound, his eyes opening in surprise when he notes the damaged roofs, the broken cobbles. It takes all my will to remain still and seemingly calm. I open my mouth to speak, but a footstep behind me makes me turn, expecting ... I know not what.

Grace hurries toward me. She has lost her veil and I notice her hair is beginning to grow again; it gleams golden in the late October sun. Her face is open in question, her cheeks red from running, but she isn't looking at me. She looks right past me to the man near the gate, who is nervously turning his hat in his hands.

"William?" Her hand flies to her mouth, astonishment dancing across her face.

I jerk my head round and re-examine the fellow for a likeness to the man I last saw languishing in York gaol. I had thought him executed by now – we all had. Can this be the same man?

The poor light of his prison did little to reveal his features, but the man before me today is a far cry from the ragged fellow I met before. Grace hurries forward, comes to a stop, and hesitates before reaching out to touch his hand.

"It *is* you," she said. "I thought you were…"

"Dead?" He laughs and, unlike before, there is humour in it. "I thought so too but it seems the king in his mercy, or perhaps in his joy at the birth of his heir, has chosen to reprieve … a lucky few, of which I am one."

He lowers his head and we do likewise, contemplating the punishments suffered by our fellows.

"But why are you here?"

Ignoring me, Grace rests a hand lightly on his elbow and ushers him into our humble kitchen. Milo and me follow behind, open-mouthed.

When Grace escorts her visitor through the door, Clara leaps to her feet, hushing the hubbub of the children. She puts the pot over the fire and removes a pile of bowls from the table before wiping her hands on her apron.

"Have a seat, sir," she says, swiping it with a cloth before he can sit, "and I will find some— we have no wine, Margery, what shall I—?"

"No matter, no matter." William takes the proffered stool, his clothes and manner incongruous in our humble company. He surveys the room, his eye hesitating on the damp wall, the broken shutters, the scattering of mouse droppings in the corner.

"Why are you here?" Grace asks again and he places his hands on his knees. His cheeks turn a deep shade of red.

"To see how you are faring. I cannot go back to ... I cannot return to Selsby now. The estate is still in Cromwell's hands. I thought ... I kept wondering how you were and I – I wanted to thank you ... for visiting me during my darkest day."

Grace puts her hands on her hips and looks askance.

"It wasn't for your benefit. You do realise that, don't you, William?"

He begins to speak but, thinking better of it, looks at the company. "Grace, is there somewhere we can talk ... alone?"

To my astonishment, she turns coy and raises her eyebrows. "It wouldn't do for us to be alone, sir. We can walk in the garden with Margery to chaperone, but don't expect clipped hedges and camomile lawn. It is more a case of sprawling nettles and hidden rabbit holes."

Regardless of her ragged clothes, she holds out her arm and he takes it. I trail in their wake, embarrassed at this strange new role. I don't know how close I should follow, or where I should look. If he becomes over familiar or threatening, what am I to do? Turn the other way, or fight him off?

In the end, the rough path is too narrow for us to walk abreast so I lag behind, keeping my eye on the hem of Grace's habit and my ear tuned to their lowered voices.

They stop to stare at the tangle of weeds beside the old infirmary door. Seeing it through his eyes, I remember it as it was before, the day I took refuge there long ago when the king's men came. The memory is cut short when William pauses and takes hold of Grace's shoulders. I pull up short to stop myself from cannoning into them. Immediately, I am on the alert and ready to intervene, but Grace seems calm and she is smiling, so I wait and listen. With a glance at me, he clears his throat and begins to speak so softly that I have to strain my ears to hear.

"Grace. I have to apologise for the way I treated you. I should never have sent you here. I was young, unschooled in the way of the world. When you refused my offer of marriage, I was … a-appalled and the news that you were to have a child was a great shock … I – I thought you a–"

"I know what you thought of me, William, but I am not. I never was. I loved Edward and he loved me. I have the papers to prove we were joined…"

"But he is dead. You are no longer–"

"No. I am no longer." She pulls away, looks at him askance. "Have you come here to propose to me again, William?"

My mouth falls open. William's face turns scarlet. He shrugs.

"It seems to me that it would provide a way out of your … our predicament. Thanks to you, since I didn't die, I am disinherited. Here, read this …"

He fumbles inside his tunic and hands her a letter, which she opens as she turns away. When she reaches the end of the path, she stops suddenly.

"They have granted Selsby Hall to Andrew!"

"Yes, but the money …"

"… is tied up in a trust until Andrew comes into his majority!"

I look from one to the other, ignorant of matters of financial law.

"Is that good or bad?" I utter, and both heads turn toward me.

"It depends how you look at it." William's smile chases the lingering marks of gaol from his features and I realise he is younger than I had previously thought. "Grace and Andrew can return to live at Selsby Hall but, until he is of age, they lack the funds to do so, or the means to make any. I, on the other hand, have a small private sum. I think we should put our resources together – for the sake of the family name, of course."

"So, you'd be doing me a service, William?"

He turns back to Grace.

"I would, yes."

He appears more confident now, his smile spreading. She puts her head on one side.

"And ... you would want the running of the estate, the position of squire, as if you were indeed the lord of the manor?"

"Until the boy reaches his majority, yes."

"No."

His smile fades and his cheeks blanch.

"I beg pardon?"

"I said, no. I will not marry you to help you regain the status you've lost. I will take Andrew back to Selsby Hall but I will go with Margery, if she will come, and the friends I have made here."

My gasp draws her attention and she steps forward to take my hand. She looks earnestly into my face.

"Margery, I know how you love this place but they won't let us stay here. We will be forced out sooner or later. Why not spare yourself the pain of eviction and leave on our own account? Come with me and we can live as we do here, but in more comfort. When I left Selsby Hall, it had a roof and a vast kitchen garden the like of which you've never imagined, and vast fish ponds; not to mention furniture and thick goose feather beds."

I look around me, at the place I have loved, the land I have worked, the ring of moorland that has cradled me for most of my life. I know it is time to leave. Blinking to clear the mist from my eye, I summon a brave smile.

"Yes, Grace. I will come with you. It is time to make a new life for all of us..."

Arm in arm, we turn back toward the kitchen but, as we reach the cloister gate, William calls after us.

"Grace, what about me? What will I do?"

Grace, her face merrier than I've seen it for many years, turns back to him.

"You, William, will visit me again when you've learned some manners and improved your skill at proposing marriage."

Spring 1538 – Selsby Hall

My life is very different now. England is different. Across the realm, the abbey bells are silent and there are great changes to the way we worship. The king has denounced the pope, and the lyrical poetry of the Latin Bible is forbidden. The idea of purgatory is laughed at now, and what need is there of nuns and monks to pray for the swift passing of souls into Heaven?

The Epistle and Gospel are preached in English now, and an English Bible is chained to the lectern of every parish church. The religious icons and idols have been smashed or burned and, while the pious are crushed into silence, Cromwell continues to entice the king to further crimes against God and all his saints.

At Selsby Hall, we remove the rood and the image of the Virgin from the church and bury them in a secret place in the garden. On that same day, I lay to rest what little religious vocation I had.

At Arden, before the king's men came, I was drifting toward a life of dedication, but now my life overflows with other, secular things and I take joy from it.

Grace, discovering a clothes press in the attic full of her old garments, provides me with petticoats and gowns. For the first time, my torso is squeezed into a tight bodice, and I feel the weight of petticoats, the pleasure of fine linen against my skin. I wear neat shoes instead of unwieldy sandals. She tucks my hair, which now almost reaches the nape of my neck, beneath a coif, and stands back to assess her handiwork.

"How do I look?" I ask when she is silent for so long.

"Nothing like Margery," she replies at last. "The clothes make a stranger of you. I wonder what Andrew will think."

We descend the stairs and seek out Clara, who emits a squeak of surprise.

"By 'eavens, Margery, your own mother wouldn't know you ..." She stops mid-sentence when she remembers that I never knew my mother and, by way of distraction, I hold out my skirts and turn in a circle as I absorb their admiration. Bessie steps forward and tests the nap of the cloth between finger and thumb. Although it is only workaday quality, I note the envy in her eye.

"I'm sure Grace can find something for you, Bessie, and for all of you."

"Of course," Grace smiles. "There are bolts of cloth in the store room; everyone can have new garments made."

The women squeal their pleasure. Bessie and Ellen link hands and dance in a ring, while I escape with Grace outside.

The sound of their excitement follows us into the sunshine. The day has just passed its zenith and we stroll through the grass, where primroses bloom in golden glory beneath the apple trees. Andrew is sleeping in the orchard, beneath the watchful gaze of a local girl who has been promoted to the position of nurse. He is approaching two years old now, and his nap times are welcomed by all of us, providing respite from his insistent games, his constant demands, and his increasingly risky duels with danger.

We pause and, as it always does when I look at him, something shifts in my heart.

"It's extraordinary how sleep transforms his devilry into purity," Grace remarks as we look down at the soft flush of his dreaming.

"He grows so fast," I murmur, so as not to wake him. "I'd like to slow him down; before we know it, he will be in the schoolroom. I've never known two years to pass so swiftly."

"It's been a busy time, that's for sure. Before my father died I was idle, immersed in merriment and the seasons passed so slowly. I had little idea of the real world then, of poverty or suffering."

"We can both be merry now," I say, tightening my hold on her arm.

"I'm not sure I want to be ..."

I release her arm and fall behind as she moves forward a few paces.

"You don't want to be happy?"

She turns toward me, her face stretched with amusement.

"Of course I want to be happy. I just don't think idle merriment will be enough for me anymore."

"Perhaps you will marry, have more children ..." I suggest, and she snorts inelegantly.

"Marry who? Cousin William? Squire Hetherton, our neighbourly lecher? I don't think so. I'd like to be useful. As strange as it sounds, I miss the days when we were on the road, when every morsel of food seemed like a banquet, when the open sky was the canopy over our bed."

"Hmm, it sounds to me like you are misremembering. Have you forgotten the cold and the gnawing hunger? Have you forgotten our aching feet, or how we fled for our lives from the king's men? Have you forgotten the price we paid ...?"

We both fall silent, and although I had not mentioned her name, the spirit of Frances rises like a wraith on the path between us. I turn away from it, the memory too painful.

"No." Grace wrinkles her brow. "I haven't forgotten and, in reality, I do not want to return to that. I just miss the purpose we had then, the sense of doing something ..."

"You've the household to think of now but ... perhaps there is something we could do to help the poor. Since the monasteries closed, the roads are full of vagrants; we are fortunate not to find ourselves in the same position. Perhaps something could be done for them."

We arrive at a crossing in the garden path, a stone seat beside a pool where fish slumber in the green depths. We sit on the edge, hands clasped.

"There is very little money, Margery. I cannot provide shelter for any more people."

"I know that, but perhaps we could open the kitchen, maybe just one day a week, to feed the hungriest, or the ailing. It could be a charitable cause in which we could persuade our neighbours to help. That old man, Squire Hetherton, would do anything for a smile from you. The closures have left so many in penury, not just the dispossessed monks and nuns, but those they fed and nursed as well. Milo says the roads of England have never been so full of wanderers."

"Now that most of them have left because I could offer no wage, there are so few staff to help us. God bless Milo and Clara and the rest but, really, Milo is little defence against violence and once word gets out, we could attract the destitute from far and wide."

"You need a husband. A rich one so we can increase the size of the household."

"William, you mean?"

I shrug. "He isn't so bad, is he?"

She leans back her head, closes her eyes.

"You marry him, then."

A bubble of laughter springs from deep within me as I imagine the proud William joining with the likes of me.

"No, thank you very much."

She raises her head and cocks it to one side.

"Do you ever think of John?"

The old flush of embarrassment heats my cheeks.

"Sometimes, but ... I was young then, it was just a girlish thing. Had he not died, I doubt we'd have ever wed. I think we were drawn to one another through circumstance rather than ... anything else."

Her palm is warm on the back of my hand.

"You talk like an old woman. Who can say what might have been? Anyway, you have all your life before you; marriage, children, we can never know what awaits us around the next bend in the road."

"As long as it isn't Thomas Cromwell."

She rests her head against mine and we fall silent, each drifting into our own thoughts, our own regrets, our own hopes of what is to come.

As we sit there, our happy dreaming is disturbed by a footstep upon the gravel and we look up to see Andrew toddling toward us, his nurse just behind. He runs up to us and tries to clamber onto my lap, leaving a smear of mud on my apron.

"So sorry, Miss Margery," the nurse exclaims when she sees it, but I wave her away before she can scold him and scoop him into my arms. He squirms like an eel when I start to tickle him, his squeals echoing across the garden. And I am reminded that the future is right here with us in the present, like an unopened parcel, an untasted treat. To attempt to predict it too precisely is to spoil it.

Author's Note

Many years ago now, I was lucky enough to study medieval monastic history beneath the tutorage of Janet Burton. I attended her first lecture with an idealistic view of the medieval period, which I saw as a crystal clear world in which the laity were shielded from personal sin by the selfless devotion of the Roman church. I signed up to the module on monasticism expecting to study a simple life, goodly men praying for the souls of their fellows. The monks of my imagination were self-denying, nurturing, healing. The nuns were Ingrid Bergman-type figures, their faces illuminated with religious goodness, mouthing gentle prayers in softly lit chapels, accompanied by strains of plainsong. A single lecture with Janet shattered this ideal and made me sit bolt upright and vow that, one day, I would write a historical novel about nuns.

Popular history tends to focus on the vast abbeys like Fountains, Glastonbury and Rievaulx, which somewhere along the way lost sight of the simple life. By the time of the dissolution, these abbeys had become immensely rich and, in some cases, were no strangers to corruption. In the case of the Cistercians, who had broken from the mainstream monastic way to adhere closer to the rule of St Benedict and had forbidden the extravagance of stained glass, patterned floor tiles and multitudinous chapels, the regulations were clearly breached. But it was difficult to avoid. By way of securing their place in Heaven, laymen endowed lavish gifts on the abbeys: gifts of land, chapels, windows etc. They paid for prayers to be said for their souls for all eternity. Ultimately, the wealth of the monasteries outstripped that of the crown. This affluence drew the greedy eye of Cromwell and his king, and the accusations of corruption had less to do with outrage and more to do with the desire to justify plundering the Holy Church.

Cromwell's campaign to close the monasteries began slowly. Picking up where his old master, Wolsey, had left off, he began chipping away at smaller, less profitable foundations or houses where moral decay had become the rule rather than the exception. Abbey treasures went straight into the king's coffers and their lands became the property of the crown, leased to the king's favourites by way of securing both their loyalty and ensuring their support for the dissolution of the monasteries. But some of the smaller abbeys closed at this time were barely scraping a living.

Arden Priory was situated in an unpopulated region on the edge of the North Yorkshire moors, the inhabitants now nothing more than a whisper on the historical record. There was nothing romantic about the cheerless life they led. The nuns at Arden were living on the edge of civilisation, closed off from the world, from family and friends, and all comforts. Assisted by just a few servants, the women undertook all manual work themselves; caring for livestock, cooking, cleaning, nursing ... everything. Even today, stripped of twenty-first century luxuries of glazing and heating, life in rural North Yorkshire can be hard; in 1536, it was extreme.

Arden Priory was founded in 1150 by Peter de Hoton, and confirmed by Roger de Mowbray between 1147 and 1169. It was never a rich foundation. One can only imagine the misery of a life of unceasing labour, meagre accommodation, glassless windows, and fasting, overworked and ill clad. In 1397, long before the dissolution, there were just six nuns at Arden: Christina and Elizabeth Darrel, Elizabeth Slayne, Alicia Barnard, Agnes of Middleton, and Elizabeth of Thornton. They were overseen by the prioress, who is named simply as Eleanor. At this time, it seems that relations between the nuns was not good. The sisters accused the prioress of pawning the church silver, selling wood without consent and providing so few candles in the quire that there was insufficient light to say the offices. They also complained that the buildings were in a state of disrepair. But this doesn't necessarily suggest the prioress was corrupt, it rather points to dire need. Janet Burton in her book *Monasteries and Society in the British Isles in the Late Middle Ages* says:

"*What emerges from their complaints is that this small community of seven women, living in the bleak environment of the North Yorkshire Moors, was suffering conditions of extreme poverty and hardship. It was life on the edge.*"

This picture of hardship, so far from my initial imaginings, has stayed with me during the ten years or so since I first heard of Arden. Being so far from the '*concourse of men*' there were few rich benefactors, so the priory would have had little chance of increasing its wealth. If there was such a degree of poverty in the fourteenth century, what was the financial state by the time of the dissolution? 'Valor Ecclesiasticus' (a survey of church finances in England, Wales and parts of Ireland made in 1535 on Henry VIII's orders) suggests that very little had changed. Poverty was always the rule at Arden.

The priory was visited by the king's commissioners on 8th May 1536 and it was suppressed the following August. At the time of dissolution, there were just six sisters, three of whom received pensions of twenty shillings each, two received ten shillings, and one received six shillings and eight pence. Sister Elizabeth Johnson, who was an octogenarian with limited hearing, was granted forty shillings 'toward her sustenance.' The church 'treasure' seized by the king's men consisted of a gilt chalice weighing 14.5oz and a flat piece of white silver weighing 8oz, and two bells valued at ten shillings. According to the 'Valor Ecclesiasticus' in 1536, the value of the house was £12. 0s and 6d. It is noted that the nuns also had an image of St Brigid, to whom they made offerings for cows that were ill or had strayed.

This suggests a reality quite different from the tales circulated in 1536 of corruption and ungodliness. Motivated by his favour of the new learning, Cromwell and his men put forward stories of nuns indulging in sexual misconduct with monks, murdering their own infants, and enjoying lewd and promiscuous lives. Even if they had the inclination, I would be surprised if the nuns of Arden would have found either the time or the energy for such practices.

The dissolution was almost universally resented by monks and traditionalists. Monasteries were a lifeline; common people relied on them from birth to death for charity, employment and for healthcare. The closures united the populace, both rich and poor, culminating in widespread protests that posed the greatest threat to the crown during Henry VIII's reign. The first rising took place in Lincolnshire in October but was quickly put down, only to spring up again in Yorkshire when the people of the north, led by lawyer Robert Aske, embarked upon a 'Pilgrimage of Grace'.

Gentry as well as common folk joined the peaceful march to persuade the king to change his mind; monks and laymen, nuns and children were among those who took to the road to preserve their way of life. The Pilgrimage of Grace was the worst uprising during Henry VIII's reign, the rebels reaching more than 30,000, far outnumbering the royal army. After initially agreeing to consider their complaints, however, the king managed to get the upper hand.

He 'invited' Robert Aske to spend Christmas at court, promising to consider the proposals, but when unrest broke out again in the East Riding, it provided the king with the excuse he needed. The Duke of Norfolk was sent to deal with the rebels. The leaders were executed, and there were widespread hangings of common people, supposed to serve as a deterrent to further protesters. Robert Aske was hung in chains on the walls of York and left there to die a long and excruciating death.

One by one, the abbeys fell, monks and nuns were turned out, some abbots were tortured and executed. By 1540, the last abbeys were closed, their lands distributed among the nobility, the remains of once-glorious buildings subjected to neglect and decay.

The plight of those affected by the dissolution has always intrigued me and I have enjoyed revisiting the period in Sisters of Arden, which is a merger of fact and fiction. The records of Arden are scanty but by piecing together what little we know with wider records of the dissolution and the Pilgrimage of Grace, I have at last been able to explore the closure of the abbeys and the uprisings that followed from the perspective of a group of insignificant nuns.

Further Reading:

Burton, Janet: Monastic and Religious Orders in Britain 1000-1300 (CUP:1994)
Chandler, John: John Leland's Itinerary (Sutton, 1993)
Hoyle, R. W: the Pilgrimage of Grace and the Politics of the 1530s (OUP:2001)
Ives, Eric: The Reformation Experience (Lion Hudson, 2012)
Moorhouse, Geoffrey: The Pilgrimage of Grace (Orion, 2003)
Schofield, John: The Rise and Fall of Thomas Cromwell (The History Press, 2011)

Other books by Judith Arnopp

The Beaufort Chronicles (three book series)
The Beaufort Bride
The Beaufort Woman
The King's Mother
A Song of Sixpence: the story of Elizabeth of York and Perkin Warbeck
Intractable Heart: the story of Katheryn Parr
The Kiss of the Concubine: a story of Anne Boleyn
The Winchester Goose: at the court of Henry VIII
The Song of Heledd
The Forest Dwellers
Peaceweaver

Author.to/juditharnoppbooks
www.judithmarnopp.com

Lightning Source UK Ltd.
Milton Keynes UK
UKHW022058010919
348916UK00003B/1013/P